Outside In is dedicated to
my sister moon Jodie and my brother Matthew.

And also to James. With all my love.

Outside In Stuart Throrogood

First published 2001 by Millivres Ltd, part of the Millivres Prowler Group,
Gay Men's Press, PO Box 3220, Brighton BN2 5AU, East Sussex, England

World Copyright © 2001 Stuart Thorogood

Stuart Thorogood has asserted his right to be identified as the author of
this work in accordance with the Copyright, Designs and Patents Act 1988

A CIP catalogue record for this book is available from the British Library

ISBN 1 902852 27 3

Distributed in Europe by Central Books,
99 Wallis Road, London E9 5LN

Distributed in North America by Consortium,
1045 Westgate Drive, St Paul, MN 55114-1065

Distributed in Australia by Bulldog Books,
PO Box 300, Beaconsfield, NSW 2014

Cover Design by Andrew Biscomb

Outside In

STUART THOROGOOD

GAY MEN'S PRESS

ACKNOWLEDGMENTS

This project would not have been possible without the insight and advice given to me by the following individuals:

John Aubusson, Steven Best, Yvonne Carron (you go, girlfriend!), George Drury, Carrie Eadie, Daniel Farley, David Fernbach, Peter Goldsmith, Daniel Gayle, Laura Jackson, Wayne Lowe, Donna Hitchen (the Northern link), Codie Larsson, Lizzie West, Fiona "PR Priestess" Williamson, Mike Williams, Keith Roddy, Carrie Jones, Clare Mowat (a true inspiration), Nigel McPheat, Shampoo, The Lovely OU Call Centre, especially the Admin team: Jo, Sheila, Sally, Tanya, Gavin, Tracy, Milena and Mandy.

And finally a special thank-you to my fantastic Auntie Val. Cheers to Bernie.

Thank you all for inspiring this fairytale of truth

PART I
The Luxury Cage

1 Mark

"Mark! Burgers! Now!"

"All right, all right!" I shouted back at Fiona as I frantically prepared the Brenda's Specials and Fries. It was a Saturday morning, the busiest time of the week at Brenda's Burgers.

Brenda's Burgers was a busy fast-food restaurant in the high street. I'd been working there for just under three months. Crap job, crap pay, but it was better than being on the dole. At least I had some sort of self-respect, and independence, especially since I didn't play in a band any more.

Oh, I'm Mark Holly, and I'm gay.

As if you didn't know.

I live with my boyfriend Andrew. He's brilliant. That's an understatement, though.

He is; brilliant, I mean. He's the best thing that's ever ever happened to me. I know I went through some shit when I was coming out, getting to grips with being queer, but that was ages ago.

All right, so it was just eighteen months back, but it seems like ages. Seems like forever most days. But you know, we've never been happier. I don't know where these people get the idea that gay men can't have decent relationships 'cos ours is going strong.

We live together in his flat. It's a nice flat; really posh. I moved in about seven months ago. We're so domesticated! It's a bit pathetic, I suppose. But nice. Nice and pathetic, that's us.

And we have the best sex, I tell you. The best. Funny really, that I'm talking like that, so openly. A year and a half ago I thought being queer was revolting; perverse...and all the rest of that sort of shit. I know better now...and I'm pleased to say so, believe me!

My family still treat me okay. Most of 'em, anyway. Well...my mum and my sister Amy are fine. My brother's still in prison.

Nick. The arsehole who almost killed me when I came out to him. Locked me in a room with...

Oh yeah, I said I wasn't going to go back over that, didn't I?

Right. Okay. Good.

Where was I? Oh, my family.

My dad's semi-okay with having a gay son. In fact, every time I see him he seems a little more friendly. But then, I've never been with Andrew when I've spoken to him. Maybe that would put a slightly different slant on matters, eh?

Who knows? Who cares? This is my life, and if I want to be with other guys, then that's what I'll do.

"Mark! Come on! I need those burgers now!"

"I'm going as fast as I can, Fiona!" I said, which I suppose was a bit of a lie. I hated working at Brenda's Burgers. Andrew said he hated me working there, too, because he knows I hate it and if I hate something then he hates it. But I hate it that he thinks like that.

He said he was going to try and get me a job as a barman at Medusa's, which is this gay club that he works at. But I turned him down. I didn't think it would be such a good idea if we lived together and slept together and worked together. That really would have been pushing it, and I wanted to do nothing that could put our relationship in danger.

Andrew's the first person I've ever loved, and I swear to you that that is no word of a lie. And when I say loved I mean *really* loved. I've never felt this way about anyone, or anything. And no, it's not just the sexual attraction, it's like...like we're intertwined with one another, like soulmates. I hate to go all mushy, but there's really no other way to describe the bond we've got. Because it's not like the way you love your parents, or your brother and sister, or even your best friend. This is something so much bigger, so much wider and deeper and stronger than any of that. And that's what Andrew and I had.

Lucky, aren't we?

"Mark!" came Fiona's frantic cry.

"I know!"

Quickly I wrapped the burgers in their grease-proof paper and dropped them into a paper bag with the garish Brenda's Burgers logo emblazoned on it. I shoved it onto the metal runners and it slid down into Fiona's waiting hands.

"In the end," she sighed, and turned back to her customer with her best 'sorry-about-the-long-wait-but-if-it-wasn't-for-my-slow-as-shit-work-colleague-you-would-have-had-your-food-by-now' expression.

I smiled slowly and called out, "I'm going to have my break now, Fiona."

"Don't be long," she warned.

"I'll try my best."

Ø

I went into the staff room and got my packet of cigarettes from the pocket of my bomber jacket. Yes, I'd started smoking. Don't know how I picked up the habit. Maybe from the gay scene. Most of my mates smoke, anyway. Except Andrew, though, and he really hates it that I smoke. I suppose I should give up really, if only for his sake. I mean, it's not really fair that I should give him lung cancer. Mind you, he won't let me smoke in the flat, I have to go outside and stand by the fire exit like a leper, an outcast.

It was a pretty nice day, for late April, so I went walking outside. I knew I was only supposed to have about ten minutes' morning break, but it usually stretched into at least twenty. Fiona didn't mind, though. She was good to have as a supervisor. Treated you all right and that. She doesn't know I'm gay, though, even though she's met Andrew once or twice. As far as she's concerned, we're just two blokes who share the rent. How wrong could she be, though? Still, it's quite funny in a way, isn't it? She reckons we're Men Behaving Badly when it's more like Carry On Camping.

You gotta laugh, though.

I walked to a nearby park and sat down on a bench. I lit my fag with a match and took a long drag. It was so relaxing, smoking; really calmed my nerves. Which was exactly what I needed after a gruelling morning at Brenda's bloody Burgers.

I thought of Andrew as I enjoyed my cigarette. I thought of him almost all the time. He was what got me through the day. No, he was what got me through everything. To be honest, I don't know what I'd have done if it weren't for him. I'd've probably gone insane fucking ages ago.

I was just stubbing my fag out on the arm of the wooden bench when a scruffy looking lad, aged around seventeen, I suppose, came up to me. He had messy hair, spots, and his clothes looked like something from 1991. "Got a spare fag, mate?" he said.

I shook my head. If it's one thing I hate, it's moochers who ask for cigarettes when they don't even know you.

"Sorry, I haven't," I told him.

"Ah, come on, man, you must 'ave."

"I said I haven't."

The bloke looked at me, eyes narrowed to slits. "Fuckin' queer," he sneered after a short pause, and then walked off, hands in his pockets, shoulders slumped forward.

Tosser.

But that was my town, see. Full of homophobic arseholes. I mean, I should know better than anyone about that, shouldn't I? Okay, so we've got Medusa's, but that's just some poky little club on the outskirts. It's quite surprising that there's even a gay club in my town, really.

Lucky there is, though. Wouldn't have met Andrew otherwise, would I?

But even Medusa's, our safe haven, our sanctuary from the (sometimes) terrifying World of the Straight has been subject to queer -bashing attacks.

Apparently (though this was before my time) we even had a bomb scare once. Fortunately that turned out to be a hoax. Unlike that terrible event in London when some psychopathic nutter bombed a gay pub in Soho.

Now Soho, that was the place to be. I'd been thinking about it a lot lately, actually. About me and Andrew moving to London. It would be cool. Real cool.

Hyper cool. Reading all the gay listings, and scene guides about the place, about the so-called 'gay village' there, it really excited me. Because unlike where I was brought up - where the word 'homosexual' is pretty much a dirty word - in London - certain parts of it, anyway; like Soho - being gay is the coolest. There are no stares, no prejudice. Me and Andrew could walk up Old Compton Street with our tongues in each other's mouths and it wouldn't even raise an eyebrow.

Yeah, London was definitely what I wanted.

But it wasn't what Andrew wanted. No, Andrew was settled. Fair enough, we'd only discussed it once, and had decided that it would probably be better if we didn't take the plunge. Not yet, anyway.

Andrew said he didn't want to leave his job. He said he was happy here, that he felt settled, like he belonged. And besides, he'd tried London, had lived there for about six months. That had been three or four years ago, before we'd even known one another existed. He'd lived in Walthamstow, about half an hour from the West End, from Gay Paradise. He'd gone berserk on the scene, apparently; that's what he'd told me. Out every night, taking every drug going, shagging each and every bloke who caught his eye. He said it'd really fucked him up.

That didn't put me off, though: I was still willing to give it a try.

But not on my own. If Andrew wasn't going to be there, what was the point? Soho may have been the Pink Kingdom, but unless Andrew was there with me, it'd be nothing; pointless; worthless.

So I'd stay in our little town, with our little gay club, and our great big fantastic relationship, and that would do me.

I looked at my watch and wondered if I had time for another quick ciggie before heading back to work.

Oh, fuck it, I thought, and proceeded to light another Silk Cut.

Ø

"Took your time," said Fiona, when I returned. I'd been gone twenty minutes. Fiona was smiling, though, so I smiled back.

"Sorry," I said. "Got lost."

"My arse." She chucked my apron at me. "Get back to work, you. And no slacking. You're lucky I don't make you stay and do overtime. Without pay!" She grinned as I put my hideous red and white apron back on. "Oh, by the way. Andrew phoned for you. Asked if you could ring him back A.S.A.P."

"Oh, right. Do you mind, Fi? I promise I'll be quick."

Fiona frowned, then sighed. "All right, all right. Christ, I'm a soft touch, aren't I? No wonder I ain't been promoted to manager yet."

I grinned. "You're the best supervisor going, though."

"Piss off," she smiled. "You've got one minute, Holly. And I mean it."

"Cheers, Fi."

I dashed off to the payphone in the staff room. It was hooked up so you didn't have to use money, though, so I suppose you couldn't really call it a payphone.

I dialled our home number.

"Hello?" came Andrew's smooth and sexy voice, and I went weak at the knees. I know: I'm pathetic. Don't worry, you don't have to tell me.

"Hiya, babes, it's me," I said. There was no one else around, so it was okay to say this.

"Mark," Andrew breathed, and I could just see him smiling. We're the soppiest, most romantic couple going, believe me. You've probably figured that much out by now, though, right?

"How you doing?" Andrew asked. "Fiona working you hard."

"Too hard."

"Good, good. I'm glad she's keeping my boy in shape. Tell her to keep it up."

"Cheeky. But you know she fancies you?"

"No! You're winding me up."

"Seriously. She said she'd love you to have her on all fours."

"And what did you tell her?"

"I told her that you've had me on all fours and that it was nothing special."

"Cheeky sod," Andrew laughed. "You're full of it, Holly."

"I know. Great, isn't it? So anyway, make it quick. She'll be out for my blood if I'm any longer talking to you."

"Okay, okay. I've just had word that I'm not working tonight. So we can have a night in together. Just you and I. Unless...you wanted to go out?"

"Where would we go?"

"Where would you want to go?"

"Dunno. Cinema, maybe?"

"Too impersonal, love. What about a video instead?"

"Or...we could go out to a club maybe?"

"What kind of club? Not Medusa's again."

"You sick of it, too?"

"Not sick exactly," said Andrew. "I just feel like a change. I mean, I work there, every time you and I go out together it's there. I know it's the only gay club around here and everything but..."

"I know, I know," I said, and helplessly the thought of the London gay scene filtered into my head again. What a thrill it would be for us both, out on the scene, a different club every night...away from Medusa's, away from the past, a new life together...

Maybe I should just move away, you know. Start a new life

somewhere else...we could go together...

The words penetrated my brain like an ice pick...like déja vu. Where had that come from?

"Oh, well, what can we do?" he said nonchalantly. "It's all we've got, isn't it?"

Maybe not, Andrew, I thought. Maybe not...

I was silent for a second; longer than I thought. Through the phone, Andrew's voice said, "Mark? Still there?"

I blinked. "Yeah, yeah. Still here. Hey, listen. How does this sound? You get a couple of vids in, and I'll cook us dinner. I'm a chef now, remember?"

"You work in a burger bar, Mark."

"Details, details. Anyway, you're a barman."

"Exactly. We're the perfect team. Okay. You sort out the grub, I'll deal with the drinks."

"And the entertainment."

"And the entertainment," he agreed.

"And then afterwards," I said, smiling craftily into the receiver, "we'll sort out some entertainment of our own, yeah?"

Andrew laughed. I loved his laugh.

"Mark we've got customers," said a female voice behind me, making me jump. I turned and saw Fiona's head poking through the staff room door. I nodded once, quickly, and gave her the thumbs-up.

"Andrew, I gotta go," I said. "I'll see you later, yeah?"

"What time do you finish? Shall I pick you up?"

I smiled into the receiver. "That'd be cool, yeah. About four?"

"Fine. See you then, babes. And don't eye those sexy straight lads up too much, all right?"

"As if. See you later, mate."

"See ya."

"Finally!" exclaimed Fiona as I replaced the handset. "Come on, you. God, I let you get away with murder, don't I, Holly?"

"It's only 'cos you fancy me."

She smiled and shook her head. "Just get out there, will you? Those burgers won't grill themselves."

Andrew picked me up at exactly four; just like he'd said.

He kissed me as I got into the passenger seat. Nothing major, just a peck. But even that was risking too much in our crappy little 'queers are lower than shit' neighbourhood. But when you're in love, you just don't care what other people think, and that's the way it should be.

"You need a shave," I said, rubbing one hand gently against the side of his face.

He smiled. "Aren't I allowed to be a slob sometimes?" he said. "Or have you got the copyright on that?"

"Cheeky fucker!" I laughed, and punched him playfully on the arm.

"So," said Andrew, pulling away in his blue Rav 4 jeep. He used to have a black Mini, but had only just got rid of it to buy his new 'passion wagon'. He'd been saving up for it for donkey's years, and it was his pride and joy. You should bloody see him of a Sunday morning! Up at the arse-crack of dawn, polishing and waxing away. Once, a couple of weeks ago, I'd joked that he loved the jeep more than me, and he'd looked at me as if I'd stabbed him in the heart. That was how much he cared for me.

"So...what?" I prompted.

"You know, how was your day, how are you...that sort of thing?"

"Being sarcastic again, Andrew?" I said, looking at him sideways, cheeky grin on my face.

He shrugged.

"I've had a good day," I said, then added, "Well, as good as can be expected in that place."

He sighed. "You really don't like it there, do you?"

"'S'all right. It's a job, isn't it?"

"A job you hate. Look, why don't you just leave, Mark? I can support us both, you know. I earn good money."

"Andrew, we've been through all this. I wouldn't feel right about you paying for everything. And besides, I want my independence. I'm almost twenty-two, after all."

He didn't say anything for a bit; neither of us did. He turned a roundabout, and then came to a set of traffic lights that were just turning red as we pulled up. Andrew chuckled suddenly, splintering the awkward silence. "Shit, we sound like a bloody married couple, don't we?"

I grinned. "Just a bit."

We didn't say anything more until the traffic lights changed back to green. "Look," I began, as Andrew changed gear, "don't worry about me. I don't mind the job, honestly. All I need is you. And it's not as bad as I make out, really it's not. There're good people there. Fiona's nice."

"Apart from the fact she fancies your boyfriend."

"Yeah," I smiled, "apart from that."

Andrew shook his head, briskly. He did that often: it always reminded me of a bird fluffing its feathers on a cold day.

He said, "Oh, just ignore me, Mark. I'm sorry I started on about the job thing again. It's just...well...oh, fuck I don't need to even say it..."

"No, what?"

"I was..."

"Yeah?"

"...just gonna say you know how much I love you. But I sound like a fucking Valentine's card! Must really get on your tits."

I leaned over and kissed his rough cheek. "Of course it doesn't."

Andrew blushed, and then cleared his throat. He was so sweet when he got all embarrassed.

"So...er...so what are we having for dinner tonight, Delia?"

"Delia! Been overdosing on the old daytime tv again have you?"

"Fuck off!"

I laughed. "Just messing. I don't know what we'll have. I'm sure I can rustle up something, though. Something special."

"What's the occasion?"

"Who says there has to be one?"

Ø

When we finally got home, I saw that Andrew hadn't been just dossing around all day. He'd cleaned the flat from top to bottom. Not that we were slobs or anything. I mean, despite what Andrew had said in the jeep, I was actually pretty tidy, although admittedly he bordered on the anal-retentive side of things, no pun intended.

"I need a shower," I said, dropping the bag that contained my hideous BB's uniform to the floor. "God, talk about Greased Lightning."

"Well, I hope you were careful with my upholstery," said Andrew, mock-sternly, but he was more stern than mock.

"Go on," he said, "you jump in the shower and I'll just pop down and give the jeep a quick polish."

I pulled my white Fila T-shirt over my head. "You and that poxy jeep," I sighed with a grin.

Andrew smiled, approached me. He put his left palm against my heart and kissed me - a proper kiss, this time.

"Mark," he said softly, "you know it's you I'd rather ride. Any day."

"Full of it, Andrew," I grinned. "Absolutely full of it. To the brim."

He swatted me playfully. "Get in the shower before I hit you properly."

"I'm going, I'm going." I turned and walked to the bathroom, already feeling the massive hard-on that I always got when Andrew and I touched like that.

Just as I pushed the bathroom door open, I turned and called out to him, "And if I catch you wanking in the back seat again, there'll be trouble, mate!"

"Up yours, Holly!" came the disembodied reply.

"Yeah, here's hoping!" I said with a smile.

Ø

In the shower, as I touched myself, I thought of Andrew...then I thought of me...then I thought of London. I thought of the two us escaping, of starting afresh, beginning anew.

I'd thought of this loads of times before - as I mentioned earlier – but on this day...I'm not sure. It was stronger than before. The lure of the big city more gripping...more...yeah, intense. That's the word: Intense.

'Course, it wasn't just about the gay scene. Like Andrew'd said, we had Medusa's, and most of the time that was enough. But the thing about Medusa's was that, at the end of the day, it was just a club. Just one little club, one little piece of land in the back of beyond that we got shoved away into. I knew what people thought of that place. The so-called 'normal' people. They thought, 'Yeah, all right, let the dirty queers have their little space. So long as they don't come out with the rest of the us, so long as they don't come out spreading their filth and disease, contaminating us...yeah, they can have their little box, their little luxury cage.'

That's not how it was in London; that's not how you got treated there; no.

And the very idea that Andrew and I would move there...

...is ridiculous, Mark, said my brain. Andrew doesn't want to move. Andrew likes it here. Andrew said so.

Which makes what difference exactly?

I wondered, then, as I soaped myself in the shiny pink cubicle, as I washed away the sweat and toil of my day, if I should maybe discuss the idea with him that night.

We'd talked about it before, sure, the idea of moving up there, but had always decided against it. Only now, I wanted it more than ever.

It was as if – I thought then – as if I was in a rut, that I'd suddenly had a glimpse of my own dreary future, of being stuck in Brenda's

Burgers forever, following orders from Fiona, someone who was two years younger than me.

'Cos maybe in London...I could find a job that I really wanted to do. Perhaps, a job in the music industry.

Ever since my band Lyar split up I'd been after something along those lines: anything. It didn't have to be playing the drums: I'd be a teaboy at a record label or something, the caretaker at some small independent studio...

...in London...

       ...with Andrew...

              ...and the gay scene...

2 Andrew

I was downstairs with the jeep for about twenty-five minutes, just giving it a quick polish. I love the jeep. Mark jokes that I love it more than him, and even though I know he's only messing, it still gets to me, still makes me think that he really does believe that. Of course, he couldn't be further from the truth, but it does make you wonder, doesn't it?

Ah, the paranoia of the truly in love. Sweet, eh?

When I went back upstairs, Mark was just stepping out of the shower. He looked so gorgeous, just in a towel, wet skin, wet hair. I stepped towards him and we kissed...yup, tongues an' all! He was a good kisser, though.

"You smell nice," I said.

"I'm wearing the aftershave you got me for Christmas."

"Why, honey, you're so sweet."

We laughed.

"Hungry?" Mark asked.

I nodded; once. "Getting that way, yeah."

"Hm. That's not quite the response I was looking for."

I looked at the clock on the wall. "It's only just gone five. We don't normally eat till around seven."

"Yeah, but I'm not normally cooking."

"No. You're normally take-away-ing."

"Watch it..." he warned teasingly.

Just then, my mobile phone rang.

"Oh..." Mark groaned. "If that's work wanting you in tonight, tell them to fuck off."

I grinned at him. "Work? On my mobile? Don't be daft; as if I'd give them my number. They always phone the flat, remember?"

I pulled the small Vodafone from the pocket of my jeans and pressed SEND.

"Hi, Andrew speaking."

It was my mate Keiran. "All right, Andy?" he said, cheerful as ever. Keiran was cool. He worked as a medic at Medusa's. We'd been good mates for yonks, ever since I started work there, which was going back a while now. We'd never shagged or anything like that, but still, I was sure there was at least some sort of mutual attraction there. I mean, I certainly fancied him...not that Mark knew, of course! But Keiran...with his gorgeous green eyes and soft Scottish accent...

But sorry; I'm getting distracted.

I said, "Keiran! How's it going, mate?"

"Cool, cool. Not so bad. How're you and Mark?"

"Fine. Great, in fact. He's cooking me dinner tonight, though. So I might have to call you around later. Give me CPR or something, in case he poisons me."

Mark smiled and mouthed the word 'Cheeky' at me. He turned and walked into the bedroom to get dressed.

"So," I said into the phone, "what can I do for you, Keiran?"

"I was just wondering if you'd thought any more about that offer I made you last week," Keiran told me. "I was gonna ask you about it yesterday, but I didn't get to speak to you properly. Too busy. Some bloody pillhead collapsed in the toilets. Code Red, you know?"

"Yeah, course. Erm...to be quite honest, mate, I haven't had the chance to get my head around it. It's quite a big offer, isn't it? And I mean...I'm not sure if I could handle moving to London again. After...well, after last time."

"Andrew, that was ages ago."

I paused for a second, remembering. The endless stream of drugs and sex and sex and drugs...never giving a damn...never knowing when to stop...just doing it again and again...pills, thrills and bellyaches, that was me.

"Yeah, I know it was," I said. "And I know it'd probably be different now...you know, with Mark and all that..."

"Exactly," said Keiran. "Look, Andy, you'd be bloody mad to turn this down. It's a top opportunity."

"I know it is. I know that, Keiran."

"Just think about it, yeah? I can't hang around forever, you know. 'Cos if you don't take this up and someone else does, you'll regret it, mate. You'll regret it bad-style."

I sighed, shut my eyes, a fragment of those old days in Walthamstow stabbing my head for a second. "Yeah, I'll think it over. Maybe I'll talk to Mark about it tonight."

"You do that."

"I will. Promise. I'll call you soon, yeah, Keiran? 'Bye."

"'Bye, mate. Love to Mark."

I pulled the mobile away from my ear and pressed END. I breathed out a shaky sigh and then abruptly, Mark's voice said, "Talk to me about what?"

I jumped slightly and looked up. A smile curled my lips as I looked at him, dressed in black T-shirt and beige combat trousers. He was frowning, with concern. "Babe?" he said.

"Oh, nothing," I told him. "Nothing important. Look, I'll tell you when we eat, yeah? I'm getting pretty hungry, actually. How about I go get us some wine and a video, and you start dinner? Yeah? What sort of wine do you want? Red or white?"

3 Mark

When Andrew left to sort out the wine and video (I told him I wanted to see the new Wes Craven slasher) I bunged on a CD (Catatonia, in case you were wondering) and went into the kitchen to sort out dinner. I wasn't doing us anything fancy: a bit of chicken and some pasta with a mushroom and sweetcorn sauce. It was mostly boil in the bag stuff, dead easy to do.

Still, I wasn't exactly Delia Smith, was I? Despite what Andrew might've thought.

Anyway, as I sorted myself out, I wondered what the hell he and Keiran had been talking about. Maybe I was being paranoid, but it just sounded so dubious.

Maybe I'll talk to Mark about it tonight.

Surely you can't blame me for being a little suspicious, can you?

I knew Keiran quite well; the medic at Medusa's. Andrew had introduced me to him a short time after we'd got it together...Andrew and me that is, not me and Keiran!

Mind you, Keiran's a bit of all right and no bullshitting. Nice eyes, nice voice , body to kill for...

But I digress, sorry.

Anyway, I'm sure it goes without saying that Andrew had no idea I fancied Keiran. Not that I'd ever do anything about it...shit, no! Andrew was my man and there was no changing that; there couldn't be.

But a boy can dream, can't he?

And then, as I slapped the two flabby pieces of white chicken on to the griddle pan, a horrible, sickening, gut-churning thought dropped into my head.

Andrew and Keiran...

...Maybe I'll talk to Mark about it tonight...

They couldn't...

...they wouldn't...

...had they?

"Nah," I said aloud, and give a little laugh in the silent kitchen, as if to convince myself that there was no way Andrew would be unfaithful, not to me.

But then the more I tried to tell myself otherwise, the more I saw Andrew and Keiran in bed together; in bed naked; naked and fucking...

I laughed again, but the laugh was as brittle as ice. In my head, I started to sing that song by Garbage... 'I Think I'm Paranoid.'

But Keiran and Andrew? Keiran and Andrew?

"Oh, fuck off, Mark," I told myself, and with a rueful shake of my head I stuck the chicken on to cook, chuckling dryly at my own immaturity.

Ø

"I couldn't remember which one you wanted," said Andrew as he came through the flat's front door, "so I just got Scream 3 again. And I got a bottle of each wine: red and white. You know, that two-ninety-nine stuff from the offy up the road? I know it's cheap, but it tastes all right, doesn't it? And it does the job."

He came into the kitchen where I stood against the work surface, putting the finishing touches on our meal. I didn't turn around, but just to have him in the room with me made me feel all lovely and warm. I heard the dull clunk as he put his shopping on the floor and then he put his arms around my waist, kissed me on the back of the neck. "Missed you," he whispered in my ear.

"Missed you, too," I said.

Andrew paused. I felt his whole body stiffen, then he drew back from me.

Still, I did not turn.

He said, "What's up?"

"Nothing," I told him and then I did turn around. I looked at him blankly. My body felt weird and hollow.

"Yes there is, Mark," he said. "What is it?" His voice was neither cold nor sharp. Instead, it sounded curiously fractured.

Then I knew I was being dumb. Stupid. Andrew and Keiran, indeed. Andrew and Keiran! I *mean*, Andrew and Keiran!

Ludicrous.

I shook my head, feeling like a wanker. "Nothing's the matter. I just missed you. That's all." It sounded stupid. He'd only been up the road.

Andrew said nothing. He cocked his head, eyes narrowed slightly. Did he believe me? I wondered. Did he?

"Dinner's ready," I said, with a too-bright smile; a smile that oozed with guilt.

Andrew just nodded.

Ø

I'd already set the table and carried the plates through, placing them down as Andrew poured the wine. Red for me, white for him. We sipped thoughtfully, and then started to eat. Neither of us said a word; but we didn't have to. There were never any tense, achy silences between us.

Then nonchalantly, I asked, "What did Keiran want earlier?"

"Just to say hi. He sends his love."

I smiled, in spite of myself. "That's nice."

Andrew smiled, and proceeded to attack his piece of chicken. "Actually," he said; (quite tentatively, I thought. There was something ominous about it, too).

My stomach tightened and I felt a chilly finger press down against the back of my neck. Quite the opposite to the soft brush of Andrew's lips.

"Maybe I'll talk to Mark about it tonight."

In a split-second, no more than the blink of an eye, I imagined what Andrew was going to say:

'You know I love you Mark; you know that...but...shit, this is hard...but, well, you know Keiran? Uh, well, er... he and I have been...'

Shirley Manson, the singer with Garbage, piped up again, from the place in the back of my mind where she'd seemed to have taken residence over the last hour.

"What?" I said, trying to sound disinterested.

"Actually, Mark," said Andrew, almost timidly. "I've got something I need to discuss with you."

4 Andrew

"Oh?" he said. His eyes seemed too large, like glass baubles. He looked almost...afraid, I suppose the most accurate word is. But of what, I couldn't imagine. I was the one who was afraid. Afraid of the past. Afraid of the future.

I smiled. "Don't look so anxious. It's nothing bad."

Mark sighed. He seemed to deflate with relief. I wondered just what it was he'd thought I was going to say.

He put his fork down beside his plate as I scooped up another forkful of pasta and swallowed it. The air felt strange and gluey.

"So what is it?" said Mark. He seemed slightly agitated.

"The thing is," I began. I felt nervous, but I didn't know why. What I had to speak to Mark about was nothing terrible. "The thing is...you know when Keiran was on the phone earlier?"

Mark tensed. Visibly tensed. Now he did look afraid.

He nodded. He looked shaken.

"Well, it was about something he mentioned to me the other night. When we were at Medusa's."

Mark looked down at his plate. He picked his fork up and pushed his chicken limply around for a second.

"Mark?" I said. "What's up?"

"Are you seeing Keiran?" he said abruptly. He looked at me, silently yet accusingly.

I felt like...I felt like he'd punched me in the face. Keiran? Me and Keiran? How had Mark got that idea?

All right, I fancied Keiran, maybe, but Mark didn't know that...and even if he did, didn't he trust me enough?

"Keiran?" I said. "You think...me and Keiran?"

Mark looked vacant. He said nothing.

"I'd ask you if this was a wind-up, babe, but I can see it isn't. You think me and Keiran have been..."

"Well, it sounded like that to me," he said. "What was it about? Earlier? All that, 'I'll talk to Mark about it later.'"

"I was just about to tell you if you'd give me half a chance."

"Tell me what?" Mark looked like he might start crying. God, I couldn't believe what was going on.

"I'm trying to tell you," I said, calmly. I drank some of my wine. I didn't want to be angry with him; truly I didn't. But it was difficult. You must understand it was bloody difficult.

I swallowed. "I've been offered a job," I said, carefully. "In London. It's a good job. A managerial position. In a gay café. That's what I was talking to Keiran about. Keiran was offered the job, but he doesn't want to move to London. He's happy here with Scott. You know, Scott? Keiran's boyfriend."

Mark looked back at his plate. He said, in a very quiet, dusty voice, "I'm sorry."

I couldn't answer him. I was choked. I felt like he'd stabbed me. That he could think that...! About me? That I'd do that to him!

"Look," I said, "I suppose...maybe I'd've thought the same thing. You know?"

Again, Mark said, "I'm sorry, Andrew."

I reached out, put a hand on his arm and squeezed it. "Let's forget it. Please. Let's just forget it."

"But..."

"Forget it."

He nodded.

"This job, though, Mark. It's good money. Much better than I'm on now. And I won't be just a barman."

"How did Keiran swing it?"

"Through a friend of his. He owns this other gay bar up in Camden. He's expanding and wants a new manager for this new place. It's in Soho - Old Compton Street?"

Mark's face changed at this new information. His eyes grew large. This time not with fear, more like with excitement and disbelief. It was not the reaction I had been expecting.

"No!" he said, grinning. "This is so weird!" Already, the memory of his accusation seemed to have evaporated.

Good.

"Weird?" I frowned. "How d'you mean?"

"I mean the idea that we're moving to London!" he cried, practically leaping out of his chair. I felt a little out of breath over the way the mood had altered so dramatically.

But then his words sank into my head and I said, "Wait, wait, Mark. I didn't say I was going to take the job."

"But you must!" He looked like a wounded animal.

"Why? Aren't we happy here? Why ruin it? Especially by going to London."

"What? Why not? What do we have to lose? What do we have to keep us here? I hate my job; I don't exactly get on too well with my family anymore, and you'll have this fantastic new manager's job. Cushy or what?" He sat back in his chair, looking all triumphant.

I shook my head. "It's not that simple, Mark," I told him, but the look on his face made me feel as if I'd just ripped the wings off a butterfly.

"What are you on about?" he said, not angry, just impatient. "Of course it's that simple. We can get out of here and start a fantastic new life. It'll be brilliant, Andrew."

"You don't know what it's like."

"Exactly. I want to see; I want to know. To find out."

I said nothing, just smiled, all watery.

"I was going to talk to you about it tonight," he said. "About London. I've been thinking about it a bit lately."

"I see."

"It sounds great. All those listings and stuff, in Gay Times and Boyz, The Pink Paper. I want it."

"Well, why didn't you say? London isn't that far. On the train."

"It's not enough."

"How do you know? You've never been there. And going up for a night clubbing on the scene isn't the same as living there. It gets inside you. It becomes a way of life. I've done it. Been there. It can screw you up, Mark."

"*Can* screw you up. Maybe it would be different this time. I'd be there with you. We'd be there. Together."

That last word hung there, somehow darkly. Like a harbinger.

I said, "Yes, but..."

"But?"

"Mark, it's weird. I know I should go. I know it's the right thing to do. Keiran told me that. *You're* telling me that. But I just think it might ruin things. It might ruin us."

"How?"

I couldn't answer.

Mark said, "You know, some bloke called me 'queer' today."

"Who?"

He shrugged. "No one. Just some twat scrounging a fag. When I told him I had none, he called me a fucking queer. I mean, he didn't even know I was gay. Probably thought I was as straight as he was. But it got to me, Andrew. It made me think."

"About what?"

"London. About getting away from shit like that."

I laughed, incredulous. "So you don't think you get stuff like that in London? You think homophobia ends here? That London's some idyllic, poof's paradise?"

"It's an improvement, I know that. Shit, Andrew! I can't believe you're even having second thoughts about this thing. A job in Old Compton Street! And not just any old job! A manager's position! Bloody hell, you must have rocks in your head to even consider turning it down. I mean, Old Compton Street! Talk about the gay Mecca!"

"Yeah. The place that got bombed because some mental cunt didn't like gays. Remember?"

"That was a one-off."

"Maybe."

"Why do you have to be so pessimistic, Andrew?

I shook my head. "I'm not being pessimistic. Just realistic."

"This could be the making of us, Andrew."

His words hurt me; cut me to the quick. "What do you mean?"

"London would be brilliant," he said, more to himself than to me. But he hadn't answered my question.

"Mark...I don't know. I did London. And it was good for a bit. But it can be destructive. Really destructive."

I felt as if my argument was getting thinner by the second. What Mark said - Mark and Keiran - made a lot of sense. But I was afraid. So afraid.

"I mean, what about this place?" I said to him, gesturing with my hands.

"Sell it. Move on. Together." Mark's eyes were warm. He reached over, touched my hand. "Andrew?" he said.

I was still and silent. Looked at my plate. Looked at the clock on the wall. Thought of Keiran. Thought of London.

Thought of love.

"I'll give it some more thought," I told Mark, giving him the best I could at this point. But I could tell he was still disappointed.

5 Mark

We didn't speak any more about London that night. After finishing the meal, Andrew washed up and then we watched the video. He put his arm around me and I rested my head on his shoulder. It wasn't long before I fell asleep, and the next thing I knew we were both in bed together.

We didn't have sex that night. The first Saturday night in a long time that we hadn't made love.

When I woke up, Andrew had left for work. Medusa's opened at about mid-day on Sunday, operating only as a bar, not a club. I knew Andrew hated having to work on Sundays. Usually he didn't, but I supposed that was just his penalty for taking the previous night off, the busiest night of the week.

The flat felt weird when I got out of bed. Too quiet almost. Too tidy. Everything just right.

So why did something feel wrong?

I went and had a shower, thought of last night. There hadn't really been that much tension. We'd spoken after the meal, just general stuff. Not London, though. Not the new job.

I couldn't figure it out. I mean, okay, Andrew might have had some bad memories, but things would be so different now; things would be so good...

I'll think about it, Mark, he'd said.

But would he?

The phone rang when I got out of the shower. It was Grace, my old girlfriend. That had been before I'd known Andrew, of course.

"Grace!" I cried, beaming into the receiver. She was wicked. And the great thing was, we were still brilliant friends after everything that happened all that time ago. S'pose you could say she was my 'faghag'.

"Hiya, darling," she said. "How's it going?"

"Fine," I told her. "Fine. What about you? How's the baby?"

She chuckled. "So far so good. Still a few more months to go yet. Keeps me up at night already, though. Kicking away. I think it's going to be a boy. A footballer probably."

"Or a kickboxer."

We laughed.

"Andrew okay?" said Grace.

"Yeah. He's working, though. And he hates working Sundays. He'll probably be like a bear with a sore head when he gets back round here."

"Ahhh," crooned Grace, sarcastically.

"How's Jason?"

"Panicking."

"Eh?"

Grace chuckled, all tinkly, like a music box. "About the baby. He's like an old woman. Worse than me! Worse than you, even!"

"Hey!"

"Men!" she sighed, and I could just visualise her rolling her eyes. "What are you like, eh?"

"Yes, but I'm gay, my dear. It's not quite the same thing."

"Whatever. Anyway, listen, the reason I'm calling is to see if you fancied going to grab a spot of lunch with me. I'm at a bit of a loose end here and I'm going bloody mad stuck in this flat."

"Cabin fever, eh?"

"Exactly. So anyway, d'you fancy it? And no, before you ask I wasn't thinking of Brenda's Burgers."

I grinned. "Where then?"

"It's a nice day. What if I sorted out some sandwiches and stuff and we go on a picnic in the park? I could do with a breath of fresh air."

I smiled into the receiver. "Sure, why not?" It was a good idea. I didn't like the idea of being at home alone any more than Grace did. And it would be good to talk over the London thing with a third party.

"Brilliant. Do you want to meet me there then, Mark? Give me...say, an hour and a half. Just to sort a few things out."

"Great. I've got some wine left over, actually. I'll bring that down."

"Woah, not for me, love. Wine's no good for the baby."

"That's all right. More for me."

"Cheeky. Look, I'll see you in a bit."

"Right. 'Bye, Grace."

Ø

"And he doesn't want to go?" she said.

"No. I've tried talking to him about it before, but that was then, you know? That was before this job had come along."

"But you didn't know about the job until yesterday, did you?"

I shook my head and took another bite out of my Scotch egg. It had turned out to be a really nice day. The sun was out, the birds were singing...well, you get the picture. The park was pretty busy, too: kids out playing, families on picnics, moochers scrounging cigarettes.

Grace looked lovely. She'd mellowed a bit over the past few months. She'd had her hair cut pretty short and had stopped wearing tight clubby kind of clothes. Maybe it was being married that had done it, or maybe being pregnant. Maybe both.

She shook her head and patted her slightly bulging belly. She did that a lot. It was a subconscious thing, she told me. "To be quite honest, I really can't see why he doesn't want to go. Like Keiran told him, it's a really good opportunity."

I rolled my eyes, remembering last night's accusation. "Oh yeah,"

I said quietly, guiltily. "Keiran."

Grace put a hand on my knee. "I wouldn't stress about that bit, Mark. Anyone would've thought what you did. Although to tell you the truth, it was Andrew we're talking about..."

"No need to rub it in."

"Sorry, but...you know."

I nodded.

"Anyway, that's not important. London is. And he didn't write it off totally, did he?"

"Just as good as."

"Mark, just talk to him some more about it. Talk him round. It sounds like he's half-way convinced."

"You reckon?"

"From what you've told me, yeah."

"But what about all that stuff he said, about the gay scene being destructive?"

Grace exhaled a thoughtful sigh. She sipped some of her orange juice. "Yeah, that sounds a bit negative. I didn't even know he'd lived in London, to be honest."

"I just think it'd be different with me there. And I'm sure Andrew's moved on quite a bit since then. He's older now. Wiser. And aren't you supposed to learn from mistakes?"

"So they say."

"Yeah." I nodded glumly.

"Don't be so down about it, Mark. You haven't really talked about it properly. Not in the light of this new job. Look...what if I spoke to him?"

I considered this for a moment, but then said, "No. I'd better do it. If I could just get through to him how much I want this. How good it would be for us."

"Don't force him into it, though."

"I don't think I could force Andrew to do anything he didn't want to do."

"Hm, I don't know about that," mused Grace. "He's so in love with you I think he'd go and live in Hell if you asked him to."

"Yeah, well the way he was talking about London last night I don't think *that* description's too far off."

Grace chuckled. "You are such a drama queen sometimes, Mark Holly."

I just grinned.

"Yeah, well it goes with the territory."

"What territory?"

"You know, being queer?"

"Ah, the nature of the beast."

"Exactly."

Grace asked, "How's everything else going, though? Apart from you and Andrew?"

I shrugged and finished the Scotch egg, poured myself a glass of red wine into a plastic cup. "Pretty shit. I hate my job."

"Another reason for escaping this place, eh?"

"One of many."

"Oh, thanks a lot!"

"You know what I mean."

"What about...family life?"

"Not so bad."

I shrugged and took out my cigarettes.

"Oh, Mark...would you mind if you didn't?" Grace asked awkwardly. "It's just...you know...the baby?"

"Oh, Christ, yeah. Sorry, Grace." I put the fags away and sighed, wearily. "Yeah, things are all right, I suppose. I haven't seen Mum for a while. I speak to her on the phone a lot, though. I don't like going round there too much. You know...what with Dad and everything."

"Is he still a bit funny with you?"

"He doesn't mean to be. It's difficult for him. I think he blames me for Nick being in prison."

"Well, that's hardly your fault."

"Maybe not."

"It isn't! Of course it isn't."

"Yeah, I know," I agreed eventually. "But it's a shame he has to be like that. It's getting better, though. Who knows? Give it a couple of decades, we could be mates again."

Grace didn't laugh. She put a hand on my leg again. "Don't say things like that, Mark."

There was a moment of silence. The shrill ring of Grace's mobile phone shattered it. She pulled it out of her handbag and said into it, "Hiya!"

A pause, and then she laughed. "Jay, I'm fine. You're such a fusspot! Huh?...Of course it went to the answerphone...No, at the park...What?...Mark...What do you mean, Mark who?...Holly...Yeah, he's fine...All right...Hang on a second." Grace took the phone away from her ear and covered the mouth piece. "It's Jason. He wants a quick word."

I smiled and took the phone. "All right, mate?"

"Not so bad. Working like a dog, but apart from that, fine."

"Got a sprog on the way, though, haven't you?"

"And don't I know it! Hey, listen, I had a look at those lyrics you wrote the other day. Not bad, mate."

"You think?"

"Definitely. Look, when are we going to get together to work on some melodies and stuff? We've really got to get on with the music."

"Easy to say, mate. But things are different now. We're both working."

He sighed. "I know. Slaves to money or what?"

"That's life."

Grace piped up: "You sound like a couple of bitter old men!"

"What was that?" said Jason through the telephone.

"She said we sound like a couple of old gits."

"Bloody cheek!"

"But she's right."

"Hey, whose side are you on?"

"Sorry. Yeah, you're right. We should get together soon. It's just I'm so knackered all the time. What with work and Andrew and stuff."

"Yeah, know what you mean."

"Just you wait till the baby comes along. All those sleepless nights, dirty nappies..."

"Oh, thanks for cheering me up."

I laughed. "Any time. Listen mate, I better go. I'll see you soon yeah?"

"Yeah, and don't make it too long. See ya."

I handed the phone back to Grace.

"Hiya, hon," she said. "Yeah...Of course I'm being careful...Yes, of course he is...What time?...Oh, cool...Oh, would you?...Yeah...That really hot Birriani...Can you tell them to make it extra hot?...Hey, I'm pregnant, aren't I? It's a craving...Cheek!...All right...I'll see you later, darlin'...Love you."

She switched the phone off. "Bless 'im."

"He's nuts about you, Grace," I said. "Totally head over heels."

"Sweet, isn't it? We're almost as soppy as you and Andrew. And that's saying a lot."

"Watch it..." I warned, but I was only joking.

We sat in silence for a bit, just watching the world go by. Then Grace said, "You've gone very quiet."

"Just thinking."

"A penny for 'em."

I smiled, slowly. "What do you reckon?"

"London?"

I nodded, and my smile expanded. "It'd be so cool." I said this more to myself than to Grace.

"Why do you want to go there so much, Mark? What's got you so convinced that London's the answer?"

"I'm not really looking for an answer to anything, Grace. It's hard to describe. Andrew knows what I mean."

"Well, obviously he doesn't."

"I just don't know why he's so bloody reluctant. I didn't realise he was so pig-headed."

"I don't think it's as simple as pig-headedness."

"Maybe, maybe not."

"Talk to him some more about it, Mark," urged Grace. "Tonight. Make him give you a definite decision. If he wants this job, he'll have to come up with an answer pretty bloody soon, won't he? How long has he got?"

"Keiran needs to know this week."

"There you are then. Talk about it tonight. Really talk. You didn't do that last night, did you? Not really talk."

I knew she was right.

She touched my hand. "It'll be fine. Andrew will see sense. If you really want this, you'll make him see sense."

"I don't want to make him do anything. I want him to go because he wants to go. It would be pointless otherwise."

"You know what I mean, though. You have to make him realise how good it would be, London and all. A relationship is give and take you know. There has to be compromise on both sides."

"Yeah, I know, Grace," I said, but I don't think I did really.

Ø

Andrew got home at seven. I'd made a bit of an effort for him, putting on a clean shirt. It was one my sister had given me for Christmas, blue silk; very nice. There were no lights on in the flat; I'd drawn the curtains and had lit candles all over the place. A Madonna ballad was playing softly on the stereo.

Andrew looked bewildered. But pleased.

"What's all this in aid of?" he said, but I thought, as if he doesn't know.

"I made us dinner again," I told him.

"Again? What have I done to deserve this?"

I shrugged. "Can't a boy make a fuss of his man every once in a while."

Andrew laughed. "You get worse, Mark. Have I got time for a quick shower before we eat? I'm a bit sweaty."

I nodded. "Don't be long."

He kissed me. "Quick as I can."

Ø

'Quick as I can' turned out to be about fifteen minutes. I helped myself to a cold beer from the fridge while I waited, listening to the water run and the sounds of Andrew's out of tune singing.

Absurdly, I felt nervous. Or maybe it wasn't so absurd. Maybe I had every right to be nervous...

Rambling on again, aren't I?

Andrew returned from the shower, fully dressed, looking gorgeous.

"Wanna go through for dinner?" I said.

"'Course. I'm starving actually. Didn't get a chance to eat anything at work. Must have had every homosexual in town in there today." He chuckled. Then as he saw the dinner table, his eyes bulged. "Shit...you've gone to a bit of trouble, haven't you?"

"Only the best for you," I said. I'd put out one of those silver platters on the table. You know, the ones with the huge shiny dome over the top.

"I don't know what to say, Mark."

"How about...let's eat?"

"Sounds good to me."

We sat down, opposite each other. "Ready for this?" I said, one hand resting on the handle of the platter's lid. The silver ring on my thumb sparkled in the candlelight, like a warning.

I lifted the lid, to reveal the still-packaged Brenda's Burgers fast food beneath.

Andrew practically collapsed into hysterics. "Fast food?" said Andrew. "How very you!"

"It's a statement," I said earnestly. I picked up one of the pre-packed hamburgers and handed it across to Andrew. He smiled at me, and the smile was full of love.

I knew then. Knew that Grace was right; I was right; Keiran was right.

This opportunity was here, and we had to take it. It was as if it had come out of nowhere, giving us a chance to begin again. That sounds melodramatic, doesn't it?

But you know what I say? Fuck it.

"Mind you," said Andrew, tucking in, "I know you say you hate your job, but the food ain't half-bad."

"Glad you think so."

He grinned.

When he'd eaten half of his burger, he said, "So what's this statement of yours?"

Slowly, I unwrapped some food for myself. I didn't answer him right away and this made the air curdle with tension. "I suppose that what I'm trying to say is that just because things aren't always great, just because we have to work in shitty jobs, or have family problems and stuff...it doesn't mean that things can't be brilliant between us."

Andrew furrowed his brow. He looked sweet and confused. "I'm not sure I get what you mean," he said.

"London," I told him, and his face altered almost at once. He looked older.

"Ah," he said, simply. The word stuck in the air.

"What?"

"I wondered if you'd an ulterior motive for all this." Loosely, he gestured to the table and the candles.

"That sounds a bit sinister," I said. "I'd hardly call it an ulterior motive."

"What would you call it then?"

Was he angry with me. I wondered, feeling slightly stung.

There was silence for a bit. The Madonna CD had finished. Neither of us looked at one another, and in the unusually uncomfortable space between speech, I spun over in my mind the words Grace had said to me earlier that day.

Talk to him about it tonight, Mark. Make him give you a decision. Really talk to him. You didn't do that last night, did you?

"You seem a bit pissed off with me," I said softly, wondering if this was all a big joke, wondering if I should forget about this crazy bullshit idea of moving to London and starting a new life.

What was wrong with me, anyway? Didn't Andrew and I have everything we needed at home? Weren't we happy together? Why throw all that away for a few bright lights and a couple of different clubs?

After all, maybe once you'd seen one gay nightclub, you'd surely seen them all, right? Didn't that make sense?

Fuckin' queer.

The words of that loser in the park yesterday.

Fuckin' queer. That's what I was at home. That's what I was to my dad and my brother and pretty much everyone else around where I lived.

A fuckin' queer.

Andrew said, "I'm not pissed off with you, Mark."

"Aren't you?"

He looked away momentarily. Absurdly, I said, "There's a beer in the fridge if you fancy it."

"That'll be nice."

I got up, fixed it for him, and as I handed it to him, I lightly brushed a stray lock of hair from his eyes. "Don't be angry with me, babe," I said.

"Mark." Andrew looked into my eyes. Deep, deep into my eyes. I felt like I was drowning. It was such an odd sensation.

"Mm?" I said, somehow feeling nervous.

Andrew blinked and drank some beer. He said, "I spoke to Keiran today."

I nodded. "And?"

He reached out and took my hand; squeezed.

He said, "And...and I told him I'd take the job in London. It's mine."

6 Andrew

I didn't get the reaction I'd been expecting, which seemed to be becoming somewhat of a regular occurrence with Mark.

Mind you, what was the reaction I'd been expecting? I'm not sure I knew. Perhaps for him to throw his arms around me; maybe even shed a tear; tell me how happy he was; that we wouldn't regret it for a second; that everything was going to be just fine from now on; London would be our saving grace.

But instead, he wet his lips and said, "I don't know what to say."

Only he didn't say it in an elated way; he was much more subdued. Like it had been an unpleasant surprise.

"Aren't you pleased?" I asked, getting to my feet. It seemed a stupid question to ask, considering how enthusiastic he'd been about it earlier, and last night. Almost like a rhetorical question: it didn't require an answer because I'd assumed it was a given that he'd be pleased.

I put one hand on his arm and traced the fingers of my other hand lightly down the side of his face. For one second I thought he might cry. But I was so thrown at that point I didn't know whether the tears would be a product of joy or sadness. "Mark?" I said. "What's wrong?"

"Nothing," he replied.

"Then why aren't you jumping around and shouting it out from the rooftops? Didn't you hear what I said? I've accepted the job. I want to move to London." Here I stopped, smiled. "With you. Like you wanted. Like you asked."

"But is it what *you* want?" he said boldly.

"Of course it is." I kissed him softly on the lips.

He laughed. "Andrew, you were so against the idea. Why did you suddenly change your mind? I thought you were dead set against it."

"I was."

"Then why the whole change of heart?"

"Does it matter? Isn't it enough that I've decided to go? That I've decided not to be a stupid twat all my life and realise that this is a great opportunity I'd be throwing away?"

He smiled. "You've never been a twat."

"Ohhh, haven't I?"

Mark shook his head and kissed me. Then his whole face changed so drastically it was like something unreal. "Yeeeaaaahh!" he cried and hugged me. "We're going to London, Andrew!" he shouted. "Shit! Oh, this is gonna be fucking excellent! And scary! But more excellent than scary, I know it!"

Now there was the reaction I had been expecting. Still, it was a bit freaky. Like he'd just come out of a coma or something.

"You and me," I said, and touched the end of his nose lightly with my index finger.

Mark, gurning away, asked, "But really, why did you change your mind so suddenly? It must have had something more to do with the job. That didn't seem to be too much of an issue before. You said it was all to do with the crap that you went through when you lived in Walthamstow."

"It was to do with you, Mark. To do with everything that happened all that time ago, when you were coming out."

Mark looked dead confused at this. "Eh?" he said.

"When you were coming out. Remember how hard it was? And all those times you denied it? Because of what other people thought about gays?"

He nodded, slowly, methodically. "You were the same though,

Andrew," he said. "When *you* were coming out. You've told me that."

I nodded. "Yeah, but I actually saw what you were going through. I remember how horrible it was to actually watch someone else wrestling with gay feelings. I suppose it's different when you're battling with it internally. It was for me, anyway. But watching you, the times when you'd run away from my flat, run away from yourself, your own emotions...it was heartbreaking. And all along I knew that if you'd just open that door inside you, how much happier you'd be."

Mark still looked none the wiser as to what I was getting at.

He shook his head slightly and said, "I don't..."

"Look," I interrupted, "basically I'm agreeing with what you said last night. Life's too short, I know. Yes, another cliché, all right, but it's true."

"Most clichés are," he said thoughtfully.

"Yes. And I know I'm not exactly London's biggest fan, but this time...well look at all that's changed. I'm older. Wiser, maybe. I'll have a decent job. And of course I'll have - "

" - me," Mark finished. "Of course you'll have me."

We kissed then. Seemed like forever, too.

"What about the flat?" he said, once we'd parted. We kept our arms around each other's waists.

I shrugged. "Sell it. Move on. We've got a place to live in London, anyway. In Camberwell. Only temporary, mind, but it's somewhere to sleep."

"You sure you want to sell this place? You could rent it out."

"No point. If we're going to do this, we might as well do it properly. Make a clean break and all the rest of it."

Mark smiled into my eyes. There were no words for a moment; none were needed just then. Right at that second, all there was in my world was this boy, and his soft skin, his dark hair and his warm eyes, and his open lips.

I love him, I thought.

7 Mark

Things happened pretty quickly after that. There was so much to do and I supposed it seemed a bit like there wasn't enough time to do it in. Well, there wasn't, really.

Andrew put the flat on the market two days after we'd had that conversation, after what was probably the biggest decision of our lives had been made. The weird thing was that even before we'd got to London, it felt as if something massive had changed in our relationship. It was almost as though we were married now; as if we'd exchanged vows without even knowing it.

Something had been cemented between us.

It was a nice feeling.

The flat was snapped up pretty sharpish, by a young couple who were expecting a baby. They reminded me of Grace and Jason. Andrew and I were both in when the estate agent arrived to show them around, and I'm sure they could tell we were a gay couple. Well, the one bedroom was a definite give-away, wasn't it? Not to mention the fact that Andrew (much to his embarrassment and my amusement) had left some lube and a packet of condoms on his bedside cabinet.

I binned my job at Brenda's the day after we'd decided to take the plunge. Was I sorry? Yeah, right. Fiona was sweet, though. "I'll miss you," she'd said, and she'd hugged me. And then she'd done something that had shocked me, but in a good way. Whispering in my ear, she'd told me, "Oh, and Mark – you and Andrew – I hope you'll be very happy together. You deserve to be."

I'd just gawped at her, not saying anything, but the look in my eyes asking her, you knew all along?

She'd laughed. "I might not have been promoted to manager yet, mate," she'd said ruefully, "but I'm not stupid enough to miss the bleedin' obvious."

That had been a little weird. Brilliant...but a little weird. But then it always was when something like that happened in my town. Homophobia had always been drilled into my head as a norm; it's just something I expected from everyone, you know? So when you come across something like that, with Fiona, it sort of takes you aback.

A week before Andrew and I left, I went round to tell my mum what was happening. I should've done it sooner, I know. This was a huge step, moving to London. Not quite as big as coming out as gay, sure, but still pretty colossal all the same.

I went round at mid-day, 'cos I reckoned Dad wouldn't be in. It sounds horrible, doesn't it, and you could be forgiven that I'd never gotten on with my dad. The sad, almost tragic thing, was that we once had, we'd once been best of mates.

But that was before he'd found out his youngest was queer. He'd almost died when he'd found out. Literally.

I won't get maudlin, though. I've done all that, and the past can't ever be changed so why stress over what might've been?

Yes, more clichés, you lucky, lucky people.

Just as I'd reckoned, Dad was out: his van had gone from its usual station outside our little terraced house. Good.

I hated thinking like that: Good, Dad's out. But what I had to tell Mum was good news, and even though me and the old man had started to build some bridges, the tension that I felt when we were both in the same room could sometimes be unbearable.

I went into the house. It always felt distant to me now. Like visiting a relative I didn't see very often. It was different if Mum came round to see me and Andrew, or if I met her for lunch or something. It was just strange in the house. The house where Mark Holly - the straight version, that is - had been raised.

Though it's an unpleasant thing to say, this was not where the gay reincarnation belonged. And perhaps never would.

"Mum?" I said. She was in the kitchen, pottering. It was what she was best at, pottering.

She turned, smiled. She looked older than she had before it all happened. Years older. And sometimes I'd think sadly, Look what I've done to her. It's all my fault.

Even though it wasn't. It wasn't my fault. It's no one's fault if you're gay. It's just the way it is.

"Hello, love," said Mum, tired eyes sparkling. She was totally grey-haired. Not one shade of black left. She used to dye it, but had stopped now. "Not much point anymore," she'd said. "Who's looking at me these days, anyway?"

I hugged her. She felt so frail in my arms. "Hi, Mum."

"How are you? How's Andrew? I haven't seen you both for a while. Is my cooking that bad?" She laughed at the small joke, but I felt faintly sickened with myself. Why hadn't I been to see her?

I knew the answer, of course I knew the answer. But it didn't seem good enough an explanation.

"I know, I'm sorry. It's just...we've been very busy."

She smiled, a little ironically, I thought. "Too busy for your old ma?"

I felt uncomfortable. "Mum...you know, it's awkward. I mean, Dad?"

The word hovered.

Mum nodded. She said, "He's better now, love. He's coping. It hasn't been easy."

And you think it's easy for me? I'd wanted to shout. Is that what you think, Mum? Well you'd better think again.

But I held my tongue. It was my inner child again. That's what

Andrew always said about me. Whenever I got really angry like that, about everything that had happened, about the homophobic attitudes in our town, he said it was my inner child acting up.

"Your inner child's pissed off, Mark," he'd tell me. "Even when you're not, that little inner child's in there ranting and raving."

But Andrew was full of shit sometimes.

"I know, Mum."

She smiled, sorrowfully. "D'you want a cup of tea, love?" she asked.

"That'll be nice," I said. The discussion was closed. We both knew the situation, both knew that my coming-out had changed things forever, and that there could be no quick fix.

"So," said Mum as we sat at the kitchen table. I lit a cigarette. "Any news, love?"

I smiled at her. I felt bubbles of excitement start to rise up through my body. My hair tingled.

"Yep," I said. "Some pretty big news, actually. Some pretty good news, too."

London, I thought helplessly, and a split-second movie of my and Andrew's new life together played through my mind.

Oh, how good it was going to be!

"Oh?" said Mum. "Sounds interesting. What?"

I took a deep breath. "I'm moving," I said. "We - that is, Andrew and I - are moving to London."

There was a silence. A silence that was neither good nor bad, but just simply there.

"London?" said Mum, and she smiled, an odd, quirky smile. Her thin, wispy eyebrows lifted like punctuation marks. "Quite a big step. When was this decided?"

"Last week," I said.

"Last week?"

"Andrew's been offered a job. A really good job. He'll be a manager in a café in the West End. And not just a grotty old greasy spoon, either,

Mum, it's one of those dead posh ones. Continental and all that."

Mum looked impressed, her smile widening and her eyes all glittery. It made me feel so warm. That's what I wanted from her: not for her to judge, not for her to preach. Just for her to be happy for me. Was that too much to ask?

Evidently not.

"That's wonderful, love," she said. "London, eh? When are you set to go?"

"Next week."

"Next week!" she exclaimed. "Mark, why so soon?"

"Like I said, it's Andrew's new job. He has to start quite early. But we've got somewhere to stay. Only temporary, but he's selling his flat so we'll have a bit of money behind us. Oh, Mum it's going to be so good. It's going to be so different to what it's like around here for us."

Mum looked at me. She seemed to understand then to understand everything...what it was like to be gay and live in a place that was about eighty-per cent homophobic. "To be honest, I'm surprised it's taken you this long to decide to move away from here. You must have bad memories."

I nodded.

"And I've heard about London, what it's like for...for your sort of people, boys like you."

I felt startled. It was like I'd opened up another part of her personality. For just one split second, the frail housewife whose knowledge of the modern world was limited at best, was gone.

She knew. She understood.

It was bewildering, it really was.

"You will be careful there, though, won't you, Mark?" she said.

"Careful?" I asked, brow furrowed.

She nodded and sipped her tea. Her eyes were tinged with concern when she looked at me. "Yes. London's not the safest of places is it? Drugs and murders and...well, look at that bomb that went off the other year. That was in a gay pub, wasn't it?"

I nodded. "Yes. But I can't live my life like that, can I, Mum? Not doing anything in case there's a danger. You might as well live in a plastic bubble if you have that attitude. And me more than anyone should know about that. Right?"

"Just be careful, that's all I'm saying, love. Just be careful."

"I will. You know I will. Besides," I added grinning slightly and lifting the mood, "Andrew will look after me."

Now Mum's smile surfaced again. "I know he will. You're lucky to have him, Mark. You know that, don't you?"

"'Course I do."

Mum said, "What about Dad? What will you tell him? You'll have to see him, you know. Explain. He'll be hurt if you don't."

I snorted ruefully. "Doubt it. Probably glad to see the back of me."

"Mark...that's not fair."

I raised my eyebrows, as if to say, Isn't it? But I kept my mouth shut.

"We went to see Nick last week," Mum told me, out of the blue.

Nick. My brother. Currently in prison for trying to beat his little brother to death. His little queer, fucking faggot bumboy brother.

In other words, me.

The mention of my brother's name pierced me. My eyes ceased to blink; they narrowed. My heart thudded.

I'd tried not to hate Nick.

Tried.

But it was difficult. It was fucking difficult. What other emotion was there that I could feel for him other than raw hatred?

And you? You still queer, eh? Still a fucking bum bandit? You must be adopted, you sick bastard. You must be fucking -

"He asked about you," Mum said. Her voice sounded low and urgent.

I drew a sharp breath. "Did he," I said. It was not a question, because I didn't care. Nick could stay in that prison until he rotted as far as I was concerned. After what he did to me. The name-calling; the violence; the pain. A year ago, he'd been sent down. The judge had called him depraved.

"He's getting counselling," Mum told me. "Seeing a psychologist. And..." She paused. There was pain in her eyes. What must it have been like for her? I wondered then. Watching the destruction of her family, the relationship between her two sons corroding so quickly and so violently?

It's not my fault, I told myself again.

"And?" I prompted, suddenly feeling an intense desire to get up and run from that house.

My childhood home.

But all it was to me now was a purgatory of bad memories.

"He wants to see you, Mark."

The words burned into my mind, like acid. Nick? Wants to see me? Why? So he can hurl more abuse at me? Call me unnatural, sick, twisted, a pervert, because I happen to have a different idea of what's sexually attractive to most blokes?

"See me?" I said. My voice was level, like the sea at low tide. But God knows how I managed it. Rage, like molten lava, began to fill me. Andrew always said that I should try not to be angry at my brother. But not for Nick's sake, oh no, for mine.

He said, "It'll eat away at you, Mark. It'll destroy you from the inside. You don't want that, do you? You don't want to let your brother destroy you from the inside by making you hate so much."

Bollocks. Andrew hated Nick, too. Hated him probably more than I did.

Mum nodded. "Yes. He wants to apologise, Mark. He wants to say he's sorry."

"Sorry!" I exclaimed. "After what he did! Sorry?"

"He's different now," said Mum. "He really wants to make it up to you."

I looked at her. "I can't, Mum. I really can't think about Nick right now. There's too much happening. Me and Andrew...the move...Nick's the last thing I want to deal with right now."

"Just think about it," said Mum. "Please, Mark."

I nodded. But I knew I couldn't go and see Nick. It would take a long, long time before that would be possible.

If it ever would be.

Ø

Andrew was home. Packing. "I put all the videos and CDs in separately," he told me. "But I wasn't sure about your clothes so I left them for you. And there was a load of dirty stuff, too. On the bedroom floor. I bunged it in the wash for you."

"Thanks," I said, half-heartedly.

Andrew looked at me. "What's wrong?" His blue eyes were full of concern.

"I've just been round Mum's."

"Did you tell her about the move?"

I nodded.

"What did she say?"

"She's pleased for us. Thrilled. But she said something that's got me a bit...shaken up."

The concern in Andrew's eyes intensified. He stood up and put a hand on mine. "What? What did she say?"

"Nick wants to see me. To apologise."

"Nick?"

"That's right. Remember Nick?"

"How could I fucking forget? And he wants to see you?"

"To apologise," I repeated. "About everything."

"Well I hope you refused."

"'Course I did."

"Good. Good."

I smiled at Andrew, but the smile was watery. "It's brought back a lot of bad memories, though."

"But that's what we're leaving behind, Mark. Look...do you want to go and see Nick? Before we leave."

"No! Goodness, no! He doesn't want to see me, anyway, not really, not to apologise like Mum said. That's just a put-on for her. He always did know how to wrap her around his little finger. Nah, he probably just wants to make himself look good. Something about his parole, I reckon."

"Forget about it."

"I will," I said, but in my heart I knew it wasn't going to be easy.

"I had a little parental confrontation of my own today," said Andrew. I looked at him wide-eyed. "I called my Mum," he continued.

"You went through with it?" I asked, stunned, pleased and curious all at once. "I didn't think you were going to."

"Neither did I," he said. "I really didn't think I'd be able to. But I decided you were right, that I should at least let her know what I was up to. If not for her sake, then mine."

I grinned, and hugged him. "And what did she say?"

Andrew took a deep breath. And began to tell me.

8 Andrew

Calling my own mother.

Doesn't sound so shocking, that, does it? I mean, what's a phone call to your mum? Not much, right? No big deal.

Hi, Mum, how are you? Oh, right. How's Dad? That's good. Been up to anything interesting lately? Oh, really? How is she? Me, oh I'm fine. Yeah, work's going well, Mark's great. Yeah, you too. Nice talking to you, Mum. I love you. 'Bye.

Nothing to get worked up about, right?

Wrong. This is my mother we're talking about here. The original toxic bitch from hell.

She'd disowned me when she found out I was gay. Wrote me off. Shed me, like a snake getting rid of its dead skin. Her only child.

"Look, Andrew, I can't pretend I accept this," she'd told me, all those years ago. Only four years, mind, but it seemed like centuries etched in stone. A lifetime since I'd felt I really had a mother.

That had been Mum at her most reasonable, too, telling me she couldn't pretend she liked the idea of having a poof for a son. There'd been worse things she'd said to me. Oh yes. Far worse.

A queer, Andrew! You're a bloody queer! I didn't raise you like that, to be a queer! God, I've failed. I've failed as a mother!

My father still didn't know. She'd never told him, was certain that he'd be unable to handle it.

And the sad thing was, I knew that she was right. There was no denying it.

So Mum came up with an idea.

When my gran died - the woman I adored - she left her flat to Mum. Mum had planned to rent it out, make a few extra quid from it. But after she found out about everything, she signed the flat over to me. Shipped me off, basically.

I'd hated the idea of that. Hated being moved away, hidden like some terrible family scandal that needed to be closed off in a cell. So I'd refused, and then Mum had said I'd disgraced the family name, which was the last straw. I wanted to go then. To get away from that hateful cow and her narrow-minded, bigoted worldview.

That was how come I'd moved to London. Like Mark, I'd read all about the gay scene there, the myriad clubs and pubs, full of guys like me. How heavenly it sounded, all that freedom. It doesn't sound much, but when you've been living a lie for years, no-one knowing who or what you are, and listening to your mother saying that queers should be shot, it was just so liberating to feel safe, to be someone and be part of something.

Of course, that was the plan, that was how it was meant to be. And for a while that's how it went.

Things got out of hand, though. So eventually I thought, 'Enough is enough' and I took my grandmother's old flat in the end, where I'd lived for the past three and a half years. Alone, until Mark came.

And now we were leaving it; selling up and moving on. The end of another era.

As one door closes, another one opens.

But in order to close it properly, Mark had said I should phone my mother and tell her what I was doing.

At first I'd refused. Why should she know what I'm up to? What fucking difference did it make? Did she phone me? Had she, even once, phoned me in the last couple of years? Had she?

Had she fuck.

But Mark had said it would be a sort of revenge, letting her know that I was fine, that I was doing okay thanks very much, and that I no longer needed her.

See, the thing is, I suppose there was a lot of inner pain there, a lot of pent-up emotional shit that I hadn't really dealt with properly; just filed it away in a dark corner of my mind somewhere.

"Phone her, Andrew," Mark had said. "At least let her know where you're going."

"What and leave her a forwarding address so she can send us Christmas cards? Yeah, I'm sure she'd love that."

"Well, just tell her you're selling the flat. What if she needs to contact you, in an emergency or something?"

"She'd probably just tell me to fuck off, Mark."

"You'll never know if you don't try," he'd said. "Remember, that's what you told me when I was coming out. Maybe you should take your own advice."

"This is a bit different, though, don't you think?" I'd argued.

"Not really. Andrew, do it for yourself. Don't do it for her, don't even do it for me. Do it for yourself."

So I did.

I waited until Mark was out. Picked up the phone, dialled the number. I didn't even know if she'd be in.

As the phone rang emptily in my ear, I tried to remember the last time I'd spoken to her. Must have been about two years ago. I'd called her for something silly - Mother's Day, I think it was. She'd been so cold towards me, my own mother. She hadn't been abusive or anything, just distant, incredibly distant. There had been tears in my eyes that day as I'd replaced the receiver and I'd sworn to myself then...

...never again. That's it. That's -

"Hello?" came my mother's voice. It hadn't changed. It sounded happy, jolly. A woman with few worries.

And perhaps that's what she was, now that she'd gotten rid of her only worry, her main worry.

Her gay son.

But that would change as soon as she found out who was on the other end of the phone. Oh yes. That would all change.

"Mum, it's Andrew."

I spoke woodenly.

"Andrew." She said the word as if tasting it, as if it had a strange flavour she had never experienced before. I wished, then, that I hadn't left the phone call until Mark had gone out. I wanted to hold his hand.

I won't cry, I told myself. I won't cry.

"Oh, Andrew. How are you?"

"I'm fine."

There was a brief, yet glacial silence. When Mum didn't fill it, I said, "I'm just calling to tell you that I'm moving. To give you my new address."

"Oh right. Moving? Where to?"

"To London, Mum. I've got a new job. It's a manager's position."

"Oh," she said. "Well done." But there was no tone of encouragement there, no hint of congratulation, not like a mother. Not like a mother at all.

"I'm selling the flat," I carried on. "I mean, there's no point in keeping it. Mark suggested I rent it out but I wanted a clean break. A new start, you know?"

"Who's Mark?" asked Mum. Her voice was soft, yet probing.

"Mark is...my mate." I don't know why I said that, why I lied. But it didn't matter, because I'm sure she knew; sure she knew exactly what part Mark played in my life.

"Okay," she said somewhat wearily. Then, "What's your new address?" She didn't add - didn't need to add - 'as if it matters'.

Fuck her, I thought. Fuck her. I'm doing this for me and no one else.

I told her the new address. Then I asked, "How's Dad?"

"He's doing well," said Mum, the cool tone of indifference never wavering. "He's fine."

"Is he there?"

"No."

The word dropped like the blade of a guillotine. It cut me. I wanted to push on with it, add something, but I knew it would be pointless. It was clear to me then that nothing had changed between us. The rift that had been formed the day she found out I was gay was wider than ever. And to be brutally honest, that suited me just fine.

Does it? whispered the self-doubting part of me. Does it really, Andrew? Wouldn't you like a mother like normal blokes have? A mother who didn't despise you because of what you are, because of your sexuality? Wouldn't you, Andrew?

WOULDN'T YOU?

No, I told myself with steely resolution, and that chilling inner voice was silenced.

"Oh. Okay then. Will you tell him I called?"

"I'll tell him."

Bitch! I thought. Tears pricked my eyes and I was horrified by them. How dare she make me cry? How dare she?

There seemed nothing more to say then. What could I say? Mum's tone of indifference, her 'I don't give a shit what you do, Andrew' attitude had wiped away any possibility of a decent conversation with her. The sad, pathetic thing was that that had been what I'd been hoping to have with her.

Dumb, sentimental fool that I am.

I felt none of the strength or power that Mark had said I would feel. I felt somewhat cheated. Mum said, "Listen, Andrew, I have to go."

She couldn't even give me the time of day, could she?

I wanted to shout back, "You bitch! You fucking bitch! Don't even want to know about me, do you? Don't even want to know what your only son has been up to in the last few years, since the day you cast him out, disowned him forever! You don't even want to know!"

Of course, the words remained unspoken. What would they achieve? She'd probably get a kick out of them, the sick cow.

"Oh. Okay then, Mum. I'll call you when I get to London."

"If you like."

"Yeah. Okay. 'Bye. Love to Dad."

"'Bye."

There was a click as she hung up first. Hung up before me. The sound clanged in my ear. She hadn't even said my name when she'd said goodbye.

Well, that was it. That was it forever. As far as I was concerned right then, I didn't have a mother.

I put the phone down and sucked in a deep breath. I wanted Mark then. Wanted to hold him tightly against me and just listen to our hearts beating together. I was so full of hate. It felt dark and primitive. I hated hating. It destroyed things. Anything good inside of me would have been eaten up by that cold, malicious, evil scorn.

But I couldn't help it, not against my mother. She deserved the hate. More than anyone I could name at that point.

If you like, she'd said. She might as well have added, but I'd rather you didn't you fucking filthy queer.

I knew I shouldn't have let the words get to me. I knew I should have brushed them off, with the utter contempt that they deserved. But it was impossible, and they closed around me, as tight as a noose around the throat of the condemned.

9 Mark

We'd planned the night before we left to be a quiet night in. We were going to get a Chinese, have a bottle of wine.

But we had a visitor.

"Who the hell can that be?" said Andrew.

I shrugged from my place on the sofa. "Search me. Go and check it out."

"No, let's just ignore it. No one knows we're in. And this is our last night here. I wanted us to just chill out."

The buzzer buzzed again.

"It's probably just someone selling something," I told Andrew. "Just go and tell them we're not interested and that'll be that."

Andrew pulled a face and I laughed at him.

"You look like a sulking child. Just answer it."

"Mark...come on. It'll ruin the mood. And what if it isn't someone selling something?"

"Who else would it be at this time?"

"It's only nine-thirty. It could be anyone."

"Oh, for God's sake." I got up and picked up the hallway phone. "Hello?"

"About time!" exclaimed Jason.

"Oh, all right, Jase," I said. I mouthed his name silently to Andrew, who, again, pulled another face and rolled his eyes.

"Get rid of him," he hissed. I waved him away and buzzed Jason up.

"So, how are you both? What are you up to tonight?" he said as he came through the door.

"Oh, nothing much. It's the big move and everything tomorrow, isn't it?"

"We're just chilling out," said Andrew. "You know." He gestured to the table that was littered with some leaflets for the local Chinese take-away and an as yet unopened bottle of red wine.

"Ah," he said. "I see. Have I called at a bad time then?"

"No, not at all, not at all. Do you want a beer? We've got some Groschl in the fridge? Or there's wine if you fancy it."

"Er, yeah, I would like a drink. But not here. That's why I've come round. To take you both out for a farewell drink."

"Oh, I don't know, mate," said Andrew. "We just wanted a quiet night in together. Get an early night. You know? There's a lot to sort out tomorrow. Getting all this lot down to London and everything." He gestured to all of the packed boxes around. Indeed, it did look like a lot. And the flat looked so weird now, with everything gone, all packaged safely away in bubble wrap and cardboard. It was like a hollow shell. Sort of eerie, in fact.

"Oh, come on lads," said Jason. "Just one drink. A farewell."

"Don't put it that finally," I said. "It's not goodbye forever, is it?"

"Even so, Mark. You know what I mean, don't you?"

I nodded.

"So come on? What do you say?"

I looked at Andrew. I knew he didn't want to go, but I was really tempted. A final drink, a big night out.

"Where d'you wanna go then?" said Andrew, trying not to sound reluctant but failing miserably.

"Your turf, of course!" said Jason. "Medusa's. One final she-bang!"

"She-bang?" I laughed, and now Andrew grinned ear to ear.

"Yeah, okay. Why not?" he said. "Ignore me. Let's go."

"Sure?"

"Said so, didn't I? Now get downstairs before I change my mind."

Ø

Well, of course I knew what was coming, didn't I? I mean, it wasn't as if it wasn't obvious or anything.

When I went through the doors of Medusa's and the lights came on and all our friends shouted, "Surprise!" I put on my best 'oh-my God-there-was-no-way-I-was-expecting-this-expression!'. The amazing thing is, I think I pulled it off.

Yet Andrew looked surprised. But that was Andrew all over.

"Wicked, isn't it?" said Grace, walking over to me and Andrew. She was wearing a long blue dress, her customary glass of orange juice in her hand. "I haven't been out clubbing for ages; I don't really like smoky atmospheres what with this 'un." She patted her stomach gently. "But how could I miss out on two of my best mates' leaving do?"

"Lucky you didn't, Grace!" said Andrew, hugging her.

"Yeah, for your sake," I added.

Everyone was there. All our friends - both gay and straight. Even my sister Amy and her husband Tim.

"I'm gonna miss you, squirt," she said, hugging and kissing us both. "Moving all the way up to the big city. Who'm I gonna tell all my problems to now, eh?" She grinned, and I thought - only thought - that I saw a tear glisten in her eye.

"I'll only be on the other end of a phone, won't I?" I told her. "This isn't goodbye yet."

"Better bloody not be."

"Don't worry," said Andrew, with an arm around my waist. "I'll see to it that he calls at least once a day."

Amy smiled. "Here," she said, handing me a package wrapped in silver paper.

"What's this?"

"Open it and see."

I did. Two bathrobes with the words HIS and HIS emblazoned on each. There were hugs and kisses all round and then more hugs. It was so lovely. To Amy I said, "Are Mum and Dad here?"

She didn't answer straightaway. But she didn't have to. I could see in her expression, even though it did not change, that they weren't coming. But the news didn't really surprise me. It upset me a bit, sure, but it didn't surprise me.

"They sent you this, though," said Amy, and she handed me an envelope. I opened it, and found a 'Good Luck' card. Inside there was a hundred pounds, all in tenners. There were tears in my eyes as I read the message, in my mother's neat hand.

> *Here's wishing you and Andrew every success*
> *in your new life together in London.*
> *Remember, we're only a train ride away.*
> *Love Mum and Dad.*

Mum had written both names, but it didn't matter. Not much, anyway.

"That's nice," I said. I squeezed Andrew's hand. "Nice," I repeated, reading the words in the card over again once more. Tears blurred my vision and I wiped them away.

"Mum wanted to be here," said Amy. She knew I was upset, but - perhaps foolishly - I tried to disguise the emotion with a too-bright grin.

"Doesn't matter," I said. "I know this isn't exactly her sort of place, is it?" Somewhat sadly, I added, "And it's definitely not Dad's."

Amy just smiled, but the smile had a trace of pity in it. No, said her eyes. Definitely not.

There was a silence then, despite the pounding Euro-Trance that the resident DJ was churning out.

The silence was ended by Andrew.

"Come on, come on. This is going to be our last night at Medusa's.

Let's make the most of it, yeah?"

Smiles broke out all round, like the sun coming out.

The party began properly then. It was fantastic. We had people buying us drinks all night. Keiran bought me and Andrew at least five tequilas each. "I'm gonna be bladdered!" I shouted over the booming music.

"So what?" said Keiran, grinning. "It's your last night out at Medusa's, ain't it? Enjoy it."

And that's exactly what we did.

It was fabulous.

Sure enough, I was more than just a tad pissed when we left; we both were. We got in a taxi and fell into bed. I was out before my head hit the pillow.

Before long the alarm clock was ringing and it was time.

Time for our new life.

Time for London...

PART II
Londinium

1 Andrew

The first week was just spent settling in. The temporary flat where we were staying in Camberwell was nice. It belonged to a friend of Keiran's who was away seeing the world or something. It was smaller than my - sorry our - old place and it did seem a bit strange when we first walked in. I suppose even stranger was the fact that we were moving into a flat we hadn't even looked at yet. I must admit that when I first turned the key in the lock I wondered just what the hell it was I'd been thinking of, moving to London. Then I remembered Mark, the thought of a new start and all it had to offer, and the feelings of disquiet vanished as quickly as they had arisen.

I started my new job on the first Saturday after we moved. A Saturday, I ask you. Talk about chucking me head first into the deep end.

Dimensions, the place was called. In Old Compton Street. Ever heard of Old Compton Street? Well, if you're gay then you must have. In the centre of Soho it is, packed full of gay clubs, pubs, restaurants, shops...you get the picture. And Dimensions, it turned out, was one of the biggest and most popular places there, aside from the fact that it had only been open a month or so. But then, maybe that was the attraction.

And I had become the manager practically overnight. You know, I'd gone from being a barman in a small gay club at the back of beyond to running a joint in the largest gay scene in all of Europe. It was off its own head. Surreal.

When I first arrived there, at the café, I started to have doubts. Was I the right man for the job? Could I really do it? Had I bitten off more than I could chew?

I suppose the underlying worry in all of it was: Would I have gotten the job if it wasn't for Keiran?

Then I thought of Mark, who was at home in our new - albeit transient - abode, fixing it up, making it nice, making it a home, and I thought: Yes. I'm here and I've done the right thing. A new beginning. That's what it's all about.

And, like all worries, it turned out to be fine in the end, nothing worth worrying about at all.

I settled right into the new job. It was weird, almost like the job had been designed for me, had been waiting there all along for the right bloke to turn up to fill the gap. The old manager trained me, obviously, a bloke named Carl who was moving overseas at the end of the month. He said I'd picked it up brilliantly, that I'd settled in better than any new employee they'd had there. And I was the new manager. Mad.

When I got home from my first night, at around one a.m., Mark was waiting for me. He'd made us tea. Nothing fancy, just Supernoodles, chips and fried eggs. But it was lovely, 'cos he'd made it. And also a bit strange, since I'd been around food all day and hadn't built up an appetite. As soon as I got through the door, though, that all changed.

Cooking us dinner wasn't the only thing he'd done. The flat looked excellent. He'd done a brilliant job of tidying up. It seemed a shame that we were only there in the short term.

"So how was it?" he asked as I came through the door, but the grin that covered my face told him before I even opened my mouth.

I told him all about my day as we ate. It was our first home-cooked meal in London. Before then we'd been living on kebabs and

McDonalds. "So you enjoyed it?" Mark said. He seemed more relaxed in our new surroundings than I did. But then I suppose that was only natural, wasn't it? He'd been the one most keen on the move.

And he hadn't experienced it before. It was all new to him, wasn't it? New to me, too, I suppose. In a way. But there was still that shadow of those old days in Walthamstow lingering around in my head like some incurable disease.

2 **Mark**

It was everything I'd expected. Perhaps more. For that first week, while we got settled in the flat and Andrew got accustomed to his new job and duties, I didn't even go out on to the gay scene properly. Just a few wanders down Old Compton Street, but that was it. What struck me most was the variety of it all. And there was a sort of anonymity about everything, too, the way it was just the norm, just people enjoying the atmosphere and each others' company. It was what I'd been looking for, it really was. It was just going to take a bit of getting used to, that was all. But surely that was to be expected, right?

I felt nervous about going into one of the multitude of gays bars, even with Andrew by my side.

For a start, those other places lacked the safe familiarity of Medusa's. But on another level, the thing that worried me was all the other gays and lesbians around. All so much more experienced at it than I was.

I got looks, from all the gays sitting outside the café's and bars. Hungry looks. Indeed, a couple of times the place felt as if it were full of nothing but eyes. Eyes that peeked and peered.

Andrew and I held hands as we walked down that street for the first time together. What a feeling it was. Just as I said, no one batted an eyelid. Because it was the norm, see. That was the great thing about it. It was normal and isn't that just what all homosexuals want? To be normal, just like everyone else. Not hated or pitied or reviled. Just accepted.

Ø

Of course, Old Compton Street was just that: a street. Some parts of London were just like back home, I knew that, full of the same senseless rage and hatred. But it was a start, all this, in Soho. A good start.

While Andrew worked, I busied myself with the flat, tidying and cooking and stuff. I knew we weren't going to be there for very long, but it seemed important to make it as homely as possible. Smaller than our old place, but 'quaint', I suppose you'd say. Or does that sound too American?

My mum would've liked it, anyway.

It wasn't until we'd been living in London for two weeks that we went to our first London gay club together. I'd popped in to watch Andrew working a couple of times at Dimensions. I was so proud of him. Although he was the manager, he was still on the 'café floor' a lot, and, as I sat there over my cappuccino and croissant I smiled at him, quietly marvelling at how quickly he'd mastered the new role. I knew then, as I watched him work, that he didn't regret the move one bit. Because unlike his days in Walthamstow, he had focus now, he wasn't just slumming it. There was a purpose and a direction to this, and that made a hell of a lot of difference.

We were free. That might sound melodramatic. But we were.

The first gay club we visited together in London was called JayJay's. It wasn't actually in Soho, but it wasn't far: along Tottenham Court Road. "It's an old favourite of mine," said Andrew as we set off after a couple of drinks in Dimensions. Andrew got a staff discount.

I'd been reading the gay press that day. Boyz and QX were a couple of the free papers available on the scene, and they'd each had little ads in for JayJay's. Tonight, apparently, was Underwear Night. If you went in just your underwear, you got in for nothing. "Do you fancy that then?" Andrew had asked me.

"Piss off!" I'd laughed back. "I'm not mincing around in just my Calvin's for anyone!"

"Not even me?"

"Well...maybe for you."

We got to JayJay's at around eleven. The place didn't get jumping until then, Andrew said. He told me that he hoped it'd be the same as last time. "Four years ago, though," he said. "Could've changed a lot."

"Maybe it won't have changed that much," I said. "It might seem different, but that could just be because you've changed, as a person."

"Maybe."

We got in the queue, which was massive, and my heart thudded with a sort of nervous excitement. It's hard to say why I was nervous. Perhaps because part of me wondered if I'd like it. Imagine the disappointment if I hated the 'big' scene. What if I got inside and longed to be back at Medusa's, back in the safety of our little town and our little scene?

And the little people with their little minds.

I squeezed Andrew's hand.

"You okay, babe?" he said.

I beamed and nodded. The music pounded through the walls of the club, which was a converted theatre. *JayJay's* screamed the sign in wild neon green, and I was reminded of that time, ages ago, when I'd first gone to Medusa's. That had been before I'd been able to comfortably deal with my feelings, though.

While we waited to go in, I took a moment to scan the people in line with us. A mixture of dykes and queers, yes, but there was a great variety of them. Separations within the separations, if you know what I mean.

You had the serious clubbers, in all their wild attire and hairdos. Then you had the old clones, in their checked shirts and big handlebar moustaches, people who would not have been clubbing if they had been straight. Too old. But because they were gay, it didn't matter. Everyone was just there to have a good time, regardless of age.

Next up you had the chickens, a term I'd heard bandied around the scene a few times during the previous fortnight. That meant you were young and inexperienced or something. It was an expression I found grotesque.

Chickens.

And the chickens will be stuffed tonight.

I didn't know which category I fitted into. Or even if I fitted into one at all.

"How do you like it so far?" asked Andrew as the queue oozed slowly forward.

"Different," I told him, continuing to look around. "It all seems very different."

"For the better?"

I grinned widely. "Oh yeah. Definitely for the better."

Gradually, we got inside the club.

Surprisingly, quite a lot of the crowd had opted for the underwear-only option in order to get in for free. Although, to tell the truth, they did seem the type of people who'd have gone dressed like that anyway, without the added incentive.

The first thing that hit me when we entered JayJay's was the size. Put it this way, if Medusa's had been a minnow, JayJay's was a killer whale. That's sort of how I felt, actually, like a minnow. Would the gay scene eat me up?

Hard dance music pounded at a volume loud enough to shift tectonic plates. I could feel it vibrating beneath my skull. It was amazing. "Wicked, isn't it?" shouted Andrew, grinning, and you could have been forgiven for thinking that it was me who'd been the more reluctant about the move. After just two weeks living in London - really, it was still only the honeymoon period - Andrew had slotted back into his old life as easily as if he'd only been gone a month.

"Is it very different to how you remember it?" I shouted back.

He shook his head, but in time to the music. "Nah! Same as ever! But it's good to be back!"

Those were the words I wanted to hear.

For Andrew to be enjoying it - even more than me - felt like a gift. It meant that I wouldn't have to worry if I'd dragged him up there against his will, or if he was only pretending to enjoy things for my sake. If he was happy, I was happy. And I knew that that went both ways.

"Let me give you a tour!" said Andrew, taking my hand.

JayJay's was built on three levels. There was the main dance floor: a huge space with two bars serving drinks (which were, as Andrew had previously warned me, murderously expensive). Then it led up to another bar, which played a trancey, ambient sort of music. This, Andrew explained, was known as the 'chill out' bar.

"You get most of the pill-heads in here later on. All off their tits."

Finally, the third level of the club provided the most evidence that it had once been a theatre; it was made up of about a dozen or so tiered galleries where you could sit, have a beer, watch the talent go by or get off with a bloke.

Lush.

Oh yeah, that was another thing I noticed that was different from Medusa's. London queers, it seemed, were far fitter than back home and, though I don't like admitting it, my eye did wander more than just once.

But I don't think Andrew noticed.

Once the short tour had finished, we went down onto the main dancefloor and just let ourselves go. I looked around at the other dancers. There was a curious sort of falseness to them all. They all had confidence, yes, more than I did. But I had the impression that beneath that confidence there was nothing but scared, lonely, isolated people. Perhaps that was what they were, away from the bright lights and glitter and loud music of the gay scene.

"Having a good time?" Andrew shouted at me. I kissed him. A quick kiss; darting. I nodded, but spoke no words. What would've been the point with the booming music? There was no way he'd understand what I was saying. The kiss was just a way of assuring him that I was fine and enjoying myself.

The club filled up quickly. But JayJay's was a popular place. I could see why.

Drugs, too. That was another big difference I noticed there, much more than back at Medusa's, where of course there were the drugs, but it wouldn't be quite so obvious. And there was only one or two people there that I knew who did them a lot. I mean, I did them occasionally. Nothing too hard, mind. Just a bit of hash every now and then. And of course, I smoked and I drank alcohol, but not in a crazy way.

At JayJay's, though, the drugs thing seemed quite different. I think...yeah, probably about a third of the people there that first night were on drugs. You could spot 'em dead easily. All dancing harder and faster than anyone else, all clutching their little bottles of water, as if the world was going to explode tomorrow if they didn't put every drop of energy into the music. And their eyes, too. That was another thing. Eyes like bloody dinner plates. There was something creepy about it all, but I wasn't going to let it ruin my night. If people wanted to do drugs, let them.

I looked at Andrew and grinned, ear to ear at one point, almost as if I was on drugs, too. But he was the only thing I needed to get me high, so that was okay.

Our first night out together on the London scene.

I'll never forget that night, not for the rest of my life. It was the best time, see. The first time is always the best; I think the same can be said about anything. The first time is always so full of excitement and mystery and intrigue. After that it's just downhill all the way if you think about it. That sounds very bleak, so you shouldn't think of things like that too often, should you?

Even if it is true.

Ø

We went clubbing at JayJay's every Saturday night after that for about a month, once Andrew finished work for the evening. Luckily, Dimensions closed at eleven, so at around midnight, after Andrew had finished everything he had to finish, we headed down there. It was so great the way all the gay places were pretty much a stone's throw away from one another.

During the week, while Andrew continued to work at Dimensions, I kept popping in every now and then to see him. I still didn't have a job of my own, though. I was far too in awe of the whole place to concentrate on anything else for a while. And not just the gay scene, either, but the whole of London.

It was such a beautiful city. I loved the buildings...and I don't mean just the landmarks, the sights and stuff, the things that all the Japanese tourists go and gawp at with their big flash cameras. Just the architecture of the normal buildings: shops and office blocks and libraries and hospitals. The detail that was everywhere. It was beautiful.

I'd only ever been to London twice, and that was only for day trips to London Zoo and the Houses of Parliament when I was at school. It was stupid, really. It wasn't as if I lived at the ends of the earth where London was as inaccessible as Paris or something. I only lived in Buckinghamshire. Just a train journey away, an hour up the road-tops.

Still, I suppose I'd never really had a cause to visit London until now, did I? I'd never really had a proper interest in the place until...well...

After the first month, I phoned Grace and told her everything we'd done so far, all about the Camberwell flat, Andrew's job, JayJay's. I told her that I loved it, that I was thrilled, on cloud nine, that I knew I'd made the right decision.

She was chuffed. But I knew that already.

Then she asked me about getting a job.

"I know I should," I said. "But what would I do?"

"I thought you wanted to look for something in the music industry," she said. "Haven't you tried that yet?"

"I haven't tried looking anywhere yet, Grace," I told her.

She was a little puzzled by that news. "Why?"

"Too busy," I said. But I thought, Too busy doing what?

"Enjoying yourself?" said Grace, answering my unspoken question.

"Yeah," I told her softly, almost guiltily. But that sounded like such a lame excuse I could've hit myself.

"Well, that's good, Mark," she said. "But you've been there a month now, haven't you? You've got to get a job sooner or later."

Her words irritated me, but only very slightly. She'd come across all motherly on me. Not surprising, though. Not with a little nipper of her own on the way.

Besides, I knew she was right about it, but I didn't want to admit it. The truth was, the idea of getting a job in London scared me, made me nervous. Back home it seemed like the perfect idea, a job in the industry I so loved and all that, but now, when I was there, the reality wasn't quite so appealing.

What would I do? I knew the music industry seemed the best bet, considering my past experience with Lyar, but how would I go about it? Advertise?

"Maybe I'll just become a rentboy," I said to Grace wistfully. "They make quite good money, apparently. Hey! We could all go on holiday to Ibiza together on my tips! You and Jason and me and Andrew!"

I was only joking, but I don't think she saw the funny side.

In fact, she was horrified. "What? Mark, you can't - "

"Joke!" I said. "Jeez, Grace, I was joking. Of course I'm not going to be a bloody prostitute."

"Oh. Okay. I just though for a moment there that..." She let the sentence float out and die.

There was a bit of a tense silence then.

"What are you doing for money?" asked Grace.

"Andrew. He's earning really good money. Much better than back home. And even then he could support us both, when he was at Medusa's."

"I know, I know," said Grace. "But what about your independence? What about your self-esteem?"

"Yeah, I know. God, Grace, give me a break, will ya? I will get a job. Andrew's suggested I go to an agency or something. See if they've got anything for me."

"Well, it's got to be better than the dole, hasn't it?" she said, maintaining her motherly tone.

"Anything's better than the dole."

"There you are then."

"Look, Grace...I was going to go the agency tomorrow. Okay? Now, when can you and Jason come down to visit? I want to take you to JayJay's! You'd love it! And it's so much better than Medusa's, you won't believe it."

"Stop it!" she laughed, back to her old self. "Don't tempt me. I can't go clubbing with the baby almost due, you know that! But I promise, as soon as it's here, I'll get Anita over to baby-sit and Jason and me'll be on the first train to Euston, okay?"

"Good."

After that, we chatted meaninglessly. After she'd hung up, I surveyed the flat and thought of what I'd said to Grace, about the agency. I hadn't been planning on going there tomorrow. Hadn't been planning on going at all. But I had to get a job. She was right about what she said about my independence. I didn't like having to rely solely on Andrew for financial support, even though I knew he was making enough money and he didn't mind paying for us both when we went out.

That wasn't the point, though. The point was that *I* minded. Sometimes it'd be nice for me to pay for us both to get into clubs, to pay for my own Travelcard on the tube, for me to buy the drinks or even to take him out to dinner.

'Course, I had my own money, from the dole, but that went next to nowhere even when I was back home.

So I decided to try the agency. Resources Plus, the place was called, and the nearest office was in London Bridge. They dealt only with office work, admin stuff, so that was okay. I didn't fancy busting my hump in some sweaty factory or warehouse, and I'd had enough of disgusting fast-food joints like Brenda's Burgers. I didn't want to work in a shop or anything like that, either. Andrew said he could sort me out a job at Dimensions, but you know my thoughts on us working together. And it'd be even worse now; he'd be my boss! I didn't like that idea one bit.

I didn't tell Andrew about my going to the agency. I suppose part of me wanted it to be a surprise. I wanted to impress him by getting a job on my own. But even more than that I wanted to impress myself.

I called the agency first and asked to make an appointment. They said they could see me immediately. That surprised me. What with being in London and all, I'd thought there would have been a huge waiting list or something. Nope. Off you go, fill out an application form, have a quick interview, do a few tests (typing and data entry; that sort of thing) and there you were.

"We'll call you as soon as something comes in that's suitable for your skills, Mr. Holly," Clare told me. Clare Mowat. That was the name of the woman who saw me. She was nice; pretty. Quite young, too. And she'd said she'd been brought up in Aylesbury which wasn't too far from where I'd grown up.

That had been on a Friday. After the interview I'd gone straight into the West End, into Soho, to Dimensions. I wanted to tell Andrew the news.

But he wasn't there. It came as a shock to me.

It was two in the afternoon, one of the busiest times for the place. Just after lunchtime and all that.

I walked through the door, expecting Andrew to be doing some paperwork at the bar with a coffee like he sometimes did, or even if he wasn't on the main floor, he'd be downstairs in the office, or stocktaking or something.

I walked up to Daniel, one of the barstaff. He was a cool bloke. Only nineteen, but dead mature for his age. He was good looking, too. And so, so, so obviously gay. Originally from Cheshire, he'd lived in London for three years and was a bit of a scene queen.

"Marky!" he shrilled as soon as he saw me. "How's it going, darling?"

We hugged and kissed each other on the cheek. Camp as old knickers.

"Not bad, not bad."

"What have you been up to today? More sightseeing?"

"Nope. Not today. But bloody hell, Dan, you make me sound like a tourist."

He shrugged and grinned. "Yeah, yeah. I know what it's like at the beginning, though. You just want to take it all in."

"That's 'cos there's so much of it, though."

"Tell me about it," he said.

"Anyway, is Andrew around? Is he downstairs in the office or -"

"Wait a second, honey," interrupted Daniel. "Let me just serve these guys. Two ticks!"

"Sure." I watched him skitter over to a middle aged gay couple on the other side of the bar. They ordered two iced teas and a couple of slices of spinach and avocado quiche.

Once he was done, he came back over, pretending to gasp for air as if he'd just completed the London Marathon. "Sorry about that, Marky. Right, what were you saying? Hang on! Don't tell me." He waved one hand queenishly in the air and pressed the other to his forehead, like the Great Suprendo about to perform some mystical mind-reading act. "You were asking where Andrew was, correct?" he said, opening one eye. The boyish grin never left his face. I chuckled at him.

"Yeah, right first time, Dan."

He smiled. "He's not here, darling."

"Oh?" I frowned, puzzled.

"He's in Camden. At our other unit. Some sort of meeting with the owner. He should be back at around five, though."

"Five? Oh, I can't wait that long. Don't worry, I'll catch him at home later."

I was disappointed. In a stupid way, I felt annoyed at him for not phoning me to say he'd be in Camden Town. He knew I popped in to see him at work sometimes.

But then I remembered the agency, that I'd been out for a while. Perhaps he'd tried to phone then. I didn't have a mobile phone so it wasn't as if he was able to get hold of me indefinitely.

"You look pissed off," observed Daniel. I looked at him expressionlessly for a second, then I smiled wearily.

"Just a bit down about not seeing Andrew," I said. "I had some good news to tell him. Well, not exactly good news, but news."

"Why not call him? I'll give you the number of the Camden place."

I thought about it, but he'd probably be annoyed if I did that. I could just imagine him sitting in this meeting room with a load of culinary bigwigs and then his whining boyfriend rings up. Yeah, right.I could just hear the lecture I'd be subjected to when he got in from work.

Daniel threw a glance at the clock on the wall. He said, "Listen, it's my break in five minutes. Why don't you have a coffee with me and tell me your news?"

"Yeah, okay."

Daniel smiled.

Ø

I waited for him to finish up a few small things - washing glasses, serving a couple more punters, making up some fresh margaritas - and then he fixed us up a couple of cappuccinos and chocolate eclairs. It was a nice day, so we sat outside at a little metal table.

I told him about the agency. He was pleased, said he'd heard about Resources Plus, that they always found decent jobs for the people on their books. I told him I'd asked for office employment, just regular admin stuff. I'd done all right at school, in word processing, RSA I and II and everything, and these days computers were so simple to use you only had to know how to turn the thing on and you'd mastered it.

Daniel said, "That's excellent news, Mark! Andy'll be chuffed for you."

"You think?" I grinned helplessly and Daniel offered me one of his Marlboro Lights.

"God, yeah."

For the rest of Daniel's coffee break, we talked about the bloke he'd met the other night whilst out clubbing at JayJay's. "His name was Taz," Daniel told me. "He had a boyfriend who was away for the weekend. Just a one night stand, but a wicked shag."

I grinned. Daniel was a brilliant bloke, and I loved him to bits after knowing him for just over a month. But he was a bit of a slapper. Still, he enjoyed himself, and he was always careful about having safe sex, so what was the problem?

"Better get back to work," he said, stubbing out his fag. "Ooh, good job your fella isn't around, darling, or he'd have my guts for garters and my spleen for suspenders."

I chuckled at that. It sounded strange, the idea of Andrew having to discipline someone.

We kissed goodbye and Daniel said again how pleased he was about my forthcoming job. I went straight home then. As I walked back down Old Compton Street, on my way to the tube station, I watched all the other gays, some with boyfriends, some alone, some in groups. They were all smiling and happy, enjoying the sunshine, enjoying their freedom; the simple pleasure of being able to go for a walk in public or have a drink together while holding hands and exchanging affection - things that straights take for granted.

It was three o'clock when I got back home. I was bored, so I watched a bit of tv. I'd forgotten how boring daytime television was, full of gardening shows, cookery shows, shopping shows, or quizzes about antiques. There wasn't even a decent episode of Jenny Jones on, for God's sake.

I wondered what time Andrew would be in. Daniel said he would be back from Camden at about five, but he probably wouldn't get home from the Compton Street unit until at least midnight. I thought about cooking him dinner, but he always ate at work anyway these days, so I usually ended up with a takeaway pizza. Or sometimes, left-overs from Dimensions.

I tried not to let it bother me, the fact that Andrew got in late from work all the time. Or the fact that he always had such a huge grin on his face as he told me every detail about his day. I should've been pleased. Pleased that he'd taken so well to our new life, that he was out there, a successful manager of a successful establishment.

I mean, it wasn't as if I was jealous of him or anything?

Was it?

3 Andrew

It had been a busy day. A nightmare of a busy day. But the thing was, I didn't mind that. I enjoyed working. Some say that the luckiest people in the world are those who actually enjoy their job. If that was true, then yeah, I was one of the luckiest people in the world.

And I had some news for Mark, too. Some brilliant news. We were moving again. Not so far this time, we were still going to be in London, of course.

That day, I'd been in a long meeting with the owner of Dimensions. Martyn, the guy's name was. He was a good bloke, dead easy going. The meeting was basically just a progress report: how did I like the place, how did I find the people, what did I think needed changing etc. etc. The nicest thing was that he seemed more concerned with my happiness rather than the way the café was being run. But I doubt that was actually the case.

Anyway, back to the moving part. Martyn had found us a flat. A permanent flat. Wicked news, wasn't it? The new place was in Newman Street, which I'd never heard of. It was just off Oxford Street, slap bang in the middle of the West End, right near Soho and subsequently right near work. Just ten minutes' up the road. The rent was reasonable, too, for a place in the West End.

Mark was going to be stoked, knowing how into the gay scene he was.

I thought a lot about Mark as I drove home that evening. Well, I think about him all the time. Today, though, I wondered about him getting a job. Not that I was forcing him to get one, God no. Financially, there was no problem. Keiran hadn't been lying when he said I'd be earning good money in London. And it wasn't just 'good' money, either. It was serious money. Really, I could afford to keep us both.

But I knew that wasn't what Mark wanted. I knew he wanted his independence. And I also knew that the novelty of the big city and the big scene would soon wear off, and that he'd become frustrated and bored with having nothing to do all day but wander aimlessly through Old Compton Street or sit at home and watch crappy American soap operas and debate shows.

It had been different back home when he'd been on the dole, 'cos he'd had his band. Once that had finished, he'd pretty much started at Brenda's Burgers straightaway because he was bored.

The thing was, though, it felt difficult when I tried to bring up the subject of working. I didn't want him to think I was nagging him to get a job. I know what that's like, and it isn't much fun.

I decided I'd have to wait for him to sort it out on his own. And with the new flat on the horizon, that might prompt him.

I couldn't wait to tell him about it.

"It's me! I'm back!" I called out as I stepped inside the flat. There were just the sounds of running water, and on the stereo Geri Halliwell was singing Look At Me.

Mark was in the shower.

I had a cool idea.

With a wicked grin on my face, I crept into the bedroom and stripped off. Then, as quietly and expertly as a cat burglar, I slinked into the bathroom. Mark didn't hear a thing, as he warbled along dreadfully to Geri.

I climbed into the shower. "Room for one more," I purred in his ear, curling my arms around him.

He jumped and turned, a look of surprise and horror on his face. "JESUS CHRIST, ANDREW!" he cried. "You scared the living shite out of me!"

I chuckled.

"It's not funny," he fumed, but then couldn't help himself and his face dissolved into that Mark Holly grin I'd fallen in love with all that time ago. "You idiot," he said.

We kissed for a moment, beneath the pulsing hot needles of water.

"You're late again," said Mark.

It was ten-thirty. I said, "I know. Forgive me?"

"Of course I bloody do! Ooh, I sound like a nagging housewife, don't I?"

I laughed. "You do, yeah. And what's with the 'ooh' bit? You've been hanging around with Daniel, haven't you?"

"Shut up," he said mockingly. He wiped his hair slick back across his head and then examined the tips of his fingers. "I'm gonna get out of here. I'm turning into a prune. I've been in here for ages."

"Well, why don't you stay a bit longer? The company's great," I said. But I was only mucking round. "Go on, you go. Open that bottle of wine that's in the fridge. I've got some good news."

Mark grinned, "Hey, snap, so have I!"

"Really?" I said. "What?"

"Have your shower," said Mark. "I'll be waiting with wine in the front room."

Mark got out of the shower and I heard the bathroom door click shut. I smiled like a maniac.

When he'd gone, I reached for the shower gel and squeezed some into my palm. I felt so warm at that moment, and no I don't mean just because of the water. Contentment. That's what it was. Total and pure contentment.

I hadn't felt so content in a long, long time. Not like this.

Strangely, I thought of Mum, and as soon as her image filled my head I expected to feel that same magma-hot flow of range, anger and resentment. But there was just calm. It surprised me.

It was like...like I'd forgiven her, almost. Except no, I hadn't. Not really, not properly. I knew that. Even if there was calm at that moment, I was sure it had to be only the eye of the storm. That anger was still there, I knew it, because it had cut too deep to be over with just like that.

I think what I'm trying to say is that things seemed to be working out for me in London this time. With Mark and the new job. A new beginning, that's what we wanted and that's what we seemed to have found. So quickly, too. That was a good sign, I was sure of it, that everything had fallen into place with such little effort.

And I think...I think I wanted Mum to know about it. I wanted to go to her, just turn up on her front door and say, "Look at me, I'm doing all right for myself, I've got a brilliant job, I'm in love and I've got a good place to live. And I forgive you, Mum. I don't hate you the way you hate me just because I'm queer. Because I'm a bigger person than all that, inside I'm a bigger person than you are..."

Perhaps one day I will tell her that, I told myself. Perhaps, one day, that's just what I'll do.

"Are you coming or what?" shouted Mark from the other room, and just like that Mum's image disappeared from my mind's eye.

Mark was sitting at the coffee table, wearing just boxer shorts. I only had a towel around my waist. He'd got the wine from the fridge and had filled two glasses. Geri Halliwell had gone from the stereo, replaced by Put Your Arms Around Me by Texas. He'd even lit a couple of candles.

The room was alive with romance.

I smiled, and actually felt tears in my eyes. It was all so soppy and sweet, and above all it was so very, very us.

"So?" said Mark. He looked eager and boyishly cute. "What's the news?"

"You go first," I said. I sat beside him on the sofa. We didn't touch, just looked deeply and lovingly into each other's eyes.

"Well..." he began, taking a slow sip of his wine. "Mine isn't that exciting. But...you know that agency you told me about? Resources Plus?"

"Uh huh." I guessed instantly what was coming. My heart turned over. All that stupid worrying about how to bring the subject up and then...

"I put myself on their books today," he said. He seemed so excited it was like he was going to explode.

"That's brilliant," I said. I shook his hand, then kissed his cheek.

"I haven't got a job with them yet, mind," he told me. "But it's a start. And Clare, the woman I spoke to, said they shouldn't have any trouble sorting something out for me soon."

"They're very good," I told him, and he nodded.

"That's what Daniel said, too."

"Well, cheers. Cheers to you."

We clinked glasses together, and then, still grinning, Mark said, "Okay then. Your turn. What's your news?"

I told him about the Newman Street flat.

"Already?" he said. "God, that's quick. Seems like we've only been here five minutes."

"Well, we have really," I told him. Then, in a softer tone, "Are you pleased?"

"Pleased? I'm ecstatic, Andrew! When do we go? God, it's all happening so fast, isn't it?"

I nodded. "As soon as we're ready. I don't want to wait too long, though. It's closer to work, see. Just a few minutes' walk away."

Maybe it was my imagination, I don't know, but I think that a little, just a little, of the excitement faded from his eyes when I mentioned work.

"Cheers," he said. "To the new flat. To progress." We clinked glasses and drank.

There was silence for a second, then I said to Mark, "I love you. You know that, don't you? I love you, Mark Holly."

He smiled sleepily. He ran a hand through his hair. "Of course I know you love me. I love you, too, Andrew."

"And you know..." I began. I let the first part of that sentence stay there alone for a second, hovering. "You know that I'd do anything to make you happy, don't you? Anything."

His smile remained on his face. "Of course I know that. And vice versa."

"We're good together, aren't we?"

"The best, yeah."

I kissed him for a long moment, while stroking the side of his face. "I want to make love to you, Mark," I said.

He kissed me back, then we looked at each other.

Mark said, "I never want this to end. Us, I mean. Together. You and me."

This declaration startled me somewhat. "What makes you say that?"

He didn't answer, just kept that same enigmatic smile planted firmly on his lips. Then he simply shrugged and said, "Never mind. Come on." He took my hand. "Let's go to bed, Andrew."

PART III
Monsters and Angels

1 Mark

I got a job!

Just a week after the agency had put me on the books, Clare called with the news that she'd found a placement for me. It was at a large company based in the Docklands; Plymouth Wharf to be exact. NJT, the firm was called, which stood for Norris, Jaybrook and Thomas. It was a financial services company, and my job was in the training sector. Basically, all the salesmen and women had to sit exams to make sure they were up to speed on a particular financial product, be it Home Insurance, Complete Car Cover, Travel Insurance, ISAs, Unit Trusts etc. etc. My job was to check the tests (or 'assessments') to make sure the spelling was correct and the alignment matched up properly. My full job title was Assessment Production Administrator. Sounds dead fancy, doesn't it? But no, it wasn't. It's scoot work, basically. But the money was quite good. Better than either the dole or Brenda's Burgers.

Having said that, though, the work really was dull. For the first week, I found it really exciting and new; being in the office environment, meeting all the new people. But after the first month, it paled and became very mundane. I suppose that's what happens with all jobs, though. Doing the same thing day in, day out. But a job was a job, and at least I had money, at least I had some independence and could contribute substantially to the rent of our new flat.

Ah, yes, the new flat. We moved in just a week after Andrew's boss had sorted it out for us. It was nice; smaller than the Camberwell pad, admittedly, but being in the West End, right there, at the heart of the action, was unspeakably exciting. For a start, we didn't have to get a tube or a bus if we wanted to go out for a drink on the gay scene. Andrew didn't have to take the jeep anywhere anymore. Soho was just around the corner, along with Oxford Street, Regent Street, Piccadilly Circus and all the rest of it.

It did have one disadvantage, though, being so close to everything. Namely, Dimensions.

Being so close to where Andrew worked meant that he was always there, practically. I'm sure he would've slept there had he been able to. I'd spoken to him about it one night, when he didn't get in until around three o'clock because he'd been sorting out some important business. I can't remember what.

It would be unfair to say he had had a massive go at me. He hadn't. But he did tell me, somewhat firmly, that being the manager of Dimensions was quite different to being a barman in Medusa's, that there was a hell of a lot more responsibility in this new role and that it was unfair of me to moan at him just because he had to work late sometimes.

He was right, I knew that. And it wasn't so bad with me working, too, really it wasn't. But my job was simple nine to five stuff, clock in, do my bit of 'quality checking' (as it was called), clock out, get my time sheet signed at the end of the week and there I am, back at home. No fuss, no muss.

After the night when I'd complained about Andrew's lateness, I decided never to bring the subject up again.

I didn't tell anyone at my job that I was gay. What was the point? And it seemed stupid to have to announce it. Would a straight guy start at a new place and say, "By the way, just so you know, I am actually heterosexual."? I don't think so. So why should it be any different for us queers?

I wasn't some mincy shirtlifter, either, with a lisp and a pout, all handbags and limp wrists. To the guys on the Assessment Team at NJT, I was just a regular, red-blooded lad. I mean, the fact that I don't mince around in hot pants and a tiara doesn't make me any less of a homosexual, but the fact that I'm homosexual doesn't make me any less of a man.

I'd sit there and make the same old quips, chuckling at the coarse humour of the straight boys at lunch whose brains seemed to revolve only around sport and tits.

It was okay.

I worked alongside two other guys, also Assessment Production Administrators. Morgan Hughes and Ned Goggins their names were. Morgan was all right. He was twenty-two, a laugh. Okay, he could be a bit vulgar sometimes, but you got used to it, and it was only in a light-hearted sense.

Ned, on the other hand, was a royal pain in the arse. Honestly, the bloke was a nightmare. He was twenty-three, the oldest of the APAs. But I tell you, he was more like twenty-three going on fifty-three. The guy was just so bloody uptight, it was hard to credit.

No one liked him, though, so that was okay. Ned had been there the longest, and it was his job to train me up. "Definite virgin, that one," Morgan had confided to me on that first day while we had a fag-break. Ned, of course, didn't smoke. I'd laughed. "Yeah," Morgan had added. "Definitely a virgin. Why d'you think he's so uptight? If he got a good lay he'd be a different person, I'm telling you, mate."

See what I mean about vulgar?

But when he told me that, I wondered what he'd say if he knew that I shared my bed with another bloke.

Oh, well. Can't worry about that, can you? Anyway, who said anyone at NJT would ever find out?

So that was Morgan and Ned.

Then there was Ben, the postboy...oops, sorry. Communications Officer, I should say.

Ben Harrow was...well, he was gorgeous. That was all there was to it. He was what Daniel would've called a 'Triple F': Fine, fit and fuckable. Sometimes, I'd just catch myself sitting there and staring at him, completely without realising what I was doing. Once or twice, I'd even got a bit of a rager up: you know, an erection? I felt guilty about it. 'Cos of Andrew. It was strange, because I'd looked at other men before, a few at JayJay's, and Keiran, the medic back at Medusa's. But I'd never really felt guilty about fancying them. I don't know why. I suppose I should've done, really, felt guilty. But it always just seemed harmless, a bit of harmless lust, that was all. It was Andrew I was in love with, wasn't it? So it didn't matter if sometimes I'd think, "I fancy that bloke over there."

It felt different with Ben, though. I kept imagining the two of us making love, and every time I did so, I thought about Andrew, and what we had together, and I went all hot and embarrassed and wanted to hug him and forget about this good looking latinate boy at work.

The good thing, though, was that Ben wasn't gay. Honestly, you couldn't hope to meet a straighter guy. Every time we were at lunch - him, me, Morgan, Ned and a few of the others - Ben was always on about footie or cricket or his latest bird (apparently, Ben had never been with a girl for longer than a week. "Too much hassle, mate," he'd say, in his broad cockney accent.)

So that was good. It meant that nothing would ever come of it, even though I fancied Ben rotten. Because he wasn't bent. Really, it was as simple as that.

The next two months flowed at a pretty even pace. Andrew got better and better and more involved with his job, I got more and more bored and pissed off with mine. It was horrible, that. I'd only been there for three bloody months and already I hated it. Was I a slacker? Or was it just that the job wasn't for me?

Probably a little bit of both. I resented Andrew because he enjoyed his job and he had thrown himself so deeply into it. That made me feel nasty, and shallow, and worthless. How could I resent the man I loved just because he enjoyed what he did for living and I didn't?

Again, that hateful question slithered into my head.

Was I jealous?

It seemed a stupid idea, ridiculous. But the more I thought about it, the more it seemed true. He always left for work before me, and arrived back at the flat hours after I'd got home, grinning from ear to ear, exultant after another fantastic day at Dimensions, gushing about how well he was doing, how well respected he was, how pleased Martyn was with the job he was doing. It made my stomach churn, when there was I, stuck at a PC all day long, checking the same things every day that meant absolutely nothing to me, all about withdrawn PEPs, and ISAs, and Investment Bonds and Pension Schemes.

I remembered my band, Lyar, when I'd spend my time writing songs and performing, and playing gigs at the local clubs; stuff I'd pour all my energy into because it mattered, because it was there and I was doing it and it was what I wanted to be doing.

Even working at Brenda's Burgers hadn't been as bad as NJT. Because at least then, even when the job and the pay sucked, I still got to see Andrew; at least he'd been only working normal hours. Okay, they might have sometimes been a bit odd, but at least he could walk away from it when his shift was up, at least there'd be someone there to take over and he could come home and see me.

It wasn't like that now. Running Dimensions sucked up most of his time. There was hardly any time for me...

No. Maybe that wasn't true. Maybe that's just me, jumping off the deep end again.

But really, we hardly ever went out, not like when we'd first moved to London, in that first month. Just under four months we'd been there, but so much had changed in that time.

One morning, I just couldn't face work. I was laying there in bed when Andrew's alarm clock went off at the same time it always did, quarter to seven. I mean, ask you! Quarter to seven in the morning. I didn't get up until eight-fifteen. I had to be at work by nine and I had to get a tube. Andrew lived five minutes' walk away from his job...sorry, career. It started to annoy me, that did, his dedication, his never-ending eagerness to get to work. When I'd come in of an evening I'd sometimes moan at the walls of the empty flat, saying how much I hated my job, how boring it was and how I wanted to write songs again, be a proper part of something. Not just some little working ant at the bottom of the big business food-chain.

Andrew would not have been able to relate to that, oh no. Andrew had it made.

Ø

The morning I decided to throw a sickie, Andrew got up and I heard him pottering around in the kitchen, making some breakfast and then the door clicked shut.

He'd gone.

I was awake by that time, so I just lay there, in the empty double bed, staring at the ceiling, and I just thought, Fuck it.

Fuck it, fuck it, fuck it.

I couldn't be bothered. I just could not bloody be bothered with it. I thought of Morgan, and I thought of Ned, and I thought of all the other hapless office drones, buzzing around like frustrated insects, trying to make management happy, all thinking they had a decent purpose in life. Bollocks, did they.

Yeah, I told myself. Fuck it.

So I got out of bed and I called my boss, Brian. I told him that I wouldn't be in that day. I put on my best 'sickie' voice and he sounded all concerned and he hoped I'd better soon and said that I was to take it easy. Don't worry, I thought. That's exactly what I'm going to do.

I had a leisurely day, all right. Had a nice long bath. Made myself my favourite breakfast of scrambled eggs and toast. Then I watched a video. Then I read a book. Then I ordered out for a Chinese meal for one, because I knew Andrew wouldn't be back from work for ages. No change there, though.

The rest of the day I just spent listening to music. Really, it was a perfect day. And, as it turned out, it made a really nice rest. A refreshing change. It was just what I needed, 'cos the next day I was sure would be easier to face and I'd go back to that hateful office building and be fine again.

But when Andrew came in, things sort of got a bit...erm, weird.

It was nine-thirty. He was in earlier than usual. I didn't actually hear him come in, it was only when he turned the stereo off that had been pumping out the chugging sounds of the Chemical Brothers at about a million decibels. The sudden silence startled me. When I turned, I saw the look on his face. Not anger, not as such. But annoyance. Annoyance that could grow into anger if it were given half the chance.

"Hiya!" I said. Absurdly, I felt like a naughty schoolchild for a moment. Then I snapped out of it, glanced at the clock and saw the time. "You're early."

"I thought I deserved an early night in. With you. Sure you had the music on loud enough, babes?"

It was only subtle, but it was there. A slightly sharp edge to his tone. Even his use of the word 'babes' failed to disguise it. Punctuating it, if anything.

Nonchalantly, I said, "Oh, did I?"

Andrew nodded, shrugged off his blue shirt. Underneath he wore just a white vest that hugged his well-defined torso. He looked somehow menacing, and yet drop dead gorgeous at the same time.

"You seem a bit...agitated," I said. "Are you all right?"

He put his fingers to the bridge of his nose and squeezed his eyes shut. "Yeah, fine. Apart from the fact that I've got a splitting headache."

"There's some Nurofen in the drawer. I'll get you a couple." I got him two painkillers and a glass of water.

"Thanks, baby," he said, and still that little term of endearment sounded odd and false.

I waited in silence while he took the medication.

"How did you get on at work today?" he asked.

"Oh, I didn't bother going in," I said casually, and draped myself on the settee in a mockingly seductive pose.

Andrew frowned. He seemed dead pissed off. Was it really just a headache? This wasn't like him at all. "Oh?" he said. "Why was that? Are you ill?"

"No. I just didn't fancy going in. Couldn't face it today. It is sooooo boring." I grinned. Andrew didn't. He looked...I don't know, po-faced, maybe?

"A job's a job, though, Mark," he said.

The words stung me. It sounded like he was lecturing me. "Yeah, but that one's boring me to death," I said.

"We all need money."

What the hell did that mean? I thought. Was he telling me off?

"'Course we do. I didn't say we didn't. I just fancied having a day off that was all. I am an adult, Andrew. I can make my own decisions, can't I?"

My heart started to beat faster. This seemed wrong. This seemed really, really wrong. I felt as though we were teetering on the brink of a row. "Don't be so childish," he said, and I just looked at him, wide-eyed, unable to believe he'd said that.

"Childish!" I exclaimed, and boom...the argument had started. "I'm not being childish, Andrew. God! Just because I fancy having a day off work - "

"It's not just that, Mark," said Andrew, cutting me off. I got to my feet.

"Then what is it?"

I couldn't believe what was going on. Where had this come from? Where had all this come from?

"You just don't seem to care about holding on to that job. Like this is all a game. Oh, I can't be bothered with working, I'll just let Andrew take care of me, let him slog his guts out while I stay here and listen to music so loud it could cause an earthquake throughout the entire West End."

I didn't answer that. The way he spoke made me sound selfish and - yes - childish. But I wasn't like that, I knew I wasn't. I knew I hadn't behaved the way he made out, and I think that he knew it, too.

"Has something happened to you today, Andrew?" I asked him. "Has someone said something to you at work? Why are you so upset?"

"I just told you, didn't I?"

"I won't accept that. I don't think you're really pissed off at me because I had the day off, are you? There's something else."

He didn't answer, just closed his eyes for a minute. "There's nothing else," he said. "I just think you should...I just don't think you're taking a very mature attitude to all this. Us being here, in London."

"What?" I snapped. "What are you talking about? I'm not one of your bloody employees, Andrew. So don't start coming on to me with all your managerial bullshit. An immature attitude? Is that what you think I've got? Because I didn't go into a job that I hate today? Because maybe I just wanted to have a little bit of fun for once?"

"That's what the weekends are for."

"Oh, really?" I said, knowing I was going over the top but unable to stop myself. My voice was getting louder. "Oh, really? When was the last time we went out clubbing at JayJay's? When was the last time we even went out for a drink together?"

"It was..." began, Andrew, trying to remember.

"Ages ago," I said. "That's when. I can't even remember exactly."

"Yeah, well it's not all nightclubs and pubbing, you know, Mark. There are certain responsibilities we've got to live up to. Some of us have, anyway."

Ohhhhh, that was it. That was it! I said, "I can't believe you just said that, Andrew." My voice had come down now, soft with hurt.

"I'm sorry." But it didn't sound like he meant it. Not one bit. He repeated, "I said I was sorry." Then a few seconds later, "Are you sorry, too?"

I shook my head, my insides all tangled with hurt, frustration and shock: shock that this had all come from nowhere, so suddenly, like a storm breaking in a tropical rainforest. "Look, I'm going to go for a walk," I said. "I need some fresh air." For a second I was tempted to add, You coming, too? but I didn't. I needed some time on my own, to reflect on what had been said.

"Mark, don't go..." Andrew trailed, but I went anyway, grabbing my jacket and slamming the door behind me.

Ø

I didn't know where I was going. I was confused. So terribly confused. What on earth had happened back there?

It was August, but the night was cool. I walked up Newman Street, and as I stepped out into Oxford Street I just thought, sod it, I need a drink.

Probably not the best idea in the world, I know, but what had gone on back there was enough to drive anyone into a bar.

It was only quarter to ten, so there was still a while before anywhere called 'time'. I went to one of my and Andrew's favourite gay haunts, Bar UK at the top of Old Compton Street. It was especially busy for a Wednesday evening. I ordered a whiskey, downed it in one, and then ordered a Budweiser. The barman smiled at me. It reminded me of my first encounter with Andrew, back when he'd been a barman, too.

"Tough day?" said the barman.

"Something like that." He handed me my Budweiser. I sat at the bar and sipped a little of it. It tasted bitter, and I knew I wouldn't be able to finish it.

A few minutes went by and I reached for my cigarettes and stuck one in my mouth. Just as I was fumbling for my lighter, thinking of Andrew and wondering what he was thinking about me, a flame appeared in front of my face. At first I was startled, until I realised some short, muscular bloke had appeared next to me and was offering to light my fag.

"Oh," I said, a bit awkwardly. "Ta."

I took a long drag and exhaled the wispy smoke. How good it felt. Calming. Relaxing. Especially coupled with the warmth of the whiskey. The stranger said, "I'm Tony. Tony Wedge." He held out a hand and I shook it. Clammy and wet. I fought back a grimace, knowing what the bloke wanted, and also knowing that now was not the time to be cruising me. Oh, sometimes I found it funny, the looks I'd get, the silly little advances by desperate blokes who actually believed they were in with a chance. But after the row Andrew and I had just had - our first proper, big row - the whole thing seemed obscene.

"Morgan," I said, without hesitation. "My name's Morgan."

"You look a little annoyed, Morgan," said Tony. He kept this stupid smile on his face, a smile I wanted to swat away.

"I'm fine," I said and turned back to face the front of the bar. Without realising it, I began to peel off the label from the bottle of beer.

"What happened?" said Tony. "You wanna talk about it?"

"Not really."

"It might help."

"Look, what is this?" I said, turning bright eyes on him. He flinched away from me a little bit. His smile faltered then, just for a second, and then it returned. He looked smug. He was well-dressed, obviously not short of a bob or two.

"Do you want a drink?" he asked, clearly struggling to open a conversation. I raised my bottle slightly.

"I've got one, thanks."

"Oh, okay." He ordered a pint of Red Stripe for himself. The young barman grinned at us both, knowing what was happening. Well, he saw it every night of the week, didn't he? The young chickens and the old chooks, all playing off of one another; the same old game.

Tony said nothing for a bit, just tapped his foot to what was playing on the jukebox: Tragedy by Steps.

Then awkwardly, he said, "So...er, how much would you, er..."

At first, I didn't know what he meant in the least. I frowned. "How much would I what?" I said.

How naive I was. Honestly, I look back now and laugh at that moment.

How much would I what?

Duh. And the award for biggest dimwit in all the gay scene goes to...MARK HOLLY!

"You know," said Tony, more awkwardly now. Actually, he seemed a little impatient. He leant closer to whisper into my ear, the scent of Calvin Klein's One heavy on his skin. "How much would you charge?" he hissed the last word. "For full sex, or even just a blow-job..."

I felt sick. Worse than sick; I felt infected. Full sex or even just a blowjob? Urgh! What did he think...

...I was a fucking rentboy!

It was exactly what he thought.

I couldn't move. I just turned, and looked at him, the total extent of my horror and revulsion as clear as day on my face.

Tony recoiled. "Look, look," he said hurriedly. "I've obviously made a mistake all right? I just thought...don't worry. I'm sorry, okay, Morgan? I'm sorry. You get a lot of...in here. I just thought. Sorry, yeah? I'm sorry."

Then he turned and vanished off into the crowd.

Repulsive. Truly fucking repulsive.

Well, of course, I'd had enough of Bar UK by that time. I just wanted to get out, out, out of there, back to Andrew and forget about it, and forget about our argument, and just get back in the flat, safely in his big strong protective arms.

I walked back out onto Old Compton Street. The place was alive; the street that never slept, that never stopped. I walked down the narrow road, listening to the cries of laughter and the pounding dance music that throbbed and swirled in the night air.

I decided to head back home, back to see Andrew to sort this whole stupid thing out. It seemed ludicrous now, that argument. Such a small thing had turned into something so big.

How?

I was just about to leave Old Compton Street when I saw a familiar figure in front of me. It was George. Not a friend of mine really, I didn't know him well enough to call him a friend. George was more of an acquaintance. I'd met him at JayJay's a couple of times, seen him around the scene on a few occasions. He was a bit of a regular at Dimensions, too, so Andrew knew him better than me, really.

As soon as he saw me, he came bounding over. George was only seventeen, but he spent all his time just bumming around on the gay scene. That's what it seemed like to me, anyway. He might have been only young, though, but he was streetwise, he knew what he was doing. He had a rich boyfriend, too, apparently, who went by the name of Peter. I'd never met Peter, so sometimes I wondered if he really existed. But I suppose he must have done, because George was always kitted out in really cool designer clothes, and he had a mobile phone and was never short of money. So where else could he have got all that from?

How much would you charge? For full sex, or even just a blowjob?

The words shuddered through me. Nah, I told myself. George wouldn't do that.

"Hi, Mark!" he said, all eager eyes and big grin. "Didn't expect to bump into you at this time of night."

"What are you talking about?" I smiled. "It's only ten-ish."

George just shrugged. "Where's Andrew?" he said. "I thought you two were joined at the hip."

"He's at home. We had a bit of a...tiff."

"Oh..." said George. "A lover's tiff. Was it to do with what happened at the café today? Is Andrew still saying it was his fault?"

I squinted at George. "What are you talking about? What happened at the café today? You mean Dimensions, yeah?"

"Yeah!" exclaimed George. "You mean...you don't mean you haven't heard about it, do you? You're joking me! What, Andrew didn't tell you? Shit, that's a bit weird."

"Yes. I mean, no. George, for God's sake, will you tell me what happened? Was it something bad?"

"Well, you could say that, yeah. There was...a bit of an accident."

"An accident?"

"Uh huh. I was there at the time, waiting for Peter. He was taking me shopping down Carnaby Street, to get a new pair of boots. These really nice black ones with flames up the side that I've been after for ages and - "

"George, for fuck's sake!"

"Okay, okay. Don't get your knickers in a twist. Anyway, I was at the bar, just talking to Daniel. The place was pretty quiet, it was about three o'clock, I suppose. And then outside these fucking yobbos started prancing around, yelling out 'fucking queers, lock 'em up, kill 'em,' all that bollocks. There was about three of them, I think, could've been four. You know the kind, Mark, not half a brain cell between them."

I nodded. I felt terribly cold then. And sick. Monstrously sick, even more so than when that horrible guy had offered me money for sex back at Bar UK.

"So of course, Daniel being Daniel just gets up and marches outside and starts telling them to...well, clear off, in no uncertain terms. And you know what Daniel's like, Mark. Rushes in where angels fear to tread, as camp and vocal as anything. And honestly, you don't have to be bloody Magnus Magnusson to see he's a poof, do you?"

I shook my head. "So then what happened?"

George winced. "One of the thugs smashed a beer bottle over poor Daniel's head. Kicked him in the face and called him a...let's see, what was it? 'A filthy little shit-stabber that should be strung up by the bollocks and shot a dozen times in the head.' Nice, huh?" George shook his head. "It was horrible, Mark. Really horrible."

"Oh, God..." I moaned. I thought I was going to be sick. My stomach churned. "It's disgusting."

"Isn't it, darling? No wonder I'm heterophobic."

It made me feel so angry. That people could do that anywhere was one thing, that people could just take it upon themselves to say what was right and what was wrong, handing out their own brand of vile, perverted justice.

Poor Daniel. My friend. My poor, poor Daniel. How dare they do that to my Daniel! How dare they!

And doing it on OUR TURF, that added an even sicker edge to it. Old Compton Street was ours; it was our place, the place we had made our own. Gays had flocked there for years, to get away from homophobia like that. It was our sanctuary, our refuge.

"Andrew felt terrible about the whole thing," said George. "Went with Daniel in the ambulance and everything. In some way - and I don't know where he got this idea from - I think he blamed himself."

"How?" I cried. Tears were squeezing out of my eyes. "It wasn't his fault, George! How could he possibly blame himself?"

"You tell me. Maybe because he's the manager of the place. Maybe he thought it was up to him to look after Daniel better...to look after all his staff. You know what he's like. Very protective."

"Yeah," I said absently.

George frowned and shook his head. "I can't believe he didn't tell you what had happened, though, Mark."

I looked up at the night sky for a second, exhaling a slow, shaky sigh. "I don't really think I gave him a chance to, George."

"Eh?"

I shook my head. "Don't worry about it. Look, I have to go. There's someone I've got to see. Something I've got to sort out."

"Andrew?"

I nodded, once, quickly. "I'll speak to you soon, yeah?"

"Okay."

I started to run.

"Take care of yourself, Mark!" George called out after me, but I hardly even heard him.

2 Andrew

Our first big row. And it was over something so stupid that, really, it was laughable.

Mark was right when he'd said that I wasn't really pissed off with the fact he'd had the day off. Of course it wasn't that. I didn't give a shit what he did, so long as he was happy, and if the job was doing his head in that much, I wanted him to be out of there. Like I've said again and again and again, 'till I'm blue in the face almost, I could afford to support us both. He didn't need to work, especially at a place he despised.

It was that business with Daniel that had freaked me out, got me all wound up. I suppose seeing Mark there, dancing away, doing nothing, without a care in the world just triggered off something. Some people say I'm too sensitive. Maybe they're right.

But seeing Daniel there, lying in his own blood, with these fucking arseholes around him calling him a 'dirty queer' and a 'filthy poof', kicking him as he lay there defenceless...it was enough to make you go out on a murderous rampage. Not that I'm in any way condoning violence, it's just that sometimes, the only sensible thing seems to be to fight fire with fire.

Wouldn't you agree?

I'd been downstairs doing some paperwork in the office when it had happened. Suddenly I became aware of all these cries of anger and

I'd rushed up. It had already happened by then, and Yvonne, the head waitress, was calling the police. I rushed outside to try and stop the bastards who'd hit Daniel, but they scarpered. Fucking cunts.

The ambulance arrived quickly, though, and I went in the back of it with Daniel. He'd be fine, they said. He'd have to spend a couple of nights in hospital, mind, and he'd have a nasty scar to show for the ordeal. But he'd live. 'Course, there might be some emotional damage, but time would just have to tell.

I hadn't gone back to work after that horrible business outside the café. I'd just stayed with Daniel while he was being taken care of. I didn't get in contact with Mark because I thought he, too, would have been at work. Maybe that was why I'd been annoyed at him when I discovered he'd taken the day off. I could've used his support, see. I could've done with him being by my side while the nurses treated the handiwork of those homophobic pricks, as they sewed up the gash in Daniel's forehead.

While the wound was sutured, Daniel had squeezed my hand. I had tears in my eyes and I thought, Shit, it's my fault, it's my fault, I should've been there, should've stopped it from happening, I'm the bloody manager of the place after all, aren't I?

Thousands of you would probably disagree with me. What could I have done? It was no one's fault but those brain-dead morons who started it all. They were to blame; them alone and no one else.

It still didn't stop me from feeling guilty, though. Like I said, maybe I'm too sensitive.

Mind you, I'd have to be a pretty hard bastard not to let something like that affect me.

When I got back from the hospital, I expected Mark to be there, on the sofa, with his supper on his lap, watching a film. I wanted to see him and tell him all that had happened and to hold him. But when I went through the door and there he was, jumping around to that booming bloody music it just made me think, Look at him. Just look at him. Not a care in the world. No problems. He has no idea what I've been through today, no idea what Daniel's been through, just look at him...

But that was unfair. Yeah, that was really unfair. But sometimes that's what life was: unfair. Was it fair for Daniel to have almost been killed today by some queer-bashing thug wielding a glass bottle? I don't think so, do you?

When Mark came back in after our row, I was on the sofa. I had my eyes closed, but I wasn't asleep. I think I was over-tired. You know that feeling you get when you're exhausted, but you can't sleep? Well, that's how I was.

"Andrew?" he said, timidly. I opened my eyes.

"Hi." That's all I said. We looked at each other for a while, a long while. His expression was odd. Not guilty, more...understanding, for want of a better word.

"I heard about...what happened today," he said. "About Daniel. I'm sorry, Andrew. I'm really sorry. I didn't know."

"How could you have known?" I asked him. "I refused to tell you, remember?"

He sat down beside me and we looked at each other. We didn't touch. "I'm sorry," he said again.

A smile broke across my face. "It's okay, Mark. I'm sorry, too. I didn't mean what I said to you earlier. About you having the day off. I was so angry about what those bastards had done to Daniel. I guess I needed to take it out on someone. You just sort of...got in the way of it, I suppose. Do you forgive me?"

"Do I forgive you? Do you forgive *me*?"

"For what? You haven't done anything wrong?"

"I stormed off like a spoilt child," I said.

"Yeah, well I called you immature."

"I deserved it." We were quiet for a bit, and then Mark laughed softly. "Listen to us. We could go on like this all night, couldn't we? 'I'm sorry'. 'No, *I'm* sorry'. 'No, I'M sorry'."

"Maybe you've got a point," I said. I smiled. "Oh, Mark!" I grabbed him against me then, holding him tight and stroking his hair. He began to cry, and I followed suit. It wasn't because we were sad. If anything it was because we were happy. Happy to be safe; happy to have each other; happy to just be us.

"Was it awful?" he asked.

I nodded against his shoulder. "It was more than awful. It was disgusting. Who told you what happened?"

"George. I saw him just now. He told me everything. Poor Daniel."

"I know."

"He's gonna be all right, isn't he?"

"He'll live. But I don't know if he'll be all right, not like he was, anyway. Imagine how emotionally damaging something like that could be."

"Yeah."

We held each other in silence for a few minutes. Eventually, I said, "I'm sorry we argued."

"Oh, let's not start that again."

"Seriously, though, Mark. I don't want us to argue like that again. I hated it. Hated having cross words with you."

We drew apart and looked intensely at each other. The love there was strong, I could feel it. It was tangible, almost, as if you could just reach out and touch it. Pick it up and hold it next to your heart.

"If you really hate the job that much, leave. It doesn't matter to me. If you're not happy there, get out. It's simple. Get up and leave. If that's what you want, Mark, it's what *I* want. You know that. Remember what I said to you, before we moved here to Newman Street, whatever I can do to make you happy I'll do. And I meant that."

"I know. I know you did."

"So leave. Chuck it in tomorrow, babes."

"It's not that bad, Andrew. Really. I said the same thing at Brenda's Burgers, didn't I, and I stuck it out there. I just needed a day off."

"But if you want to leave..."

"I'm fine."

"Yes, but..."

And before I could finish, Mark just pulled my face against his and kissed me hard. Then I became aware of his hands unfastening my belt, unbuttoning my trousers and freeing me from my boxer shorts. He finished the kiss and just said, "Andrew...shhhh..."

Then he went down on me, taking my erection in his mouth, gently suckling. I groaned in pleasure. I can't remember the last time he sucked me off. He sucked harder and harder and, gently, I put my hand on the back of his head, stroking the nape of his neck as I pushed into the sweet warmth and wetness of his mouth. "Ah, Mark," I said. "Oh, Mark. Baby. Oh..."

I came a few seconds later, and we both moaned in pleasure. "Oh, Mark, baby, I love you." My eyes were half-closed as I enjoyed that divine feeling of orgasm.

He looked up, peering up at me from beneath his dark fringe. "I love you, too..." he said.

3 Mark

As it turned out, I did decide to leave NJT after all. Two weeks after the night we had that row. It wasn't a rash decision, not really: I'd thought long and hard about it. But in the end, I decided it just wasn't for me; it just wasn't me, full stop. Like Andrew had said, he was fine about it and we both realised that it was the music industry I really wanted to work for, and although I could've stuck it out at NJT while I looked for a job in the profession I craved, there didn't seem much point.

On the day I left, they'd sorted out a big card with GOODBYE AND GOOD LUCK on the front. It reminded me of the day Andrew and I had left for London, the party at Medusa's. Ben had signed the card, too. You know, gorgeous Ben?

See ya, mate. All the best. Ben.

I wondered if he'd have written that if he had known I was gay. Probably not. He'd probably have written something like, Fuck off, ya nonce. Don't come back. Ben.

Clare, from the agency, called me a few times after I left that place with new jobs for me. But I turned them down. She got a bit huffy with me at one stage. "Mark," she'd said. "If you're not going to bother going to these placements then I may as well take you off the books."

I just told her fine, take me off them. Office work wasn't for me, anyway. There was only one thing I wanted to do, and that was work in the music business. I craved it. It was like a drug. I kept thinking more and more about Lyar, about the old days. We had been good, you know. It was a shame that we'd split up; a real shame. We might not have done had it not been for me being gay, but...

But I was gay, and it wasn't my fault if certain individuals couldn't handle that, was it?

One day, while Andrew was at work, I listened to Lyar's demo CD. We'd made it ages ago, had handed it round to record companies without luck. As I listened to it, to the songs that I'd helped to create, I got all sentimental, smiling wistfully back to those carefree days, when I didn't really have any responsibility to speak of.

'S'pose I didn't now, really.

Still, things felt different in London, and as time went by the novelty *did* start to wear off: all the bright lights and the gay scene, the double decker buses and the flocks of foreign tourists. It all became a bit...common-place. Andrew had said that would happen, though. "Give something long enough and it will get mundane, Mark."

But I just hoped it wouldn't be a case of familiarity breeding contempt.

Ø

It wasn't until mid-October that I got another job. If you could call it that. Handing out flyers at the end of the evening at JayJay's. It was really shit money, so it sort of felt more like a hobby than an actual job. I'd been offered it by the bloke who ran the club. His name was Melvin O'Riordian. Seemed like a basically decent bloke...I guess. He was in his mid-forties, but was something of a chicken-chaser. Renowned for letting underage kids into the club in the hope he could shag them later. That was the rumour, anyway. It was a laugh, though, handing out flyers. It meant I got to go to JayJay's every Saturday night, stand there at the front entrance and take everyone's tickets.

Then I could go in, enjoy the club, come and stand at the door at five in the morning and hand out the promotional crap for the next weekend.

I made some really cool friends at JayJay's, and pretty soon all the punters got to know me, too. It was a laugh, and much better than sweating my balls off in that horrible office.

Andrew rarely went clubbing, of course, but I didn't mind that too much. Not that I was going off him or anything, never! I was still head over heels in love, but I could go out and do my own thing and see my own friends without feeling I needed him with me for survival on the gay scene. I guess you could say I'd found my own way.

Another good thing about being a so-called 'door whore' at JayJay's was that I got to eye up the talent. I'd gotten much more relaxed about that. Before, I'd always felt like I was being unfaithful to Andrew by looking. But I reckon he did it as well, and just so long as we were looking but not touching, it presented no threat to our relationship.

Some people say that gay men are naturally promiscuous, but I personally think that's a bit of an unfair generalisation. We look, sure. But so do straight people. All those women at hen-nights with a male stripper gyrating in front of them, everything hanging out. They're all married or have boyfriends or fiancées, don't they? And there they still are, 'oohing' and 'ahhing' and shouting 'get yer cock out!' But it doesn't mean they're going to jump into bed with the bloke, the same as I wasn't going to jump into bed with every good looking guy that smiled at me, winked or pinched my arse in a friendly, flirtatious way.

Daniel worked as a doorwhore, too. He'd recovered well from the attack outside Dimensions a few months earlier. Physically, anyway. There was still some psychological damage there, though, I'm sure. It was only subtle, mind. He was just a bit edgy and suspicious of everyone, a bit nervous. Couldn't say I was surprised, though, the poor bloke. And the worst thing was, the police had never caught the evil bastards, despite articles appearing in Pink Paper and Boyz. Daniel, it seemed, had turned into a little bit of a scene celebrity because of it. And knowing Daniel, he played right up to it.

I was pleased. It really helped his confidence, I reckon.

Things with Andrew and I were going well. We'd come to an arrangement which allowed us both to do our own thing and still maintain a healthy, loving relationship. He sometimes came out clubbing with me, and we had a blast, but the thing is, you've got to look at it from two different viewpoints.

First you had Andrew, who'd been out there clubbing it years ago, when he lived in the East End. He'd done it every weekend back then, and now he was more into running Dimensions. Going wild on the scene was something for him to do occasionally, which suited him well.

I, on the other hand, was in the situation Andrew had been in back in Walthamstow. It was all new, and I wanted to suck it all in, take it all inside me. The difference with me was that I wasn't going to let it destroy me, let it make me go off the rails, 'cos I had Andrew, and all of Andrew's experience, to watch out for me.

All in all, life was good.

One Saturday night in late November, I had the night off from JayJay's. Andrew and I had been planning on going clubbing together: it would've been the first time in ages - you know, the two of us - and I was really looking forward to it.

But there was a problem. Andrew had the 'flu. He'd even had to take a couple of days off work, so you can imagine how ill he was. I took really good care of him. Cuddled him all up on the sofa with the duvet, got him some Lemsip from the chemist and these Night and Day things. Then I made him some tomato soup and some really nice bread rolls. I was the proper little mummy taking care of her son. He laughed. "You don't have to do this," he said, all bunged up and sniffly. "I've only got 'flu."

"Shut up and eat your soup," I told him. "I'm going to go and get some videos for us to watch tonight."

"What about the club?"

I snorted. "Andrew, you're in no state to go clubbing. You've got to stay in and rest. You've got the 'flu."

"Maybe so, but you haven't."

"Yeah, but I can't exactly be out there having a good time while you're in here sick."

"Yeah, Mark, but I'd hate to sit here with you next to me, knowing that you'd rather be out there having a whale of time."

I frowned. "Mm, good point." I thought for a moment, then shook my head. "Nah. I wouldn't feel right about it, Andrew."

"Mark."

"What?"

"Go. Phone Daniel and see what he's doing."

"I know what he's doing. Working. They can't give everyone the night off at once, you know."

"Well, what about someone else? Come on, there's loads of people we know. You'll probably see someone there. Where were you planning to take me tonight? JayJay's?"

I shook my head. "No. I thought we'd try somewhere different tonight. I was thinking along the lines of Elysium."

"Yeah, haven't been there for a while. Go on then, what are you waiting for?"

"Andrew, I wouldn't feel right about it. I don't mind staying in, honestly. It'll be...cosy."

Andrew gave me a look of disbelief.

I thought about going out. Then thought about staying in. Then thought about what Andrew had told me.

"I'll get my jacket," I said.

Ø

It was Christian I went out to Elysium with. You haven't met Christian yet. I'd known him for a couple of months and we'd hit it off instantly, sort of like me and Daniel. That was the good thing about the gay scene. Because it was all pretty much in one area, every queer knew every other queer or, at the very least, a friend of every other queer. So all our friends were each other's friends. It was cool.

I'd arranged for Christian to come to the flat and we'd walk down to the club together. He wanted to say hi to Andrew, to see how he was feeling. "Is he taking care of you all right?" Christian asked the afflicted one.

"Too well," sniffled Andrew, all bundled up on the settee. "I didn't realise he was such a mother hen."

"Ah, bless," said Christian.

"We won't be back too late," I told Andrew. I kissed his forehead, not his lips. "Don't want to catch your germs!"

"Charming!"

While we walked down to Covent Garden, which was where Elysium was located, Christian said, "You're lucky to have Andrew, Mark."

"I know."

"You make such a nice couple. Safe. Relaxed. It sort of...represents everything good about being gay."

I looked at him with a half smile. "That's a weird thing to say."

"Not really. It's true."

"Oh, well...cheers, Chris."

We got to the club. Elysium was smaller than JayJay's, built on two floors rather than three. But that didn't matter, because it meant it got more crowded, which was cool. The people there were pretty much the same mix, though: you had all the different varieties of homosexual, the queens, the chickens, the chooks and the clones.

It was fun, being with Christian. He was a real character. He didn't have a boyfriend, said he didn't believe in them. He just enjoyed his friends, and shagging around a bit. Little bit like Daniel in that respect, I guess.

We got into the club and went for it, really went for it. The music at Elysium was harder than at JayJay's, really big beat stuff, like Fatboy

Slim and Armand Van Helden.

We'd been there for about three quarters of an hour when Christian pulled me to a corner of the dance floor and shouted into my ear, "Here. Try one of these."

He pressed something into my palm. Something small and round.

An E.

Drugs.

They were there of course, all the time on the gay scene. Maybe more than on the straight scene, I didn't know. I mean, I knew Christian had popped more than the odd pill in his time, Daniel, too, and George.

But with Christian, it didn't stop with the occasional pill, I knew that. He did everything: coke, ketamine, acid...all of 'em.

It was okay, though. I didn't mind what anyone else did, it was up to them, right? Let people get on with their own lives, that's what I say. Live and let live and all the rest of it.

I'd never really considered taking drugs - well, not hard drugs, anyway. I mean, okay, I might have done a few of the softer ones, hash and stuff. And of course, there was the fags and the booze. But they didn't seem to count. Maybe because they were the legal ones. Still just as damaging, though...I guess.

It just...I dunno. Taking Ecstasy seemed like such a big leap, though, from those other things. That's what all the hype was about. You read about it in the newspaper all the time, don't you, people dying after taking an E at their eighteenth birthday party. Their first ever pill and - bam! - six feet under. Look at that girl...what's her name? Leah Betts, that's it. Splashed all over the media, she was.

"Well?" Christian shouted in my ear. "Take it. Don't worry, I don't want any money or nothing."

Still, I hesitated.

Christian rolled his eyes. "Come on, man. Don't be such a poof!"

I thought of Andrew, and what he'd said, all about drugs fucking him up years ago.

And suddenly, I felt an overwhelming desire to swallow the bloody thing. I don't know why, honestly I don't. I really can't explain where that feeling came from, and how suddenly it came.

It was just there, on that November Saturday night, with the music pumping around me and everyone having a good time, and with Christian in my ear, I just thought, Yeah, why not? I'd had nothing to drink yet so I wasn't pissed or anything. It was a conscious decision. I knew what it was I was taking, I knew the risks involved. And sometimes, I think you have to take a risk. Experimentation, I thought. Yeah. That's what it is, and just like that, those doubts were gone.

"It's good stuff," Christian assured me. "Mitsubishis always are. And these baby's are choc-full of MDMA."

But I didn't know what the hell MDMA was.

"Have you taken one?" I shouted at him, only just audible over the booming bass-lines.

He nodded, a big grin from ear to ear. "Oh, yeah. Yeah, mate. This shit is gooood."

And he seemed fine. So why not me...?

Perhaps I wouldn't have taken it had I not been in a club. Perhaps the mood just took me over, making me feel reckless and carefree... But no, I'm kidding myself by saying that. It wasn't as if it was my first time in a gay club, or even my first time in a London gay club. The time was right; the moment was right, and that's all there was to it.

I'm not trying to glamorise drugs or anything. They're bad for you. But at the end of the day it was up to me.

So I grinned and popped the pill into my mouth, this surge of adrenaline and excitement whizzing through me as I did it. I felt like such a rebel. Christian handed me his bottle of water and I took a short swig. The pill tasted foul as it went down my throat.

"You'll feel like a princess in about half an hour, darling," he said, smiling that crazed smile.

"Don't leave me on my own," I said.

"Don't worry, sweets. I'll look after you."

After that, as we continued dancing, I couldn't stop thinking about the drug I'd taken. I felt so anxious about it. I mean, yeah, it was my idea, my own stupid fault for taking it, so who did I have to blame? No one. But I just kept thinking, What if it's rat poison? What if it's bleach? Who knows what sort of chemicals I've just chucked down my neck?

Christian seemed to realise how tense I was, and he'd come up and shout in my ear, "Don't look so worried, love. It's just a pill. I've had loads of them in my time. I'm on two right now. Don't worry. If you think about it too much, you'll never come up on it, Mark. Just relax and forget about it."

Forget about it. Right.

But slowly, it happened. It was so weird. Amazing, but weird. First I started to tingle, my whole body...up from my toes, then right to the tips of my hair. It felt like my hair was alive in fact, like each individual strand was alive. A sea anemone exploring strange waters. And indeed, the waters around me seemed very, very strange.

The music got louder, the beats deeper. It was like I was sinking, and yet flying at the same time. I could feel my eyes grow wider, and my heart pump faster. I touched my hair and my scalp prickled. This is amazing, I kept thinking. This is amazing. Where have these pills been all my life! This is amazing.

Like I said, I'm not trying to glamorise drugs, really I'm not. I'm just being honest here, trying to tell you what it was like that first time. And the truth is, that the first time I tried Ecstasy it *was* amazing. It was out of this world.

I just remember thinking, I love this place; these people; this music. I never want to go home. I never want to leave, for this to end. Never, never, NEVER!

The lights flickered, and they looked strange and beautiful, like things from another planet, touching the faces of all those around me, all those gorgeous, beautiful, wonderful people.

That was another thing I remember, too. I fancied everyone. Everyone. Every bloke in there, fat, ugly, skinny, short... whatever... they were all gorgeous as far as I was concerned. At that moment... I'd've fucked 'em all. Or let them fuck me.

"You all right?" asked Christian, beaming. "You're up aren't you?"

"Buzzing my nut off!"

He laughed. "That's my boy."

I smiled back, and really let myself go on the dance floor. It was impossible not to, impossible to stop dancing. My whole body felt so warm, and yet chilly at the same time. The sort of chilly you get when you're dead excited about something; you know, that lovely sort of goosebumpy feeling.

Like I said, I'll never forget that first pill.

About forty minutes after the E came up, when the love-rush really reached its maximum peak, I started flirting with some guy in front of me. To tell you the God's honest truth, I can't remember what he looked like. Not properly. But at the time, he was like the most gorgeous thing on two legs. That's how I felt, anyway. It was as though I'd stopped thinking in the natural order of things – I felt things more than I thought them.

That's what it does to you, though, the E. Nothing is ugly or horrible or nasty...everything is just there for you, all brilliant and magical and sparkly, there for you, there for the taking. It's amazing.

Anyway, this guy.

I was dancing behind him, and he was inching closer and closer towards me so that my front was touching his back. Then he'd jerk forward a little, like teasing me. It was funny. Seemed so at the time, at least. If I hadn't been off my tits on illegal substances, I would've thought differently.

But the mood had possessed me. All there was then was that moment, that club, that bloke. So when he grabbed my hand, I thought, Okay...yeah, I like this.

And then when he tried to kiss me, I thought, Okay...yeah, why not?

It was the same when he put his hands down my boxers, still kissing me, harder and harder. So what? So what? I told myself.

Then when he asked me if I wanted to go back to his place, I thought...Fuck it, what's one night?

Andrew'll never know.

4 Andrew

To be honest, I hadn't been totally thrilled with the idea of Mark going out with Christian. Oh, Christian was all right, he was a nice guy and everything. But he did a lot of shit that I didn't exactly approve of. I don't want to come over all high and mighty, give you the holier-than-thou rundown or anything.

It's just that Christian did drugs...serious drugs. And I'm not talking about just the odd pill one Saturday night a month, or the odd joint here and there. No. He did it a lot more than that, and it didn't stop with just taking the crap, he sold it, too. Something I really didn't like.

It wasn't just drugs, either. He was into rent. Did it quite a lot, actually. Now, shagging around is one thing, that's okay if you're not in a proper relationship. A lot of people did it on the scene. But getting paid for it, that was something else all together, something that left a really bad taste in my mouth.

But I was probably worrying about nothing with Mark. He was a sensible bloke, he knew what was right and what was wrong. For God's sake, he was twenty-one. It's just that I had trouble forgetting about those old days in Walthamstow. I, too, started off with all good intentions and a firm belief that the dark underbelly of the gay scene would have no effect on me. Wrong. It had soon swallowed me up.

But look, I don't want to go on about that. Because I know what you're going to tell me. Just because it happened to me, didn't mean that Mark was going to go the same way. And even if he did, I'd turned out all right, hadn't I?

Although that wasn't really the point.

When Mark left with Christian to go out to Elysium (not one of my favourite gay clubs, by the way, but it did make a nice change from JayJay's every now and then) I just sat there and watched telly, trying not to worry. I do worry too much, I know that. But when you're as deeply in love with someone as I am with Mark, you just can't help being concerned.

The 'flu medication I was on made me drowsy, so at about midnight I had no choice but to turn in. I knew I wouldn't be up until about twelve noon the next day. Medicine always did that to me. But I imagined Mark would probably sneak in when he got home and just slip into bed beside me. The thought was warming. What better way is there to wake up other than beside the man you love?

Ø

Except I didn't. Wake up beside Mark, that is. At first I thought it must've been too early or something. But no. The alarm clock told me it was quarter past eleven in the morning.

So where was Mark?

I sat up, and my head felt all thick and fuzzy. It was as if I was trapped in a load of raw cake dough. I closed my eyes and took a couple of breaths. I always go like that after taking medicine. The drowsiness just knocks me for six.

I got out of bed, and my body ached, as it does when you have 'flu. Damn, I thought, wishing the illness would piss off so I could get back to normal, back to what counted.

I put my dressing gown on, and tied it tightly around my waist, padding through to the flat's small livingroom.

Mark was there, on the settee. He still had his jacket on from last night, and was smoking a cigarette, staring out at nothing.

"Hey," I said. "What are you doing here?" It was meant to be a joke, but Mark didn't respond for immediately. Then he jumped slightly and turned his head.

"Huh? What?"

I noticed, with a small amount of unease, that the hand holding the cigarette was shaking slightly.

"Have you only just got in?" I asked.

Mark looked at me confusedly. "Huh? Oh. Yeah, about an hour ago."

"Did you have a nice time?"

"It was okay, yeah. Yeah, good. I'm just really tired now, though."

"I can imagine. Did you go back to someone's flat or something?"

"What makes you say that?"

I was startled by the briskness of his response.

"You know, for a chill-out? After the club let out?"

Mark looked blank. He seemed very confused, like his mind was elsewhere.

"A chill-out," he said slowly, woodenly. "Yeah, that was it."

"Oh right. Whose?"

"Whose what?"

"Whose flat was the chill-out at?"

"Huh? Oh, some mate of Christian's. Didn't really know him that well. It was...quite shit, actually."

I nodded slowly, then said, "Mark?"

"What?"

We stared at each other for a moment, as if we both wanted to say something but had absolutely no idea what that something was.

"Do you want a coffee?" I said.

"Yeah. Please. A coffee'd be nice."

I nodded and got him the coffee. "I feel much better now, by the way. Thanks for asking." I chuckled, to show him that I'd been joking.

Mark was silent. He took a long drag on his cigarette, and then coughed.

"Bad for you," I said.

"So's everything," he answered, and there was a bite to his voice. I ignored it.

I made myself a cup of Lemsip; disgusting stuff but it eased the 'flu. "So," I said, taking my place beside Mark on the sofa. "Any gossip from last night? Did Christian get off with anyone? You know what he's like."

"Christian's all right."

I paused, then said carefully, "No need to snap."

"I didn't snap!"

"Oh-kay," I said slowly, getting a little riled myself. I took some more Lemsip and winced. "Ew, that's foul."

Mark said nothing, took another drag on his cigarette. It had finished and he stubbed it out.

I thought, Something is wrong here; something's not right.

But what?

"So was it a good night?" I asked.

"You asked me that already."

"Oh, did I? Sorry."

"What's up with you?"

"I might ask the same of you."

"Oh, come off your high horse for once, Andrew."

I was stunned! Where had that little eruption come from?

"What's that meant to mean?"

"You're always lecturing me, you are, Andrew." He didn't shout it, didn't raise his voice one bit. But there was a darkness to those words. A darkness that was not him at all, didn't suit him in the least. But it was there.

Why?

"What do you mean, I'm always lecturing you?"

"Just because you've lived in London and done it all before, you think you know best, don't you? That I'm just the stupid kid from the sticks who doesn't know shit from clay about the big city. Isn't that right, Andrew? Isn't it?"

I sat back on the sofa, shocked to the core. I wasn't like that. I knew I wasn't. So why did Mark seem to think so? And why had my innocent remarks sparked him into such anger...?

And then I knew. It was like a light-switch being flicked on in my brain.

It all seemed so obvious when you thought about it: the snappiness, the shaky hand, coat still on, staring into nothingness...

Of course, everybody has a different come-down from drugs. Some people don't get come-downs at all.

But I got them.

And, clearly, so did Mark.

"I'm sorry," he said, hollowly. He lit another cigarette with a barely steady hand, coughing again as he took that first drag.

"Sorry for what?"

Just a shrug. "Dunno..."

"Mark..." I trailed.

He just looked at me.

I took a deep breath and said, "What did you take last night, Mark? Was it a pill? E?" There was no tone of lecturing in my voice; I wasn't about to come across as the stern parent telling their kid that drugs are evil and terrible and they'll destroy your life. That never does anyone any good. If someone's gonna do the drugs thing, they're gonna do it.

Believe me, I know.

Mark refused to look at me. He just sat there, hunched forward, puffing his fags, legs trembling.

"Mark," I said. I put a hand on his shoulder. I thought about Christian then, wishing the little shit was right there so I could plant my fist in his face. What had he done to my baby? What had he done?

"Mark, look at me."

Mark turned his face towards mine and I took it in both hands as gently as if it were porcelain. His skin was rough with stubble.

I looked into his eyes. Red; puffy bags underneath them, pupils still dilated. He was pale and his face was covered with a light film of sweat. "What did you take, Mark?" I repeated, voice soft; soothing; lulling.

He swallowed. His expression was...glazed.

"Ecstasy," he said at last. "Christian gave it to me."

"Fuck," I breathed, and closed my eyes. Damn that little bastard!

All right, all right. Maybe I was being a bit biased to blame it solely on Christian. Mark was a big boy, he could've said no. Unless Christian slipped it into his drink or something. But that thought was too frightening for words.

"What kind was it?" I asked. "D'you know?"

"Mitsubishi, I think he said."

"And you took a whole one?" I asked, horrified. "The whole pill?"

Mark nodded. Puffed more fag.

Christ! I thought. The first time he takes an E and he has a whole one. Wonderful. It must have blown his fucking brains out.

I remember the first time I'd taken a pill. It had only been a half – a white dove, I think – and I'd been tripping for hours and hours. A whole one – let alone a whole Mitsubishi – would've had me caned for days.

"How do you feel now?" I asked.

Without looking at me, Mark said, "Like shit. Andrew, I feel horrible. I feel..."

"Empty?"

He nodded. "Empty," he repeated, and even his voice sounded empty. Vacant and hollow. "It was good at the time, Andrew. It felt amazing. It *was* amazing. But now...it's like I have nothing left. Everything just seems worthless and pointless."

He looked at me now and it was like looking at a ghost. Fragments of what should've been there.

I tried to be reassuring. I said, "It's just a come-down. You'll feel better soon."

Of course, sometimes come-downs could last for days. Take a pill on a Saturday night, feel brilliant for a couple of hours, and often you wouldn't recover completely until about Wednesday. Was it worth it? Was it bollocks.

The thing about Ecstasy – about any drug, really – is that it doesn't really give you extra pleasure or energy, it only borrows it from elsewhere. It's like taking out a mortgage on your senses.

Buy now.

Pay later.

I know I sound like some kind of patronising Public Services announcement there, but there's no getting away from the truth.

Drugs. Are. Shit.

"I feel sick," said Mark. He closed his eyes and put a hand to his forehead.

"Have you got a headache?" I asked.

He nodded.

"I wish I hadn't taken that fucking thing. Everything seems so out of sync. On the way back here I felt like...like everyone was watching me. I was even convinced that some little old lady was a policewoman, that she knew what I'd done. I was so paranoid. It was awful, Andrew. It *is* awful."

"I know," was all I could say. But the situation scared me. I felt as if I were looking at myself four years ago, back in Walthamstow. It was like something was beginning, like history was repeating.

Something is here. Something has come.

I remembered my worries from the previous night, when Mark had gone out with Christian, what I'd thought. Well, it turned out my concerns had been justified hadn't they?

A flotilla of unsettling questions filled my head:

Was it starting? Was this it? Was Mark going to go the same way I once had? The hard drugs, the casual sex, the trail of destruction? Was he?

He said, "I'm sorry, Andrew. I feel like I've let you down."

There was guilt in his eyes. I put my arm around his shoulders and held him against my chest. He didn't cry, as I'd expected him to.

For long moments we sat there in silence.

"I won't do it again, Andrew," he said at last. "The drugs. I swear I won't do them again. I just thought I'd...try it. I know that sounds stupid, but..."

"Shhh.Don't worry. It's okay to try these things sometimes. It makes us stronger people in the long run."

"I don't feel very strong right now. I feel like shit."

"That's what happens. We all do it, and we all learn. Okay?"

He nodded against my chest.

When he looked at me again, those same traces of guilt were still in his too-wide eyes. I kissed his forehead. "Why don't you go to bed?" I said. "Sleep it off, yeah?"

"'Kay." He got to his feet. "I'm sorry, Andrew," he said again.

"I know. It's all right. Sleep it off, okay? We can talk some more when you're better."

He nodded again, solemnly. Then he turned and disappeared into the bedroom, leaving me alone to think over what had happened and to pray that it really was just going to be a one-off.

5 Mark

There was more to it, though, wasn't there? More than just the E. But as far as I was concerned, that other part was something Andrew was never going to find out about. How could I tell him that I'd slept with someone else, even if that someone else had turned out to be nothing more than a one-night stand?

I'd woken up that Sunday morning in bed beside a tuft of blond hair. That was all I could see of the one-night stand. Snoring so loudly he woke me up. I felt horrible as soon as I opened my eyes. Dirty. Ashamed. And yes, like Andrew said, empty. I couldn't remember very much about the night before, just vague, shapeless details.

The club. The pill. Kissing some geezer. Getting in a taxi. Getting fucked. Or was it me who did the fucking? Or had there been no fucking at all?

See what I mean? Hazy, all of it hazy. I felt like I was in a mental fog.

The bloke lived in a place called Rotherhithe, in South East London. I'd slipped out of his flat early that morning without a clue where I was going. Eventually I found the tube station and bunked the train to Whitechapel, and from there on to Euston Square. I had to walk all the way down to Newman Street, as paranoid as shit, scared out my mind and convinced that the Drugs Squad were watching my every movement. Thing was, I didn't really realise it was a come-down until Andrew said so. How could I have known, though? Remember: it was the first time I'd ever tried hard drugs.

But like Andrew'd said, I slept it off. When I woke up, I didn't feel empty anymore. I still felt horrible though. Guilty. I had a shower, but I couldn't wash the guilt off. What had I done to Andrew? How could I have been so reckless by jeopardising our relationship like that?

It wasn't you, Mark, I tried to console myself. It was the Ecstasy. It was that crap. It wasn't you.

Bullshit. Of course, it was me. I mean, sure, it would be great if we could just blame everything on something else. It would be great if there was always a scapegoat for every situation, every eventuality. But of course there isn't.

We all have a choice.

That Sunday evening, after my first ever one-night-stand of shame, Andrew and I cuddled up on the sofa and watched a film. It was a weepy one: Beaches, with Bette Midler. We both cried like a couple of old queens. It was safe, though. Away from the brightness and bitchiness of the gay scene.

I remembered what Christian had said to me the night before.

You make such a nice couple. Safe. Relaxed. It sort of...represents everything good about being gay.

Did it?

With Andrew's arm around my shoulders and my head against his chest, listening to our unified breathing and heartbeats, it all seemed very true.

If only I'd known what was waiting around the corner.

∅

Christmas arrived. It was lovely. Andrew and I got a real Christmas tree for the flat and the place smelt absolutely fantastic. London was magical at Christmas-time. All the shoppers and lights in Oxford Street, the restaurants with all their Christmas menus. Brilliant. There was such a sense of togetherness about the whole thing; it was utterly heart-warming.

I got Andrew some Tommy Hilfiger underwear and the latest Jennifer Lopez CD.

He got me a gold chain with a crucifix on it. I was absolutely awe-struck by it as I opened the little box on Christmas morning. "Andrew!" I exclaimed. "You can't afford this. This is too…too extravagant."

"Do you like it?" was all he'd said, smiling that relaxed smile of his.

"It's…fantastic."

"Well, then. That's all that matters."

"You can't afford…" I began, but trailed off. Truly, though, it was beautiful. I put it on straight away. "I'll never take it off," I told Andrew, and I knew I wouldn't, either. It was such a wonderful gift…like an engagement ring or something.

For Christmas dinner, we had Daniel round with Steven, his latest boyfriend (or latest casual fuck, as the case might have been). Andrew and Daniel did all the cooking, coming up trumps with a brilliant turkey dinner and all the trimmings. In the evening, we also invited George round for drinks. He brought with him the mysterious Peter who we all finally got to meet. (Incidentally, it turned out he was lovely, even if he did spoil George rotten).

I actually got to speak to my dad on Christmas day. Mum phoned, just to say Merry Christmas, and then she said my dad wanted a word. I couldn't believe it. I was dead nervous, which was weird. Like I told you earlier, my dad and I had always gotten on really well, and now I was nervous about speaking to him on the phone. It was nuts. But we had a short chat, only lightweight stuff, you understand. "How's life treating you?" etc. But it was good speaking to him. I guess it's true what they say about 'Goodwill to all men'. Even if some of them happen to be poofs.

Ø

Andrew was pretty busy during the festive season, though. As you can imagine, Dimensions was packed out pretty much every day and every night right through to New Year. Though of course, when you considered the Millennium celebrations that had taken place the year before, it seemed pretty tame in comparison.

We spent New Year's Eve in JayJay's. It was fab, a really fun night. And no, before you ask, I didn't take any more pills, just a little bit of speed, which left me with no come-down whatsoever. Plus it left me more aware so that I wouldn't end up falling into the sack with the first bloke who pinched my arse.

Speed was all right. So was E, I guess. I just didn't much fancy taking it any more after that night in Elysium.

Andrew still hadn't found out about all that by the way, and that was the way I intended things to stay.

Once Christmas was out of the way, things got back to normal. I was working on the cashtill at JayJay's by that time. Yeah, I got promoted. It was still a bit of a shitty job, I know. And by no means did I want it to become a career. But it did for then, just while I got my whole 'wild-on-the-scene' phase out of my head. I mean, it wasn't as if I had a kid to look after or anything, was it?

Oh, right, that reminds me. Grace had her baby in December. Two days before Christmas Eve, a bouncing baby boy. No, they didn't call him Jesus. Didn't even call him Mark, in fact. They called him Rupert.

I don't know what they were thinking, to be honest. Rupert. I mean, for God's sake, that poor little kid. Of course, I didn't say that to Grace. I was all, "What a lovely name, Grace. Strong. Intelligent. I love it." I do think I'm quite a good liar, though.

Grace said she'd love to come down and see me and Andrew now that little Rupert had finally appeared. But I knew it'd be ages before she visited. It wasn't exactly a barrel of laughs bringing up a kid: I know that from my niece, Melody.

Oh, well. There was plenty of time for me to show Grace and Jason around the scene...once they got used to being parents, of course.

Working on the front desk at JayJay's meant that I couldn't go in and enjoy the club at any time, unlike when I used to give out flyers. People arrived throughout the entire night. Of course, sometimes whole hours would go by and no one would come in. But that was always in the early hours of the morning, and by that time, the club was heaving anyway. It was still a laugh, though, the job. I'll say that much. I was good friends with all the staff and I knew all the regulars. It made me feel great; popular. The first time in my life when I'd really been that popular. At school, I'd always been kind of a loner, and my only friends back home had really been the guys in my band, Lyar. But that's because I hadn't really belonged in those places: at school and at home. Those weren't really my people. Not like in London, on the gay scene.

Ø

One night while working at JayJay's, I had a bit of shock. It was at the start of the night. I was going about my usual routine, taking people's money and flyers, doling out the change etc. It was a busy night, busier than usual, in fact. We had a top-name PA in that night. Some pop singer called Lacey Williams, who'd practically come out of nowhere and taken the charts by storm. So as you can imagine, her first live performance in one of the country's biggest gay venues had aroused quite a bit of interest.

It was frantic to begin with, queues stretching on for what seemed like miles. I served everyone quickly, as I had learned to do, getting them all through as fast as possible. A few of my friends came in, and I let them in for nothing, as you do. Then a bloke came up, holding out his discount flyer and a tenner.

I paused for a second, recognising him from somewhere but trying to work out just who he was and where I knew him from. He was

145

smiling in a way that told me he recognised me also.

And then...it dawned on me.

I knew who it was.

"Ben?" I said, confused. Ben Harrow, the gorgeous postboy from NJT, the bloke who I'd fancied. Also the bloke whom I'd been sure was as straight as a die.

He grinned that gorgeous grin. "All right, Mark?" he said. His voice was the same: cockney and butch. But now he had blond highlights in his otherwise jet-black hair.

He was still drop-dead gorgeous.

This is not really happening, I told myself.

You bet your life it is, Mark.

"Hi," I said, voice stumbling slightly. Stumbling with shock, I guess.

"You're working here now, are ya?" he said. His grin did not fade.

"Uh huh." I nodded. Ben? I thought. Here? At JayJay's?

Was he gay?

It seemed ridiculous. Like a contradiction in terms. Ben Harrow equals gay?

Had the world gone mad?

He must be here to see the act, I told myself. That's it. Yes. He's here to see Lacey Williams. She was an attractive woman, after all. Had everything in all the right places. Just the sort of girl a lad like Ben would go for.

I remembered one of his crude jokes from my NJT days.

What do you call a hooker with a runny nose? Full.

There you go. Straight as a die, like I said. Yeah, that was it. He's only here to see Lacey Williams, to ogle at her tits and all that.

He said, "So, er, are you gonna take my money or what?"

Behind him, the massive queue began to get restless.

I blinked, pulling myself out of the trance I seemed to have slipped into. I took his tenner and handed back the change - two quid. Ben grinned. "See you around, Mark," he said, and then he vanished through the archway into the pounding music and the swirling dry ice.

I watched him go, unable to believe what I'd just seen. Ben? At JayJay's? It was utter madness.

Well, of course I couldn't leave things like that. I wanted to talk to him, to find out what he was doing there. Had he really just come to see Lacey Williams? Or did he bat for my side after all? The latter seemed to defy belief.

To Carrie, who was working alongside me, I said, "Cover for me, will ya, Caz?"

Carrie was wild. She was twenty, with long blonde and black hair, and she had a diamond stud in her nose. "What? Mark, look how busy we are!"

I studied the surge of people, all desperate to see Lacey, and of course, enjoy their usual Saturday night's worth of clubbing.

I sighed. Of course I couldn't desert Carrie. It was only the two of us working the front desk, after all. And why did I want to go, anyway? To chase after some bloke, even though I had Andrew? What was I playing at? Did I want a repeat performance of that night at Elysium, when I'd taken that pill? 'Course I bloody didn't.

But still...this was Ben. Ben Harrow. And I didn't want to chase after him for the obvious reasons. It was more curiosity that had gotten hold of me, than lust. Well...sort of.

"Yeah," I said to Carrie, somewhat glumly. "You're right."

"Look, this lot'll be cleared in an hour or so," she said, as we both continued to serve frantically. "Then you can go off. It'll be quiet then, so one of us can have a break. We'll take it in turns, yeah?"

I smiled at her. "Yeah. Cheers, Carrie."

Carrie just beamed.

Ø

She was right, of course. Things did go quiet after about an hour and a quarter. The majority of the punters who turned up that night were all inside, having a ball. "Go on, then," said Carrie. "Hop it. Have an hour of fun and then come back 'ere so I can nip off for a bit."

"Brilliant. Don't worry, I shouldn't be too long."

"I said an hour, Marky boy. No longer, yeah?" Carrie raised her eyebrows. She was wicked, Carrie, but I tell you this: I wouldn't have wanted to have crossed her. No way.

I jumped off my stool and slipped out of the side door of our booth, disappearing inside the large, smoky club. I walked past the coat-check girls, saying hi to them as I went, and then hurried down onto the main dancefloor. The music was so loud. Pumping, throbbing, vibrating. It was awesome. To me and Carrie back upstairs it was just a dull thud. Down here it was so loud it was almost unbelievable.

I needed to find Ben. Insane, I told myself, as I scanned the faces of the crowd. This is totally insane. Why are you looking for him? What do you want to start, Mark? What about Andrew?

I'm just curious, I told myself. I'm just curious as to what the bloke's doing here, that's all.

The music pounded on. It was relentless.

I knew the DJ, Wayne, quite well. Tonight he was really on top form.

I pushed through the bodies and couldn't get Ben out of my head. How gorgeous he was!

A Triple F, Daniel would say. Fine, fit and fuckable.

Yum.

Then I thought of Andrew. So trusting and loving and caring. He who'd do anything in his power to make me happy. That's what he'd said, that's what he'd told me. And there was I, chasing after someone else, practically drooling over them.

I'm just curious, I told myself. I'm just -

And then I saw him. Standing by the stage he was, leaning against it, tapping his foot. He seemed relaxed and casual. Not at all like the crazed dancers around us. He looked almost as if he was…waiting for something.

Or someone.

I walked up, smiling like an idiot. I had on a checked shirt and dark blue combats, he was wearing light-coloured jeans and a white T-shirt that showed off his muscles. A Triple F if ever there was one.

He recognised me and his eyes lit up.

And suddenly, I felt unbearably foolish. He beckoned me over with one finger. I was irresistibly drawn to him.

"Hi," I shouted into his ear.

He just beamed.

"What are you doing here?" I asked.

"Same as everybody else, I suppose."

I wondered if there was some sort of hidden message in those words.

"This doesn't really seem like your kind of place."

He shrugged, but didn't answer. It was so infuriating! Part of me wanted to shake him and shout, "Just tell me, will ya? Are you queer or what, Ben?"

Of course, I didn't.

He said, "Mark, do you want a drink?"

There was time before I had to go back to Carrie. At least half an hour. So I said, "Yeah, okay."

We went up to the middle bar, the so-called chill out room. The music wasn't exactly quieter up there, but it was easier to talk. And I felt that Ben and I needed to talk.

I wanted him, I knew. I was a terrible person for it, because I had Andrew, and that should have been enough. But it was pure lust, see. That was all there was to it: lust. I loved Andrew, and I fancied him like mad, sure. But I wanted to sleep with Ben.

Oddly, I felt like I had when I'd been coming out, about the conflicting feelings between straight and gay. Only now my feelings were battling between Andrew and Ben. The feelings swung one way and then the other. Like a dead man hanging from the gallows, swaying in the wind.

Ben got us a Budweiser each and we sat at one of the small tables in the corner.

He said, "You're shocked to see me here, ain't ya?"

I nodded. "To say the least."

Ben's grin widened. "Can't say I'm surprised to see you here, though, Mark. I always thought you were...you know."

"Bent?"

"For want of a better term, yeah. Bet you didn't think the same of me, though, did you?"

I shook my head. So it was true! Unbelievable. Un-fucking-believable.

Ben Harrow was gay.

Even with him sitting there in front of me, smiling about it, coming out to me, it still seemed like some kind of joke, like a set-up.

Ben ran a hand through his hair. My heart fluttered with the wanting of him.

And you know what it all reminded me of, the whole unlikely situation? It reminded me of when I first met Andrew, when I had all those weird, conflicting thoughts spinning around in my head. The Budweiser. The banter. The little shocking comments. All of it.

I remembered how I'd felt when Andrew had first invited me round to his flat.

"How about you come round to my place tonight?"

I remember the first time he admitted he fancied me.

"I like you, Mark, I really like you, but if you're not interested..."

The first time I kissed him.

"It's nothing to be ashamed of, Mark."

And the way I'd felt, all hot and uncomfortable, scared and excited. And here I was, feeling the same way over Ben.

Only it was different this time, wasn't it. Oh yes. This time it was very different.

"You look a little worried, Mark," said Ben. "Have you got to get back to work?"

"Not yet."

"Good."

The music, ironically, had changed to a High NRG cover version of the old Abba hit Gimme Gimme Gimme (A Man After Midnight).

"So...you're really gay then?" I said. It was a dumb question, I know. He'd just admitted the truth to me, after all.

He nodded. "Queer as fuck, yep."

"But..."

"I know. I'm the typical straight boy at work, aren't I? All loud jokes and sexist remarks. It's just a front, though, Mark. It isn't the real me. This is the real me." He held his arms out as if to show he wasn't hiding anything.

Helplessly, I thought, my God, he's gorgeous.

"Are you still working at NJT?" I asked.

"Oh, yeah. Still there. A job's a job, isn't it? How long you worked here for?"

"A few months. The pay's not great, but it's a laugh. You know?" He nodded.

Ben leaned across the table then, arms folded. He put his face close to mine and my heart started to thump. I didn't move, though. Didn't pull back. "I must admit, though," said Ben, "I don't come here very often." He looked around the chill out room. "Not really my sort of club. I prefer the music a bit harder."

"Oh, yeah? Where do you usually go?"

"Frenzy. Up in Brixton? D'you know it?"

I nodded. Frenzy was a place I'd heard of but had never actually visited. Perhaps that would change now.

"Are you seeing anyone at the moment, Mark?" asked Ben. "Have you got a man in your life?"

Without any hesitation whatsoever, I said, "No."

Oh, why did I say it? Why why why why WHY?

I don't know. Really and truly, I just don't know. I was horrible. I know that. I was horrible and hateful and ugly. Why had I lied?

Why hadn't I told him about Andrew?

The answer was simple. Because I wanted to have sex with Ben. There's nothing else I can say.

I wanted to go to bed with Ben Harrow.

That was the whole sordid truth.

I was as bad as all the others, wasn't I? Just another one of those bitchy, drug-fuelled, sex-crazed scene queens who don't give a flying fuck about anyone but themselves. As long as they got a shag at the end of the night, nothing else mattered.

What was wrong with me? I had a boyfriend who loved and trusted me and there was I completely denying his existence so I could get laid. Disgusting.

Ben smiled and proffered a packet of Royals. I took one and he lit it. He said, "I'm not seeing anyone either."

It sounded like an invitation. But an invitation to what? His bedroom?

"So...how long you been out then?" he asked.

"Two years, give or take."

"Your parents all right about it?"

"Sort of."

"Ah. I'm not out to mine at all. It might be different if I still didn't live at home, but I do."

I nodded, understandingly.

"I'm glad I saw you tonight, Mark. I always wanted to ask you at work if you were gay but it's not really something you can just drop into the conversation, is it? Not at a place like that."

"No," I agreed. I felt horrible. About not saying anything about Andrew. I wondered then if I should mention him after all. It would've been the right thing to do, wouldn't it? But did I do it? No.

I was worthless; I was scum.

Ben smiled, like a viper. "You live alone, don't you, Mark?" he said.

"Uh huh," I said, amazed that my voice remained steady.

That's what I'd told everyone at NJT. But it hadn't seemed so bad lying about that there, because it was just easier than saying I lived with another bloke. Oh, sure, I could've said Andrew was only my flatmate, but telling everyone I lived alone just seemed easier. And of course, I hadn't wanted any of the lads to know I was gay. Didn't have that excuse with Ben, though, did I? Not now.

He put a hand over mine. I didn't pull back. "I like you, Mark," he said. His eyes were very bright. Actually, I wondered if he was on E.

"I like you, too." My voice was measured.

There was a moment when the world seemed to stand still. My head felt empty. Then the feeling passed and I stood up, too quickly, and knocked the table. The bottle of beer tipped over onto the floor. "Shit!" I exclaimed.

"Don't worry about it," said Ben.

I smiled. I felt like such a moron. "Listen, I have to go back to work. Carrie'll be spitting chips. She needs a break as well." Actually, I still had a few minutes, but I thought I'd better get out of there ASAP. I didn't like the way the conversation was going.

"Sure, sure," said Ben. "It was good seeing you, though, Mark. Hopefully I'll see you again?"

"Yeah."

"Look. Take this." He reached into his pocket and pulled out a business card. He handed it to me and I looked at it. There were two numbers, home and mobile, and below that, an E-mail address.

"Cheers," I said.

"'Bye." He turned to walk away, but then stopped, came back towards me.

And then before I could do a thing about it, he pulled me against him, pressing his mouth against mine. His tongue slipped past my lips.

I should've stopped. Should've resisted. Should've done

anything except that...

I kissed him back. Yeah, I kissed him back - kissed him back with a passion that even Andrew and I hardly shared.

When we pulled apart, fire danced in our eyes.

"Call me," said Ben.

And then he was gone.

6 Andrew

Things were going well, for both of us. Christmas was brilliant. Mark and I were so happy. He got me some cool designer underwear and a CD by one of my favourite singers, Jennifer Lopez (J.Lo - cool stuff!). I got him a gold crucifix. It had been expensive, sure, but it was worth it for Mark. I loved him so much. I know I'd been a bit worried after that night out he'd had with Christian, but it'd turned out to be nothing. Just a bit of experimentation in the end, and that was harmless. I suppose you've got to try these things really, haven't you? How else will you know otherwise? No matter how much advice people give you, there's no substitute for finding out for yourself.

Things at the café were going well, too. In fact, after Christmas, I got a raise. It was untrue! But totally fantastic. Martyn said it was due largely to the way I'd handled the Christmas rush so well.

It was all working out just as Mark had predicted. A new start. New friends, new job, new confidence. And the love we felt for one another had only increased. That was the amazing thing. Before we'd moved down to London, I'd been on at Mark about how destructive the scene could be, about how it fucked you up and all that, but it turned out that London had been the best thing for both of us.

He still worked at JayJay's, and to be honest, when he started doing that - handing out flyers - I didn't think it'd last long. But once again, he'd proved me wrong. I knew he didn't think of it as a proper job, but it would do as a stopgap until something really special came round the corner. And I knew it would.

It was only a matter of time.

7 Mark

I wasn't going to call the number. Really, I wasn't. Okay, I know I sound like a wimp. I know you probably think I'm a bastard, a real, one-hundred-per cent, Grade-A bastard. I had Andrew, didn't I? And wasn't Andrew everything a gay man (or straight woman, come to think of it) could want? He was good looking, good in bed, had a good job, an all-round nice bloke - and above all, he loved me, loved me like no one else ever had before. And there was I, fancying someone else.

Ben Harrow.

And you know something? You're right. I am a bastard. I'm a total cunt for doing what I was doing, for thinking what I was thinking. A total and utter cunt.

There are no excuses for me.

I called Ben while Andrew was at work. I couldn't believe I was doing it, and yet I still did it. Something inside my head was pushing me on. Something bad. It was almost as though there was this little demon perched on my shoulder whispering, "Go on, Mark. It's just a shag. What can it hurt? Just a shag. And Andrew won't find out. Not if you're careful, Mark. Not if you're smart."

I took the business card out of my pocket. It was a bit crumpled now. I rang the mobile number first, 'cos I knew he'd be at work. It was Tuesday lunchtime.

He answered.

Oh, God.

"Hi, Ben? It's Mark."

"Oh, hello, Mark." He sounded slightly amused. "What's up?"

"Nothing. I was just bored and I found your card so I thought I'd give you a buzz."

"Oh, thanks a lot!" He laughed.

"You know what I mean."

"Yeah. I think so, yeah. So...how have you been?" he asked. It had been over a week since I'd seen him at JayJay's.

"Oh. All right, I guess. Haven't been up to much."

"Wish I could say the same, mate. I've been working my arse off all week."

"All week?" I exclaimed. "It's only Tuesday."

"Yeah, but you know what it's like in this place. Busy, busy, busy. I hate it."

"Why don't you just leave? Like I did?"

"I need the money."

"Ah."

"So...what are you doing tonight, Mark?" asked Ben.

Tonight, I thought, mentally running over what I probably would be doing. Sitting alone, watching telly till around one, when Andrew got in. Then he'd tell me all about his day, I'd listen, then we'd go to bed. Without sex, most probably. (Andrew was always too knackered to do anything these days).

To Ben I said, "Not a lot." Then I added a bit of a dangerous question: "Why?"

"My parents are away for a week. They've gone skiing. I was just gonna watch a couple of videos tonight. You'd be welcome to come round if you want. Have a couple of beers and that. I've even got a bit of gear if you fancy."

I hadn't smoked pot for ages. The idea was appealing. And even more appealing was the idea of Ben. Naked.

I knew I shouldn't have gone. I should've said no right then and there, on the phone. Or better still, I should've told him about Andrew, confessed everything, said that I'd lied, that I had a boyfriend and that I was very much in love.

But I didn't. I wanted him too much.

I tried to tell myself that it was just like that time with the bloke at Elysium, when I'd been off my nut on E, not knowing what I'd been doing, not realising the consequences it could have. But this time was so different. I was sober now. Completely composmentis. Oh yeah, I knew what I was doing all right.

"Okay, sure. That'd be fun. Whereabouts do you live again?"

"Tottenham Hale. I can meet you at the tube station if you want. Think you can find your way there okay?"

"I don't see why not."

"Cool. About six-ish? Or is that too early?"

"Six is fine." Andrew never finished work until late anyway, as I've said. I'd just tell him I was going round George's or something. It'd be fine. Sure, I hated lying to him, and I knew I was a bastard, but at the end of the day, I was determined to make sure this thing with Ben was a one-off. A quick one-night stand and then things could go back to normal and that would be that. I mean, I wasn't planning on staying at Ben's all night. God, no.

"Brilliant. Okay, well I'd better get back to work. See you at six then."

"Yeah, all right. Six."

We said our goodbyes and I put the phone down. I sat on the sofa and breathed out a long, ragged sigh. What was I doing, what was I doing? The question kept spinning round and around in my head. I was horrible. I was nothing. Andrew didn't deserve me.

It was all true. But when I thought about not going to Ben's that night, I felt...no, not sick, exactly, but...yeah, disappointed, that was it.

I just had to go. I had to see what would happen.

I remembered the kiss in JayJay's.

I thought, Had to see what would happen, Mark? Had to see what would happen? Bullshit, Mark. BULL. SHIT. You know what's going to happen...

It will just be a shag, I told myself with steely resolution. Maybe not even that. Maybe just a blow-job, or a quick wank. Nothing much. Nothing to get upset about really.

Ø

At about three o'clock I went round to Dimensions, to see Andrew. As I'd expected, it was really busy. Daniel was at the bar, as usual. "Hello, darling!" he gushed. "What can I do you for? Don't tell me. You want Andrew, yeah?"

"Got it in one."

Daniel giggled. "Oh, love. It really is a many splendoured thing, isn't it? He's in the office. Go on down."

"Thanks, Dan."

I went down to the office. Andrew was sitting at his desk, doing some paperwork. Around the walls of the office were flyers for various gay nightclubs and bars in the area. "All right, stranger?" I said, walking in. I felt like crap. Total crap. I knew I was about to lie my head off to him.

"Hey!" he beamed. "How you doing? I was just thinking about you."

"Betcha say that to all the boys."

Christ, what was I doing?

"You busy?" I said, stupidly.

Andrew gestured to all his paperwork. "Swamped. Who would've thought being a manager was going to be so stressful! See what Daniel got me?" Andrew indicated to a small squashy red cube thing on his desk. "An anti-stress device," he explained.

"Cute," I said, fondling the bizarre object.

"What have you been up to today?" he asked. "Anything interesting?"

"George phoned me a little while ago. Asked me if I wanted to go round his tonight. Peter's away on some business course or something."

"George getting lonely is he?" said Andrew, with a grin. I felt weak and shaky. I hated lying to Andrew, especially over something like this. I thought, briefly, about the evening ahead, about what I was really going to get up to. With Ben. And my heart thudded like a bass drum.

"You don't mind, do you?" I asked, knowing that he wouldn't.

"Of course I don't mind. You go. Have a good time. I'm not gonna be in until late, anyway. Not with all this lot to get through." Once again, he gestured to the paperwork on the desk. "And even then I doubt I'll be good company. Bath and bed, that'll be me."

"Okay, then."

"Come here and give me a kiss."

I smiled, stooped down and kissed him for a long moment, my hand on the back of his neck.

"What time did you say you'd be at George's?"

"Six, I have to meet him."

"Ah. I would take you in the jeep, but - "

"Don't be soft, Andrew. I'll get the tube. As always."

He grinned.

"I better go," I told him. "You're busy."

"Mm, unfortunately."

"See you later," I said.

"Yeah. See you later."

We kissed again, and then I left the small office. I went back upstairs, said goodbye to Daniel and walked into Old Compton Street.

All the way back to the flat, I thought about it all: what I was doing, how I was doing it; I thought about Andrew and Ben. And most of all, I thought about me. What kind of person was I? Why was I doing it? Did I have something to prove? And if so, what?

I got indoors and took a shower, as if washing away the guilt and shame I felt, just like the morning after Elysium, in November. It was stupid, though. The water and soap didn't get rid of anything. It just moved it around, to a different place. I mean, I hadn't even done anything yet. Hadn't even slept with Ben.

I'd kissed him, though. I'd taken his number. Then I'd called his number.

I got out of the shower and put on a pair of black jeans and a grey woolly jumper. Aloud, to the four walls of the flat's small living room, I said, "I love you, Andrew."

Who was I saying it to? Myself? God?

I didn't know.

But Andrew wasn't there, was he? The one who mattered, the one who counted, the one who needed to hear those words. He was at work, busy, working his arse off to support us both.

I am scum, I thought for the umpteenth time. But you know what? Calling myself scum didn't make me want to call Ben and tell him it was off, tell him that I couldn't see him again. No. Insulting myself just sort of justified everything. It was like, if I knew I was doing wrong, if I admitted that part to myself, the idea of cheating on Andrew with another lad didn't seem so bad. It's weird, it's difficult to describe. I'm sure I sound like I'm babbling, trying to vindicate myself, but there is a sort of logic to it, if you think about it. *I* thought so, anyway.

I left the flat at five o'clock, went straight to Tottenham Hale. I had to change tubes a couple of times but I was used to the whole underground system by then, so there was no problem.

I got to Tottenham Hale at five-forty. I had twenty minutes to kill before Ben turned up. I waited, had a cigarette. As I smoked it, I wondered about him, wondered what he wanted to get out of this evening, wondered what sort of gay he was. A slag? Or someone who wanted to settle down?

Or perhaps, a bit of both, like me. Because wasn't that how I was? On the one hand I wanted to settle down with Andrew, live together as a happy couple and be in love and all the rest of it.

And yet, on the other hand, I wanted to have sex with Ben. And it wasn't the first time, was it, eh? What about that other guy, the one I can't even remember. Yeah, so I might have been under the influence of something at the time, so what? It still happened, didn't it? I still did it, behind Andrew's back, didn't I? For God's sake, I didn't even go to him and tell him what had happened back then, that I was sorry. Didn't even bother to try and explain. Nope. Just shoved it right under the carpet, didn't I? How sordid.

Now there was I, on a chilly February evening outside a tube station, waiting for corrupt shag number two to come along.

Oh, nice guy, Mark, I told myself. You're a real star bloke.

An icy breeze whirled through the air, frosting my heart.

And then Ben turned up, and just one look at him was enough for every doubt in my head to go flying out the window. Momentarily, at least.

He looked beautiful. Masculine, sure, but there was an essential beauty to him. His black hair, still with the blond highlights, had been split into curtains that fell into his luscious eyes. He had a slight growth of stubble on the lower half of his face that somehow made his lips seem even more full and vastly more kissable. He wore white jeans, a black Reebok sweatshirt and over that a dark blue denim jacket.

He smiled, my heart melted, and it no longer seemed so cold outside.

From my mind's eye, Andrew's image faded, and then was gone. Ben Harrow was so damned gorgeous he occupied every part of my concentration. There was simply no room for anything or anyone else when he was around.

"Hi, Mark," he said. "Good, you're early. I like that." He winked.

I just laughed.

"Come on," he said. "My house is this way. I'm freezing my fuckin' bollocks off out here."

See what I mean? You'd never guess he was gay, would you?

We started walking. "Haven't got a spare ciggie, have you, mate?" asked Ben. "I've left mine indoors."

"Yeah, course." I gave him one, and lit it.

"Ta. Bloody hell, what a day, though! It's so busy in that place, I tell ya."

"Yeah, I remember," I said, thinking back to NJT and cringing inwardly at the memory.

"Some bloke got sacked today for pissing around on the e-mail. You know Henry Goodwood?"

I nodded, remembering a tall lad with dark hair who'd worked over in Finance and Planning.

"Yeah, well poor old Henry got caught with some porn on his e-mail. Sacked straight away. Got called into the office with old Risotto Billotto, you know."

"No way!" I exclaimed. Risotto Billotto, otherwise known as Lorraine Billotto, was one of the big managers, and a fearsome bitch. I'd always hated her when I'd been there. "What happened to Henry?" I asked.

"I don't know the ins and outs of it, mate, but he was escorted straight off the premises, didn't even get a chance to say goodbye to any of his mates. She's a bitch, that Billotto. I reckon she's a dyke. Probably getting her end away with that fat whore Helen from Accounts, eh?"

We both laughed at the thought of that.

"You really don't like working there, do you?" I said, and the words reminded me of Andrew. How many times had he said that to me about some of my jobs: Brenda's Burgers; NJT.

I forced myself not to think about it.

"I hate it, mate. It's not so much the work I mind, it's the people. They're all so up their own arses. And everyone there is so homophobic. I mean, you've seen what it's like. You know. But you got out."

"So could you."

He shrugged. "Probably. But I might as well stay there, at least until something better comes along. I'm saving up for a new flat. The sooner I move out of home, the better. I hate living at home, Mark."

"Sounds like you hate a lot of things."

"I don't hate sex," he said, without any hesitation. His words threw me. He chuckled. "That's shocked you, ain't it? Don't worry, I like to shock."

"I'll say. I couldn't believe it when I saw you at JayJay's. At work you seemed so -"

"Straight? Like I said, you have to be in that place. But it's okay. It's not as if I'm some handbag holding shirt-lifter, anyway, is it?"

"No."

He nodded, just as we came to a small semi-detached house. "Right. Here we are. Home sweet home. The place is a bit of a tip, so excuse the mess."

"'S'all right. You should see my place."

"Where in London do you live?" asked Ben, as he got his front door key out of his jacket pocket.

"Oh...Newman Street. Just off Oxford Street? I don't know if you know it."

Ben whistled without pitch as he put the key in the lock. "Shit, Mark. That sounds expensive. Off Oxford Street? So it's right in the West End?"

"Uh huh." I started to feel a bit uncomfortable. Damn, why didn't I just lie? I thought. I should've said Camberwell or somewhere.

"Jesus, how do you manage to pay for that? You can't earn that much at JayJay's, surely."

I improvised quickly. "No, I don't. Certainly not enough to live there. No, it's a bit of a long story actually. The flat...used to belong to my grandmother. My Mum inherited it when Nan died, and then said I could live there. I wanted to move to London to find the gay scene and all that. You know what it's like. Living in a small town and everything. Not the easiest of places to be if you're queer."

"I suppose not, no," said Ben. "But I've always lived in London. The whole gay world's always been just a couple of tubes away."

"Lucky."

"Yeah, I guess. It certainly makes coming out easier, I reckon."

"You're probably right."

We went inside. It was a nice little house, well-decorated. "Go through to the living room," said Ben. "You want a beer? I've got Fosters or Red Stripe."

"Red Stripe, please," I said.

He nodded and went into the kitchen while I made my way into the living room. Everything reminded me of when I'd first started seeing Andrew.

Ben came in with the beers. I'd sat myself down on the brown settee and as he handed me my can, already opened, he kissed me. Only gently, just brushing his lips against mine. My flesh prickled. He brushed a hand down the side of my face, but said nothing, just kept that lush half-smile on his mouth.

"What do you fancy watching on video? I've got quite a few good ones."

I drank some of the beer. It was nice and cold.

"Oh, I don't mind, Ben. You can choose. Is it all right to smoke in here?"

"Yeah, course it is. Mum and Dad smoke like chimneys, anyway. Here." From a coffee table he handed me a heavy glass ashtray.

"Okay, I'll choose." He smiled, and went to the large tv set. From a stack beside the video, he took a blank cassette and slid it in.

"This is a good one," he said, sitting next to me on the settee. Right next to me. Our legs touched.

He clicked PLAY on the remote control in his hand. The screen flickered black for a few moments, then it changed to the image of two young, naked, good-looking men kissing each other vigorously.

"Porn?" I said, with a smile. I looked at Ben. He was grinning from ear to ear, as if he'd just told me a hilarious joke.

"You don't mind do you? This is a wicked tape. Hardcore. Illegal in Britain."

"How'd you get hold of it?"

"Oh, I have my ways, don't worry about that. Look, watch this bit." He pointed at the screen. I looked and watched as one of the two young men was bent over a dining room table and then slowly fucked by his partner.

"Looks nice, doesn't it?" asked Ben, somewhat darkly. "Yeah, that looks really fucking nice."

I nodded. The whole thing was sordid and obscene, it really was. And yet it turned me on something rotten.

Casually, I said, "I've never watched a porno before."

"You haven't? God, that's a shock. Coming from a gay man."

"I guess."

"Look. Here comes another one." I turned my attention back to the screen, to see that a third naked young man had entered the room and the guy getting fucked had started sucking the newcomer's cock.

"You ever been part of a threesome, Mark?" asked Ben, all nonchalant.

"Can't say I have, no."

"Oh, you should give it a try, mate. It's fab. What are you, active or passive?"

"Never really thought about it," I said. "Both, I suppose. That is to say, I've done it both ways."

"And which do you prefer?"

I had to think about it. I enjoyed fucking Andrew, sure. But when he took me, it was better, because...I don't know why. It made me feel wanted, and loved, and safe. And he was so gentle when he did it. It was never anything like, wham, bam, thank you man. And it wasn't just sex either. I know this'll sound rubbish, but it was making love. Sure, the first time he'd gone inside me, it'd hurt like shit. Christ, I remember, it had felt like he'd been impaling me with a red hot poker. But over time, that had changed. Nowadays I just felt bliss.

To Ben, I said, "Passive, I suppose."

"Yeah, you're like me, mate. Passive to the last. I've never been active, and to tell you the truth I don't think I could be. The idea of doing the fucking...it just doesn't appeal to me. It's a bit of a problem sometimes. When I go to gay bars and shit, and pick people up, they always reckon I'm gonna want to fuck them. 'Cos I'm so..."

"Butch?" I suggested.

"Yeah. But you can go both ways?"

"Yeah, sure. I don't mind it that much at all to be honest. I just prefer to be the...receiver."

Ben laughed. "That's a good way of putting it."

I smiled.

We watched the porno for a few more minutes, without saying anything. It was so surreal as the lads on the screen groaned and moaned as they were sucked and fucked and rimmed and, at one point, even fisted.

It was sick, and yet, at the same time, it was arousing.

Ben said, "What about sucking? You like giving blow-jobs? Or being sucked off?"

Perhaps if I hadn't just finished off my entire can of Red Stripe, I would've thought the question disgusting. But no. I actually found it funny. "Oh, both ways," I said. "If a cock's clean, I've got no problems taking it in my mouth."

"Yeah, same here," he said. "And rimming?"

"Never done it," I said.

"Would you want to?"

"Dunno." I lit another fag.

We watched the porno again, in silence for a bit. The scene had changed to a beach. One young bloke was lying on his back, his legs up against a dark-haired lad's shoulders as he was fucking slowly in and out. They were both moaning in pleasure.

"Nice huh?" said Ben. And his voice was a low, seductive whisper.

I nodded and exhaled a stream of smoke. It floated in the air, wispy and grey, like a spirit escaping from a grave.

Slowly, Ben's hand moved to my thigh. He squeezed gently. I turned and looked at him. He was staring at his hand as it moved slowly up my thigh and then to my crotch. He applied a slight amount of pressure and my erection began to grow.

"I want you," he said.

I want you, Mark, I really want you...but if you're not interested...

Who'd said that?

Andrew. Two years ago.

Ben looked up. He smiled. "I want to do all those things on that video with you, Mark. Do you like me? Do you want me?"

I nodded. I felt numb. Emotions anaesthetised by lust, by the mutual attraction that crackled between us like electricity.

The air was still and silent save for the sounds of the porno vid. I wanted Ben...wanted him so badly.

And I could have him. Right then, in that moment, I could have him. He was there; right there for the taking.

"You're gorgeous, Mark," he said. "I always fancied you at NJT. Always wanted you to fuck me."

I couldn't say anything.

Ben slowly put his face to mine. His kissed me, gently at first, and then I felt his tongue in my mouth. I put my hand on the back of his head and pulled his face against mine. His tongue went deeper into my mouth, to the back of my throat. We kissed deep and hard; it seemed like we did it for a long time, but it couldn't have been more than a few minutes.

"You're a good kisser," he said when at last it ended.

I just smiled. Words seemed somehow inappropriate.

"Do you want to go upstairs? To the bedroom?"

I nodded.

"Come on then."

He squeezed my crotch once, then took my hand, leading me upstairs. We went into his parents room. I felt a little nervous.

"I've only got a single bed," said Ben. "It'd be better in here for us. More room." He grinned. "Don't look so nervous, Mark. My parents are away skiing remember? God, there's no way I could've had you round here if they were home. No way in hell."

"I gathered that," I said.

Ben closed the bedroom door. He turned to face me and we kissed again. He slid a hand up underneath my top, toying with my right nipple for a moment. "You're gorgeous, you are," he said.

"So are you," I replied, lamely.

"You reckon."

"'Course."

He grinned, and then took his top off.

What a body! Shit, shit, shit! What a fucking body! You have no clue, no clue at all what his body was like. He must've worked out. He must've done! It was so defined, so sculpted. He could've been a model; really, he could've been a top fashion model. It was difficult to credit that someone as gorgeous, someone as fit as Ben Harrow, was rotting away in some shitty little office. He could've had the world at his feet had he wanted to, on looks and physique alone.

"Take off your jumper," said Ben. "Please."

I did as I was told. "Nice," he said, eyeing my chest. "Mm." He ran a hand over it, tweaked my left nipple this time. We kissed again, naked chests pressed against each other. It was wonderful. As we pulled apart, he fingered my gold crucifix; the one Andrew had bought me for Christmas. "That's nice, too," he breathed.

I felt a twinge of guilt, but pushed it away.

Ben brushed a stray lock of hair out of my eyes and we stared at each other, his dreamy smile remaining on his lips. Actually, the whole situation seemed to possess a dream-like quality. But maybe that was me trying to make everything seem okay. Maybe I was just saying to myself, It's a dream, that's all it is, just a dream. And dreams aren't real. And things that aren't real can't hurt anybody. Certainly not Andrew.

Maybe I was full of shit.

"Beautiful," said Ben, and he stroked my face again, still smiling.

I wanted to take the crucifix off, because then the thought of Andrew would seem even less real, like some made up figment of my imagination. But I didn't take the chain off.

I watched as Ben began to strip. When he was naked, he said, "Like what you see?"

"Yeah."

"Good." He stepped towards me, kissed me quickly on the lips, and then he took hold of my right hand, taking my index finger in his mouth. He sucked gently, like he was giving a blow-job; eyes closed, groaning slightly.

He took my finger out of his mouth, pulled me against him again so our bare chests were touching. I was so hard I couldn't stand it, my erection straining against my jeans, straining for freedom.

Ben slipped my finger - wet with his saliva, - between the cheeks of his arse, up into the tight hole. He said, "I want you to fuck me, Mark. Yeah. I'd like you up inside me. Just like the video. That's what I want, Mark. That what you want, too?"

I nodded. It was what I wanted, too.

We kissed again, then Ben slowly went down on me, kissing my naked torso as he went. When he reached my waist, he unfastened my belt, and savagely pulled down my jeans and boxers. He sucked me off for what seemed like ages, and just as I was close to coming in his mouth, he released me. "Not yet, babe," he said. "Not yet."

He stood up and put my hand on his arse. "In me," he said, voice low and dark. "I want you in me. Want you to fuck me. Tell me that's what you want to do, Mark. Tell me."

I swallowed. "I want to fuck you, Ben."

He smiled like a snake.

"Come on then. Fuck me."

"Have you, uh, got any..."

"Sure." He nodded once; picked up his jeans from the floor and from the pocket he pulled out a couple of extra-strong Durex condoms and a packet of Wet-Stuff lubricant.

He lay on the bed as I got myself ready. I lubed myself up first then him, fingering him deeply. "Uh..." he said. "Oh, yeah. Feels good, Mark. Go inside me, baby."

I pushed into him, slowly at first, but then he urged me to go harder, and deeper. He wasn't particularly tight down there.

"Yeah. Fuck me, Mark. Harder. Fuck me!"

Ø

It was amazing, the sex. Really amazing. It wasn't exactly better than anything Andrew and I had done before. It was just different.

Afterwards, we slept for a bit. Ben held me close to him, as if he'd been the active one. It was nice being with him. There was no more guilt. No more shame. Just me and him, laying there silently in his parent's bed.

Ø

We nodded off for a bit.

When I woke up, it was almost eleven o'clock. I couldn't believe it. I hadn't planned on being asleep that long. I'd been meaning to head back home at around nine-ish. Oh, shit, what was I going to do?

Ben was still asleep, and I got out of bed, went into the ensuite bathroom. As I sat there, naked on the toilet, tears crowded in my eyes. I felt sick. Part of me wanted to just stand up, get dressed and run.

But I didn't; I couldn't. My whole body was just suffused with this horrible dull nausea.

I thought of Andrew, as the tears rolled down my cheeks. It was so awful, the whole situation. How could I have done that to him?

Just as before, there were no answers. No excuses. Nothing but the blatant, disgusting, horrible truth. I felt as I had when I'd come out, all knotted up and confused and disgusted with myself. Because there were no answers. There were NO ANSWERS.

I touched the chain around my throat, the crucifix, Andrew's Christmas present to me. His face filled my head, and I tried to brush it away, to get rid of it somehow, to pretend that the man I loved didn't even exist.

It was useless. His face stayed there, dancing in my mind, his lips moving, asking a single word : "Why?"

Why, Mark? Why did you do it?

I thought: I hate myself.

In the bedroom, I heard the bed creak as Ben stood up. Quickly, I wiped the tears away. I didn't want him to see me crying. He'd find out the truth, find out about Andrew and all of my lies, and then he would hate me, too.

I thought of the sex. I asked myself if I regretted it, asked the most truthful, honest, decent core of my soul if I regretted it.

And the answer I got scared the living shite out of me.

Because that answer was no. I didn't regret it. No matter how much I would've liked to; no matter how much I know I should have regretted it...I didn't. The obscene truth was that I'd have done exactly the same thing again. Like I told you, the sex had been wonderful. Unmissable.

Unregrettable.

"Hi," said Ben, as he stood in the doorway of the small ensuite. He was smiling sleepily.

"Hi," I replied softly.

"How are you?"

"Fine."

"Thanks for that. That was brilliant."

I just smiled.

Ben said, "Are you hungry?"

"Not really."

"No? I'm starving. Do you fancy some pizza? My treat."

Oh, God. Oh, God. That's what Andrew had said to me. Once upon a time.

It was too much. It was all too, too much.

"I'd better be heading back home," I said.

Ben looked perplexed at that. "Home? At this time? You might as well stay the night. Don't you want to stay the night with me?"

I did. But I knew I couldn't.

"Please?" he said.

"I can't..."

"Why? What's keeping you? You haven't got to go to work, have you?"

"No."

"Then you can stay, can't you? Go on. I don't want to stay here on my own tonight. Not when I can have you."

But you can't have me, I thought. I touched the crucifix. Tell him, Mark, whispered Andrew's voice in my head. Tell him about me Mark. Tell Ben that you've got a boyfriend, and I'll forgive you, I'll forgive you, Mark...

"I can't stay with you tonight," I told Ben.

"Why? You still haven't given me a reason."

"It wouldn't be right."

"Why wouldn't it be right?"

I stared at Ben. There seemed to be real hurt in his eyes. I felt like such a shithead.

"I don't know," I said.

"Look, you're just feeling tired," said Ben. "That's all it is. Have something to eat, have a beer. You'll feel better. You'll want to stay then."

I didn't say anything. Whatever I told him would sound stupid. And I didn't want to tell him about Andrew. Even though it would've been the right thing to do, for everyone involved, I didn't want to tell him.

I remembered what I'd told myself before I'd come to see Ben that night.

It will just be a shag. Maybe not even that. Maybe just a blow-job, or a quick wank. Nothing much. Nothing to get upset about really.

And I'd also sworn that I wouldn't stay the whole night with Ben, hadn't I? That if I didn't sleep with him for the whole night it would all somehow seem okay.

And yet the idea of spending the night locked in Ben's arms was nice; warming. But what of Andrew? Shouldn't I have preferred the idea of staying locked in his arms for the whole night. Of course I fucking should have.

I said to Ben, "Look, Ben, I promised I'd meet my mate for a drink tonight at Bar UK." Yet more lies. Lies upon lies and then lies again.

"Bar UK closes at eleven," he said. "The same as everywhere else. Just phone your mate and say you fell asleep. It's the truth, isn't it?"

The truth. What the hell did I know about the truth?

"Yeah, I suppose you're right."

"Of course I'm right. Look, just phone him will you? You can use my mobile. I'll get it for you."

"I...okay."

Just one night, I told myself. It's just one night and that's it. Then I'll go back to Andrew and I can forget all about this.

Pathetic. I know. Pathetic.

I got off the toilet and followed Ben into the bedroom. He took his mobile out of the pocket of his jeans and handed it to me. "You call your friend," he said. "I'll go down and phone for some pizza. Or do you want Chinese?"

"I'm not hungry."

He shrugged. "Suit yourself." He slipped his underwear back on and vanished out of the door. "I'll be in the living room when you're finished," he called back up to me.

I didn't answer. With a barely steady hand, I dialled the number of the Newman Street flat. The answering machine clicked on. Either Andrew wasn't home yet, or he was in the bath.

I felt a shudder of shame run through me as I listened to Andrew say,

"Hi, I'm afraid Mark and Andrew aren't available to take your call at the moment, but if you'd like to leave a message, we'll get back to you...if you're good looking enough. Cheers!"

There were three quick beeps, indicating that we had three old messages, and then a long drawn out beep.

Mustering a cheerful, lightweight tone, I said, "Hi, Andrew, it's only me. I'm, er, still at George's. We fell asleep and I'm gonna crash here tonight. I've had a bit to drink as well, so...I'll see you tomorrow, okay? I hope you had a good day at work. Love you."

I pressed END on the small mobile phone and took a long, calming breath. I was grateful that it had only been an answering machine. Lying was easier if you only had to do it to a cassette.

I felt better for having told Andrew I wouldn't be home that night. Not much better, mind you, but it was a start. Once tomorrow came, I could put it all behind me.

From downstairs, Ben called, "Mark! Everything okay?"

"Fine," I said. "I'm just coming."

Slipping back into my clothes, I plodded downstairs. Ben was waiting for me in the living room, on the sofa, in just his Calvin Klein boxers. "All right, sexy?" he said, that irresistible grin planted firmly on his mouth.

I smiled loosely back at him.

"I've ordered the pizza. A large Hawaiian. You might get hungry once it arrives."

"I doubt it."

"Mm, we'll see. Kiss me."

I did as he asked.

"Mmm, nicer than pizza any day."

I smiled weakly.

"So you're staying, yeah?"

My stomach felt tangled. I blinked. I swallowed. Agitatedly, I ran a hand through my hair. "Yeah," I said at last. "Yeah, I'm staying."

8 Andrew

"Hiya!" said Mark as he came in that Wednesday morning. "God, am I glad to be back. That George, he can really talk, can't he?"

I turned away from the kitchen counter where I'd been making myself a cuppa. "Mark! I didn't expect you to be back so early."

"Couldn't wait to see you, could I? I'm sorry I stayed out so long. I didn't mean to. We'd, er, had a bit of gear as well; George found Peter's secret stash. Knocked me right out. You didn't mind me crashing there, did you?"

I smiled at him. "Of course I didn't. I know what it's like. And to be honest, the tube isn't exactly the nicest of places in the middle of the night, is it?"

"It isn't the nicest of places at any time," said Mark.

"True!" I laughed. "Coffee?"

"Excellent, yeah. I've got a bit of a hangover, actually."

"You should've stayed round George's a bit longer."

"I wanted to catch you before you left for work."

"Ahhh."

Mark smiled. "Shut up," he said playfully. "What time did you get in?"

"Not till after midnight. There was shitloads on at work."

"You got my message okay then?"

"Soon as I got home, yeah."

He came up to me, wrapped his arms around me and said, "I missed you, Andrew." He spoke softly.

I chuckled. "What was that for?"

"I just told you," he said, his face buried against my chest. "I missed you."

"You only saw me a few hours ago."

"So?"

"Nothing. Listen...why don't I take the day off work? We'll spend it together. Just you and me."

He pulled away and looked at me. "You can do that? I thought you had shitloads on."

"Last night I did, yeah. But I've got through most of that now. So what about it? We'll have a nice day. Go for a walk. Get a bite to eat. Just us."

He smiled. "I'd like that."

"Yeah?"

"Yeah."

"I'll phone in then."

"And say what?"

"It doesn't matter what I say. I'm the boss, remember?" I laughed, and Mark smiled his sleepy, boyish smile.

Ø

I called Rebecca, the assistant manager, and told her I wouldn't be in that day, that I had some personal business to sort out. She said it was fine and that she'd hold the fort. Rebecca was good like that. Well, everyone at Dimensions was. I had a good bunch of employees under me.

We went for a walk first. We popped into a nearby branch of Tesco's and bought some stuff for a picnic: just a few sandwiches and cans of Coke and shit. It was a chilly day - I mean, it was February - but it was bright. You know those really nice bright winter days? We went to Soho Square and ate our food.

Soho Square was cool. In the summer, obviously, it was crowded with shiny, happy gay and lesbian couples. In the winter, it was less crowded, but there was still a nice atmosphere. Mark and I were like a courting couple as we sat there on a bench, with our prawn salad sandwiches, Cokes and Doritos. It was so sweet and touching.

After the picnic, we went to the Odeon cinema in Leicester Square and watched a film together. Then we headed to Bar UK and shared a pitcher of one of their cocktails. Kinky Bitch's Broth, it was called. Hilarious.

"I'll cook us dinner," said Mark as we were leaving the bar.

"Oh. I thought we'd go out somewhere. I'll pay. There's that new Italian place in Victoria. Supposed to be good. The pizza there's meant to be killer. Daniel told me."

Mark wrinkled his nose. "Ugh, no thanks. Had enough of pizza for a while. No, I don't really fancy going anywhere," he said. "I wanted to cook you dinner, anyway. To say thanks for today. It's been lovely."

"It has hasn't it? Just the two of us."

"Chilling out."

We kissed. It was six-thirty.

"So dinner?" asked Mark. "What do you fancy? Anything you like."

"Except pizza."

"Yeah. Except pizza."

"Okay...what about spaghetti bolognaise. With Caesar Salad."

He grinned. "You've got a thing about Italian food at the moment, haven't you?"

"Just as long as I don't have a thing about Italian men, eh?"

"Huh?"

"It was a joke."

"Oh. Yeah, I know. Come on; let's go to Tesco's. I'll pick up the ingredients."

Stuart Thorogood

Ø

We got all the stuff: mincemeat, pasta, ready-made Caesar and a bottle of red wine. Mark paid for it all, even though I told him I would.

"You've paid for everything today," he said. "It's my turn."

"Guilty conscience?" I joked.

"No. Just because I want to treat you doesn't mean it has to be for any particular reason, does it?"

"Of course not."

"Well, good."

We went back to the flat. "Right," said Mark. "You sit yourself down and I'll get dinner started. D'you want a glass of wine?"

"Oh, go on then, twist my arm."

"Cheeky."

Mark poured me a glass of wine and I switched the stereo on. Tori Amos, one of our favourites.

He'd just started to sort out the Caesar Salad when the phone rang. "I'll get it," I said. I looked for the receiver. It was one of those cordless phones, and I had to dig it out from behind one of the sofa cushions. It was always ending up there for some reason.

"Hello?"

"Hi...Mark?"

"No, hang on a second, I'll get him. Who's calling?"

"It's Ben."

"Okay, wait there." I covered the mouthpiece with one hand. "Mark? It's someone called Ben for you."

9 Mark

"What?" I said, shocked to the marrow of my bones. "Oh, right. Hang on." I finished up what I was doing at that moment and then dried my hands on the tea towel. I was shaking, but I tried not to let it show.

I didn't know why I'd given Ben my number. It was stupid. It was mad. Why hadn't I realised that he might phone when Andrew was home? Christ, why did I never consider the consequences of anything?

But when Ben had asked me if he could have my number as I was leaving that morning, I felt like I couldn't refuse. What could I say? 'Oh, sorry, I haven't got a phone'?

Yeah, right. After I'd called him?

So I'd given him my number. And as I didn't have a mobile, it had to be my home number, didn't I?

I took the phone from Andrew's hands, rolling my eyes as I did it. I'd just pass Ben off as some annoyance who bothered me at JayJay's. Something like that, anyway. What else could I do?

Tell the truth? whispered my mind and my heart. It's not too late for that, is it, Mark? Is it…?

"Hi, Ben," I said. My voice stayed even.

"All right? Who was that?"

"That was Andrew."

"A friend of yours?"

"That's right, yeah."   I swallowed. I was blushing, I knew it. Andrew went into the toilet.

Good. That gave me a bit of breathing space. Ever so slightly, I turned up the stereo. Tori Amos was singing Winter.

"You left quite suddenly this morning, Mark. You could've stayed longer."

"You had work to go to, didn't you?"

"Could've bunked it."

Shit, I thought. What is it with all these people wanting to take the day off just to spend it with me?

"So can you come round tonight then? My parents are still away. We might as well take advantage of it, eh? Or…I could come round to yours if that's easier?"

Oh, yeah. Come on over, mate. That'll be just peachy.

The toilet flushed and Andrew emerged once more into the living-room.

I faltered for a second as I tried to think of an answer for Ben. What was this turning into? It was like a soap opera. A soap opera from hell, and I had the starring role. As the two-timing bastard.

"No…"

"No what?"

"No not tonight. Saturday?"

"What about your work? JayJay's is always busiest on Saturday, isn't it?"

"I'll bunk it."

"You sure?"

"Yeah, said so, didn't I? Saturday'll be wicked."

"What time?"

"I'll ring you."

"Okay, cool. Look forward to it, Mark."

"Yeah. 'Bye."

I hung up.

"Who's Ben?" said Andrew.

I put a hand to my head and groaned loudly. "Oh, just some sad twat from JayJay's. He got my number from someone but I don't know, for the life of me, who. Probably Daniel winding me up, or Carrie or someone."

"Or George," said Andrew. "You know what he's like."

"Yeah," I said absently. "Could've been George I suppose."

"Well, as long as you don't do anything about it, eh?" He was laughing.

"As if!" I exclaimed. "The bloke's rancid."

"Good. And I take it you're not gonna be bunking off work Saturday?"

"'Course not. That was just a front. Be fun to wind him up a bit. I mean, I'm spoken for, aren't I? He shouldn't try and touch other people's property."

"You're mean."

"I know. But you love me for it, don't you?"

"Shut up, you," he said. "And get back into that kitchen. I'm starving!"

"Bitch!"

Ø

We had a lovely evening, the perfect way to round off an excellent day. Well...apart from that phone call, anyway.

The meal was cooked to perfection; the wine good; the company great.

And the sex afterwards...well, it was the best we'd had for a long long while. Who knew? Perhaps my encounter with Ben had been a blessing in disguise. Perhaps it had shown me exactly how special the relationship I had with Andrew was.

Andrew left for work earlier than usual the next day, to compensate for his time off. Honestly, the man was so conscientious.

It was so laudable. Once he was gone, I called Ben. I'd made an important decision that night, while laying beside Andrew. Long after he'd fallen asleep, I'd just stared up at the ceiling, the events of the last few days rolling around and around in my head.

That Saturday, I wouldn't phone in sick at JayJay's but I'd still go round to Ben's.

Once there, I would tell him everything. I'd apologise; tell him I was sorry that I'd led him on; and then leave and forget about it. Forget about it all. I knew I wasn't going to feel particularly good about any of it, but it had to be done.

Ø

"Hello?" he said, on the end of the phone. He was at work. I could hear the hustle and bustle of the NJT office burbling faintly around him.

"Ben, it's Mark."

"Oh, all right?"

"About Saturday…you still up for it?"

"'Course. I want another seeing-to, don't I?" He laughed, as if he were joking. The thing was, I knew he wasn't.

I want you to fuck me, Mark. That what you want, too?

I shivered.

"How does three o'clock sound?"

"Oh, fine. Yeah, that'll be good. Think you can remember the way back to mine?"

"Yeah, course. You only have to show me once." I laughed, feebly.

"I believe that. Okay, I'll see you then. Saturday, at three. Can't wait."

His words made me want to cringe. I knew I was going to hurt him. Perhaps hurt us both.

The rest of that week passed uneventfully. I just sat around the flat doing nothing. Well, apart from thinking about the situation I was in. But it was impossible not to think about that.

When Saturday came around, I was dreading it. But I knew I had to go through with it. Things had got too out of hand too quickly and now I had to nip it in the bud, stop it all for good.

When Andrew left for work that morning, I gave him a long kiss goodbye. I pottered around the flat for a bit, had a shower, shaved, got dressed and at two I caught the tube at Tottenham Court Road. My heart was beating like a tribal drum.

What was Ben going to say? How was he going to react? What was I even going to say?

I honestly couldn't answer any of those questions.

It had turned quite chilly by the time I got to Tottenham Hale. It was almost March.

I arrived at Ben's house dead on three. I knocked on the door and he answered, wearing a black tank top and beige jeans. His hair was wet, as if he'd just stepped out of the shower.

"Hi, sexy," he said. I wanted to say, Don't call me that.

"Hello," I said. There were slivers of ice in my voice, but I don't think Ben noticed. Once more, everything seemed to parallel the days when I'd started to see Andrew. The day I'd gone round to his, to tell him that I definitely wasn't gay, that everything was a mistake.

"I'm not gay, Andrew. I'm not. The other night...I'd been drinking. Or something. Too many ideas in my head. I'm not gay, though. I don't fancy men, I fancy women. And I'd appreciate it if you'd stop asking people about me. I'm sorry if you're attracted to me but I'm just not gay..."

"Come in," said Ben. I walked past him into the house. He pinched my arse as I went. "Phwooar!" he said.

"Don't," I whispered.

He chuckled. The chuckle sounded like marbles being dropped on a hard floor.

"Go through to the living-room, Mark," he said. "I'll be through in a minute. I was just getting something to eat. D'you want some? Cheese on toast? Or we've got some beans I could bung on for you."

"No, it's all right. I've already eaten." I hadn't, but the thought of eating anything made me want to puke. My stomach was too unsettled for that.

"Do you ever eat?" he joked.

I didn't answer.

"A drink then? I've still got some of that beer left. Or we could have some of my old man's Jack Daniels."

"Bit early for me," I said. "Have you got any Coke?"

"Yeah, sure. Make yourself at home; I'll be through in a minute. Stick a porn on if you want."

I seriously had to wonder if that last part was a joke. Somehow, I didn't think so.

"So what sort of week have you had?"

"Oh...you know. Nothing much. Bummed around Soho a bit, that's all. It's been a bit of a slow week I suppose."

Ben snorted. "Wish I could say the same," he called back.

"Working?"

"Uh huh. Working my arse off for those fuckers."

While Ben sorted out his food and the drinks, I lit a cigarette nervously, wondering what I was going to say to him. It wasn't going to be easy.

But it had to be done.

A minute later, he returned with a plate of food for himself and a drink for me. "I'll have a drop of whiskey in a minute," he said. "Got a spare fag?"

"Yeah." I handed him one and lit it, then sipped my Coke.

Ben sat down beside me as he ate his food. Our legs touched again and he squeezed my knee, smiling at me cheekily. He winked at me.

Shit, how am I gonna get through this? I thought.

I just sat there. "You're quiet," he observed. "What's up?"

"Nothing." I was getting cold feet fast. I had to take a hold of the situation. Take the bull by the horns.

"Good. Now come here and give me a kiss."

I did it. Shouldn't have. Should've stopped right there. Held up the red card to him. But no. I kissed him. But then pulled away, before it had really finished.

He sensed something was wrong then.

Good, I thought. Keep going Mark. Keep climbing. Don't stop. Don't turn back now.

"What's wrong?"

"Ben...we need to talk."

"Later," he said. "Afterwards." He kissed me again then, practically forced himself onto me. His tongue went in my mouth.

I pushed him back, a little roughly, I suppose.

"No, now!"

"What's wrong with you?" he frowned, a trace of anger in his deep brown eyes.

"Ben..." I began. "There's something...something I didn't tell you about me. I..."

"What?"

"I've...I wasn't totally honest with you before. At JayJay's. That night I saw you?"

"How? How weren't you honest with me?"

"Remember when you asked me if I was with anyone? If there was a man in my life?"

Ben nodded.

"Well...there is. I've got a boyfriend. We live together in Newman Street."

"Ah. Let me guess. Andrew, right?"

"Yeah. The guy who answered the phone."

"How long have you been with him?"

I swallowed nervously. "Two years." My stomach churned. Ben was going to get upset now. I could see it coming, like a storm cloud on the horizon.

But he had a right to, didn't he? I was the one who'd lied, who'd crapped on everyone.

"That's a long time," he said.

I nodded. I felt so ashamed.

Ben didn't say anything for a bit. I looked at him. "I'm a bastard, aren't I?" I said at last. I got up. "I'm sorry, Ben. I should've been honest with you from the beginning. I've led you on."

Still, Ben didn't say anything.

"I'd better go," I said. I got to my feet.

But Ben grabbed me by the wrist. "Mark, you don't have to. Stay. It doesn't matter that you've got a boyfriend. He'll never have to find out. Not if we don't want him to." There was a smile on his face. A dark smile. He looked like a cobra ready to strike.

Something inside me turned cold.

Ben stood up and faced me, the smile still suspended on his Latinate features. He said, "Most of the blokes I'm seeing are involved with boyfriends. No big deal." He shrugged.

"Ben…"

"Look, it's just sex. I'm not looking for a relationship at the moment. Just a casual shag every now and then. What harm can that do?"

I felt queasy. This was not the Ben Harrow I had known and lusted after. There was a seediness to the way he spoke.

"Look, Mark, it doesn't bother me that you've got a boyfriend. People get too hung about sex. This Andrew's the one you're in love with, not me. So what if we get together every now and then? It'll just be…our little secret."

The queasiness inside me intensified. This was just too perverse. I didn't want to be in this situation at all.

In many ways, Ben's attitude was worse than mine. Sex was

supposed to be something beautiful. The way he spoke made it feel ugly and dirty. It made *me* feel ugly and dirty.

Ben grinned and made a grab for my crotch. I pushed him back, with more force than I'd anticipated. He fell back onto the sofa and now anger twisted his face into a threatening mask. "What the fuck did you do that for?"

"You know why, Ben! I just told you, it can't be like this for me. I want a one-man relationship. I don't want to sleep around."

"Oh, well it didn't stop you the other day, did it? What do you think you did then? Andrew still existed when you were fucking me, didn't he? When you had your fucking cock up my arse, Andrew was still there, wasn't he?"

"Stop it, Ben."

"Why should I? You initiated this, Mark. You pushed the button for all of this. You started this game."

"And now I'm ending it."

"You cunt."

"I know. I know I am. I said I was sorry. I didn't mean for this to happen. It just sort of did." I knew how pathetic that sounded, but what else could I have said?

Ben stood up; he tried to kiss me again. When he spoke his voice was softer. "Mark, don't go, eh? Just stay for tonight, and then that'll be it. I promise. You won't hear from me again. Let's just go up to the bedroom and - "

"Ben, I said no," I told him, firmly. "I'm gonna go now."

"Mark - "

"Goodbye, Ben."

I turned to leave the house. Adrenaline coursed through my veins. "Mark, come on..." said Ben, and he pulled me round by the arm just as I was about to step through the living room door. "Just one more time, yeah?" He smiled wryly. "For old times' sake?"

It all seemed like such a sick joke.

"Fuck off, Ben," I said. "I'm going."

"Mark…"

"'Bye."

I walked out of the house, banging the door behind me. It was over; I'd done exactly what I'd set out to do. In a way, I was proud of myself. But it was a misguided sense of pride. For wasn't it my fault, all this? Like Ben'd said, I'd started this game; I'd pushed the button.

And even though I knew I'd done as much as I could to put things right again, it still did nothing to ease the feeling of dread that lay heavy on my heart.

As I walked back to the tube station, I knew that I hadn't heard the last of Ben Harrow.

Ø

I went to work that night, as usual. But I was noticeably off, not my usual self at all. Hardly surprising, considering. Even Carrie noticed. "What's the matter, Mark?" she said, when the queue was relatively quiet. "You seem a bit weird tonight."

"Weird?"

"Yeah. What's the matter? You and Andrew haven't fallen out or anything, have you?"

I smiled. "No, Caz, nothing like that. Just got a lot on my plate at the moment."

"Pressure getting to you, eh?" she smiled.

"Mm, something like that, yeah. I'll get over it, though."

"That's the way to look at things."

I just smiled.

I still couldn't shake Ben's image from my head. It was horrible. I thought that once I'd gone to him and explained the situation things would get back to normal. But they didn't seem to show any signs of doing so. I guess what was bugging me most of all was the fact that Ben had my home phone number. I mean, after the way things had gone back at his, I wouldn't have put it past him to call Andrew and tell him everything. I probably deserved it, sure. But that didn't mean I wanted it to happen.

After work I went home to find the flat in darkness and Andrew in bed. It was four in the morning. I stripped off, climbed into bed and laid an arm across his bare chest. He responded by turning over and holding me close against him. I felt safe then; safe and relaxed. Christian's words echoed in my mind:

"You sort of represent everything that's good about being gay".

Oh, yeah. Sure I did. What did I represent that was good about being gay? After the way I'd behaved, the things I'd done, what good did I represent about anything?

I wondered if I would ever be a good person again.

As I lay there, beside him, in the darkness of our bedroom, I felt an emotion so cold and horrible that it threatened to overwhelm me.

Fear.

Fear, cold and heartless, seized my heart in its icy talons. I'd wrecked everything. Or, at least, put everything into a position where it could be wrecked. Through cheap and meaningless sex, I'd placed everything Andrew and I had together right in front of a wrecking ball.

Christian had said we made the perfect gay couple. That had turned out to be a bit of a faulty judgement hadn't it? The perfect gay couple? Maybe one of us was perfect - Andrew - but I was a long way off. Perfection could not touch me now. I was tainted.

I closed my eyes, trying for sleep. Though I don't know how, eventually, it came. But when it did, it was plagued with nightmares; nightmares about greed, betrayal, lust and forbidden desires.

10 Andrew

February ended and March began. It was my birthday on the sixth. My twenty-fourth. I couldn't help but feel like an old man. Twenty-four, for God's sake! Twenty-four!

"It's hardly one foot in the grave time, Andrew," Mark told me wryly, the night before the 'big day', as he kept referring to it. "Anyway, you don't look a day over thirty."

"You're seriously asking for it, boy."

He just smiled cheekily.

My birthday fell on a Saturday, which meant that I would've had to work all night. As you can imagine, and as I've probably already mentioned, Saturday night in Soho wasn't exactly a quiet time.

But I arranged it so that I wouldn't have to go in that morning until mid-day. Spend a little time with my boy.

He was lovely; so sweet.

First, he woke me up with breakfast in bed. The lot. Scrambled eggs; toast; hash browns; bacon; orange juice; coffee. And there was a single red rose in a little glass vase.

"Good morning," he said. And he kissed me on the forehead, then on the mouth.

"What's all this?"

"What do you think?"

"You didn't have to go to all this trouble," I said, tucking in. He knew how much I loved my breakfasts, though. And it wasn't very often that I got to enjoy a big fry-up like that in the mornings.

The phone rang, just as I had a mouthful of scrambled egg.

"I'll get it," said Mark. He reached over to the bedside cabinet and picked it up. "Hello?" he said, smiling like he had a secret. "Excellent timing. Yep. He's up. Wait a second."

He kept smiling and handed me the phone. "Who is it?" I said.

"See for yourself. Or rather, hear for yourself."

I took the phone. Absurdly, I thought it was going to be my mother. "Hello?"

It was Rebecca, the assistant manager at Dimensions, launching into a terrible rendition of 'Happy Birthday'.

"Stop, stop!" I laughed. "For the good of humanity, Bec, please stop!"

"Charming! Well, happy birthday, anyway, you old git."

"Cheeky mare."

"Whatever. Anyway, I have a gift for you."

"Oh yeah?"

"Yeah. The gift is...drum roll, please...that you don't have to come into work today. At all!"

"Oh no...really. I don't mind."

"I don't care. It's your birthday. You're taking the day off. Mark and I have been in discussions all week."

"So you've both been planning my life behind my back, have you?" I said, just joking.

"You bet your sweet arse we have. Someone's got to."

"You're probably right."

"Now, finish your breakfast. And I don't want to see hide nor hair of you today, all right? Dimensions is off limits to you."

"Oi, let's not forget who's the manager, shall we?"

"Yeah, I am. For today, at least. Anyway, it was Mark's idea. If you want to moan at anyone, moan at him."

"Don't worry, I will," I told her, tipping Mark a wink. He smiled back at me, and then blew me a silent kiss.

"Anyway, I've got things to do, birthday boy. You enjoy your day, okay? And make sure Mark waits on you hand and foot, like he said he was going to. See you tomorrow."

"Okay, Rebecca. Thanks again."

"No probs. 'Bye."

When I put the phone down, I looked at Mark. He was beaming. The world was in his eyes. "You're a crafty sod, you are."

"You love me, though, don't you?"

"Well, duh. Come here."

He leaned across the bed and we kissed. "It's awfully lonely in here on my own," I said. "I reckon I need some company. Some naked company."

"Oh, really? Who'd you have in mind?"

"Someone not a million miles away from here."

He smiled back at me. I loved those stupid little bits of banter we'd toss back and forth. It was sweet and schmaltzy. Two words that went very well with our relationship.

He stood up and took off his clothes. I loved watching him strip. There was something so erotic about just watching him get naked. He got into bed beside me and I turned his face towards me, kissing his mouth. "The breakfast'll get cold," he murmured.

I smirked. "Fuck the breakfast."

"Hey! I took ages slaving over that."

"I know. And I think you're lovely for it. But there's something a lot tastier in the bed other than the scrambled eggs."

"Fair point."

We made love then; slowly; tenderly.

Afterwards, we slept for a while, entwined with one another. And I knew it was going to be a good day.

Ø

We got up at around one, having made love once again. I opened my cards then. Cards from Daniel, George and Peter, Rebecca and all the staff at Dimensions, Grace and Jason (oh yeah, and Rupert), Christian and a few of our other mates on the scene.

And, of course, Mark. The silly idiot had only gone out and got one of those huge novelty cards, hadn't he? For My Boyfriend, it said on it, with a huge picture of two kittens snuggled up together.

Inside, he'd written, Andrew, there are no words...much love forever, M. xxx.

I cried. Honestly.

For a present, he got me something I'd wanted for ages: a lava lamp. It was brilliant; dead camp.

I received nothing from my mum or dad. Perhaps stupidly, I had hoped at least to get something from Dad. He didn't know about me being gay. He had no cause to ignore me.

Oh, well. I'd sort of desensitised myself against being hurt by my parents. It was something I'd come to expect, d'you know what I mean?

Mark took me to lunch (although, actually, it was more like tea) at a trendy restaurant in Covent Garden called Lizzie's. "Bit better than Brenda's Burgers this is," I remarked.

"Only slightly."

After the meal, we went to Bar UK and had a couple of drinks while I decided where we could go during the evening.

"It's completely up to you, babes," said Mark. "You choose. Birthday boy's decision. All right? But please, not JayJay's."

"Fair enough. Okay...let's see. Why don't we try somewhere different for a change? I mean, how many Saturday nights do we get to go clubbing together, eh?"

"That's what I was hoping you'd say."

"Overground's supposed to be good. Mind you, that's in Kent. Bit of a trek. What about...hey, I know! There's that place up in Brixton. Frenzy. I've heard good things about that club. Yeah, I quite fancy that. What do you reckon?"

"Sounds good to me, yeah."

"It's cheap too."

"Andrew, money doesn't matter. It's your birthday. Today everything is on me. Got it?"

"Got it. Hm, I could quite get used to being a kept boy, you know."

"Don't push it, mister," he laughed.

Ø

We had a couple more drinks at the bar and then went back to the flat to get changed. Once we got there, he presented me with yet another gift. "Mark, you can't afford all this..." I trailed, as he handed me the bag with the Armani logo.

He put a finger to my lips. "You let me worry about that, all right? Here. Just open it and tell me what you think."

I did, and found a gorgeous forest-green silk shirt. "It's your colour, I reckon," he said.

"Mark..." I couldn't get this stupid smile off my face.

"Try it on."

I did. "Perfect fit."

"Thought so. Daniel helped me choose it, though. So he has to take some of the credit."

"Baby," I said. And I kissed him, sliding a hand underneath his T-shirt, feeling his firm chest. We separated from each other, eyes bright as laser beams.

"Later..." he said.

Ø

On the tube up to Brixton, I started to get excited. I hadn't been clubbing for ages, and when I did it was only to JayJay's. We'd been in London for eight months now. Almost a year. Wow.

Frenzy was gonna be wicked. It was cool to be going to a place outside of our usual haunts, away from Soho, Old Compton Street and all the rest of it. Different. Special.

We queued up and a few people recognised me as the manager of Dimensions, which was a bit weird.

Mark put his arm around my waist and leaned his head against my shoulder. "Not tired are you?" I joked.

"Hardly. It's been a good day, hasn't it?"

"It has; it's been brilliant. Thank you so much. But it's not over yet, is it?"

"Not by a long shot."

Frenzy was a pretty big club. And it was busy, too. Like everyone had turned up for a huge party for me. Mark and I danced sexily together, right up close against each other's bodies. Like that dance that had been all the rage in the early nineties: the Lambada.

"This is fucking excellent!" Mark yelled at me. It was like that first night in JayJay's. It all felt new and fresh.

After a couple of hours dancing, we went to get a drink. There was this cool place in Frenzy, down near the foyer. It was known as the Frenzy Boudoir, and there were all these huge beanbags and inflatable chairs in there, while a DJ played classic hits from the eighties. Around the walls were framed photographs of pop and film stars, many of them autographed.

Unlike the chill-out room in JayJay's - where the music was still brutally loud and made it next to impossible to hold a conversation - the Boudoir was more like a regular bar, where you could have a chat, or just sit with your lover, watching the gays drift in, meet up, separate, leave. It was relaxing. And it made a change from the pulsing madness of the club's inner sanctum.

I sat on one of the immense beanbags and Mark went to the bar to get the drinks. He insisted.

When he came back, he handed me my Red Bull and Vodka, and then sat between my legs while I stroked his hair. We probably made the picture of romance. Or the picture of soppiness, depending on your point of view.

We sat like that for a good twenty minutes. Just enjoying each other's company, listening to the cheesy trash sounds that the drag DJ churned out.

Then this bloke came up to us both. He was smiling. Pretty good looking. Nice brown eyes. He was dressed well, too. "All right?" he said to me. "You must be Andrew, right?"

I was puzzled. The newcomer proffered a hand, which I shook. "Er, have we met?" I asked, confused.

"No. We spoke on the phone, though. I'm Ben. A friend of Mark's. All right, Mark?"

Mark looked up from his position between my legs. "Hi," he said stonily.

Ben smiled. "I'm gonna get a drink," he said. "You two okay for one?"

"Er, yeah I'll have another," I said. "Thanks."

"No problem. Mark?"

"I'm fine." He answered a little crossly.

"Suit yourself," said Ben. "What'll you have, Andy?"

Few people called me Andy. It felt a bit weird that a perfect stranger had done so. "Same again, please. Red Bull and vodka."

The bloke nodded and went to the bar. When he'd gone, Mark turned. He looked anxious. "Andrew, let's go," he said. His voice was a bit hushed. A bit urgent.

"Why do you want to go?"

"That bloke's weird. I told you, remember? He's always bugging me. Come on, let's go. At least let's go back onto the dancefloor."

"But he's getting me a drink now. Come on, he doesn't seem that bad, babe."

"You don't know him like I do. He's weird. He'll be bugging us all night."

I looked over at the bar where Ben was now being served. "I feel a bit nasty just upping and leaving. He seems nice enough."

"You've only said two words to the bloke. Come on, Andrew. Please."

"It's only one drink. Look, I'll have that and then we'll go downstairs or something."

"Andrew."

"Mark, come on. It can't hurt. He won't bother you if I'm here, will he? What's he gonna do? Come on to you?" I chuckled, but Mark's face stayed rigid. He seemed almost afraid of something and it did make me wonder. Was this Ben fella stalking Mark? I know that might sound really dramatic and over the top, but you should've seen how rattled Mark looked.

In any case, by that time it was too late to leave. Ben came back over with the drinks. Mark turned away from me, clearly in a huff. But I have to admit I thought the way he was behaving was a bit...well, a bit immature, to be blunt.

"Here you go, mate," said Ben.

"Ta," I said, taking the drink.

"You sure you don't want one, Mark?" There was a sense of irony to his words.

"I said no, didn't I?"

"Mark," I said. "That's a bit rude."

Mark said nothing.

"Don't worry about it," said Ben. He kept smiling this amused little smirk. I felt odd. There seemed to be more to this encounter than met the eye. But what?

"So," I began, "how long have you known each other?"

"Oh, quite a while," said Ben. "We met at NJT, back when Mark worked there."

"Really?" I said. "I thought you knew each other from JayJay's."

"Oh, we've seen each other there a few times, haven't we, Mark?" said Ben. "I don't go there that often, though. This is my regular haunt. It was quite a shock for Mark to see me at JayJay's. Always thought I was straight, didn't you, Marky?"

"Uh huh," he said flatly.

"You all right down there, Mark?" asked Ben. "You don't seem very pleased to see me." He smiled, but the smile was as thin and sharp as a paper cut. And his words seemed to carry with them a hidden undercurrent.

"I'm fine," said Mark. Then he turned round, staring up at me. There was a pleading look in his eyes. "Andrew, can we go? I'm...really tired all of a sudden. Come on. I've had enough."

He really didn't want to stay. There was obviously something about this Ben character that had upset him.

"Yeah, okay," I said. "I'm a bit bushed myself, actually. Been a long day."

"Oh, that's a shame," said Ben. "We were all getting on so well."

"Yeah, I know. But it was nice to meet you. And, er, thanks for the drink." I held up the glass and gulped a quarter of it down.

I stood up, and Mark got to his feet also. "Bye, Mark," said Ben. "It's a shame you couldn't stay longer, eh?"

"Yeah," he said. "A real shame."

"Still. I'm sure we'll see each other around sooner or later. You know what the gay scene's like. Everyone's always bumping into each other, aren't they?"

"I suppose so," said Mark, guardedly.

Ben kissed Mark on the cheek, and then me. "See you later, Andrew," he said.

"Yeah."

We turned to leave, walking past Ben.

"Mind you," he said, in an unnecessarily loud voice, "it is something I've come to expect from Mark. Running away from me. Happened just the other week. Isn't that right, Mark?"

I stopped, froze in my tracks as my brain processed those words and tried to make some sort of sense out of them.

Running away from me....happened just the other week...

Mark turned too. His face was austere; jaw unyielding. "Fuck off, Ben," he said, poisonously. "Just fuck off."

"That's not very nice, is it, Mark?" said Ben. His smile was horrible. It was ugly and gaping. "That's not very nice at all, Marky. It's not very nice to walk away from people, is it? Huh? Wouldn't you agree, Andrew?"

"Look," I said, firmly now, "I don't know what your bloody problem is, mate, but - "

"My problem? You want to know what my problem is, eh, Andrew?"

"Yeah," I said, voice getting louder, "I want to know."

"Why don't you tell him, Mark? Tell him what happened. Tell him what we did."

"He's mad," said Mark. "See, Andrew? I told you he had a screw loose. Let's just go."

"Yeah, you know all about screws, don't you, Mark? Eh? You certainly knew what you were doing when you screwed me, didn't you?"

"You're not right in the head, mate," I told him.

"No. I don't think I am. Otherwise I wouldn't have let your boyfriend fuck me, would I?"

"He's lying, Andrew," said Mark.

"Yeah, that's right, Mark. You just keep telling yourself that. You might start to believe it soon."

"You fucking little shit," I said. I stepped forward and pushed Ben. "Yeah, Mark told me you were a bit of a headcase."

Ben laughed. He sounded insane. "You're drunk, Ben," Mark told him. "Just go home and sleep it off or something. Leave us alone."

"Oh no, Mark. I'm not leaving you alone. Not until you admit to this poor sod the sort of boyfriend you really are."

"You bastard!" shouted Mark, and then he exploded into white-hot rage, surging forward and smacking Ben square in the eye. "How dare you? How fucking dare you?"

"Me?" said Ben, putting a hand over his face. "Me? I wasn't the one playing away from home! I wasn't the one who cheated on my bloke! It was you, Mark. You've got no one else to blame."

Mark was seething by this time. He was shaking with anger. He went to hit Ben again, but Ben was ready this time. He blocked Mark's arm and then jerked his head back in one sudden movement before ramming his forehead into Mark's face. Mark fell back into my arms. Blood was gushing out of his nose. He resembled the mangled wreck that had collapsed into my flat after his brother had beat the shit out of him. "You bastard, you bastard!" he was shouting at Ben.

I couldn't think. Honestly, I couldn't. The situation was so bizarre. We'd attracted quite a crowd by that time, people gathering around us; gasping and gawping.

I heard one guy say to his boyfriend, "Ooh, lover's tiff. Jealous rages. They're terrible things. That'll be one relationship down the pan, you know."

The clubbers knew. They had an extra show that night. How they enjoyed it. They circled us.

"Tell him!" screeched Ben. "Tell him, Mark! Tell him how you fucked me! How you begged me to let you fuck me! Tell, Andrew, Mark! Tell him!"

"Let's go, Andrew," he said.

I felt chilled.

Security people arrived then, breaking it all up. It all seemed like a bit of a haze. Ben was thrown out of Frenzy; I remember that much. And then some medic was taking care of Mark asking if he was all right. I felt deadened. Unable to react fully.

Ben's words rotated in my brain like some dreadful recording. Words about Mark fucking him, about cheating, playing away from home.

It was true, what Ben had screamed.

Tell him how you fucked me, Mark...

I knew it was true. You only had to take stock of that fight between Mark and Ben to know that. Mark had cheated on me. Slept with someone behind my back. Slept with Ben.

No, I thought. No no no no no no no...nooooooooooooo.

My stomach turned as cold as deep water in an ancient lake...

It was true.

And as I stood there, in the Frenzy boudoir, with medics and security and excited clubbers swirling around me, I thought, Happy birthday, Andrew. Many happy returns.

11 **Mark**

So what now?

Once I'd convinced the medics at Frenzy that I was okay, Andrew and I left the club and caught a cab back home. We didn't speak to one another. It was clear that Andrew knew what I'd done. I thought about lying to him, saying that Ben was a mental case, that he didn't know what he was talking about, that he was trying to ruin my life by making out I'd had an affair with the greasy little freak.

What was the point? Andrew wasn't stupid. He'd looked into Ben's eyes, and he'd looked into my eyes, and he'd seen the sickening truth.

That's how I felt: sick. Hollow and sick. It was my worst nightmare, all of it.

Everything was crashing to the ground.

We got into the flat. We hadn't said anything to each other since leaving Brixton. Andrew seemed to be deep in thought.

"Andrew...?" I ventured.

"Yeah," he answered softly. He went to the fridge, pulled out the bottle of whiskey Daniel had bought us for Christmas. It was still practically full.

Andrew hardly ever drank at home.

He got a glass out of the cupboard. A single glass. Filled it and downed it. He winced as the burning liquid went down his throat.

Nervously, I said again, "Andrew..."

He sat down on the sofa, rubbed the bridge of his nose. It was like that time when we'd had that argument, after Daniel had been attacked outside Dimensions.

"Andrew. I'm so sorry."

It sounded utterly pitiful.

"So it's true then, is it?" he said. He looked up, wet-eyed. "You and Ben? You slept with him, did you?"

I nodded, mechanically. "Only once. I swear to God, Andrew, it was only this one time."

"And that's supposed to make me feel better is it?" He spoke softly, yet savagely.

"No...I guess...no."

"No. You're right. It doesn't make me feel any better."

"Andrew..."

He stood up, abruptly. "I'm going to bed."

"O-okay."

He walked past me. I grabbed his arm and we looked at each other. "Andrew, I'm sorry."

"Sorry that you got caught?" he said, and then he pulled free from me and went into the bedroom.

When he'd gone, I sat down on the arm of the settee and cried like I'd never cried before.

Ø

I didn't go to bed that night. It would have felt like an insult to Andrew. I just crashed out on the settee. When I woke up, the flat was empty. He'd gone to work.

I felt ill. I didn't know what to do, where to run, who to turn to. I thought of Ben. I bet he was laughing his head off now, wasn't he? Given me what I deserved. The thing was, though, I did deserve it.

I looked around the flat in despair. I wanted to run away. But what would that solve? Christ, I'd really fucked up.

I thought of my brother, Nick. He'd slept around and it had cost him his marriage. Looked like that sort of thing ran in the family, didn't it?

But I didn't want to go the way of my brother. I wanted to fix things, make it up to Andrew, make it right. How? How was I supposed to do that? Maybe it was too late. Maybe some things couldn't be fixed if they were broken well enough.

Oh, please, I thought. Please don't let it be too broken to fix this time.

I picked up the telephone and called Grace. I needed to talk to someone, someone away from London and the gay scene.

How ironic.

"Grace, it's Mark."

"Mark! This is a nice surprise. How are you? How's Andrew?"

"Grace, listen. I have been so stupid. I've done something terrible. Really terrible." My voice quivered.

"Mark, what is it?"

"I've...oh, Grace, it's so horrible. I feel so ashamed!"

"Mark, calm down and tell me what's wrong. It can't be that bad."

"It *is* that bad, Grace." I took a deep breath. "I've cheated on Andrew. And he's found out."

Silence. Then a sharp intake of breath. "Oh, Mark," she said.

"I know."

"But why? Why did you do it? God, I thought you were so happy together."

"We are happy together. I just...I just had a moment of weakness."

"And that's it? That's your excuse? Oh, Mark, how could you do that to Andrew? he's such a nice bloke. I don't understand it. I mean...were you drunk or something?"

Oh, how easy it would be to say I was drunk, that I hadn't been in total control of my senses. But the whole thing had been calculated and planned. I'd known what I was doing all right when I caught the tube to Tottenham Hale, when I'd met Ben, when I'd...when I'd fucked him.

"No, Grace," I said. "I wasn't drunk. But it was only meant to be a one-off. It was a one-off with Ben. I wasn't going to see him again after that."

"And what difference does that make, Mark? Once was enough. Christ, I can't believe you've been so stupid. What has Andrew said?"

"Not much. He only found out last night. And now he's gone to work. He's so hurt, Grace. I don't know what to do."

"Well, I don't know what you want me to tell you," she said. She was angry. But what had I expected? Andrew was the nicest guy in the world, and I'd crapped all over him.

"Grace, I don't want to lose him."

"Then why the hell did you go with this...this Ben, or whatever his name is?"

"I don't know."

"Well, you're going to have to do some serious apologising, Mark. If you want to keep Andrew, you're going to have to get down on your knees and you're gonna have to beg. But even then, I'm not sure if that's going to be enough."

"No," I said. "Neither do I."

Ø

I thought about going to Dimensions to see him. But I knew he wouldn't talk to me at work. Not about this. So I waited until he got in.

Late, as usual, at twelve. I'd gone out and got some fish and chips in. I had to do something to get out of the flat. I was going mad. Mad with guilt, shame, worry and a million and one other negative emotions.

"Hi," I said when he came through the door. He looked knackered. "I got some fish and chips in for our tea. I got you cod and - "

"I'm not hungry," he said, cutting me off. "I had something to eat at work."

That was feasible. He often did that.

"Oh, okay. D'you want some wine or something?"

"No thanks. I'm just gonna have a bath and then probably go to bed. All right?"

"Okay." I looked at the plate of fish and chips resting on my lap. I only just managed to resist picking it up and throwing it against the wall. I couldn't stand it! Couldn't stand this horrible feigned indifference of Andrew's.

It was worse than the silent treatment.

"Andrew, don't be like this."

"Be like what?"

"Pretending that nothing's happened."

He turned and looked at me tiredly for a long moment. "Mark. I just want to forget about it. You've said you're sorry and I believe that."

I couldn't understand him. That's it? I wanted to say. But speech eluded me for a moment. Andrew's explanation didn't seem acceptable. I didn't deserve his forgiveness so easily. I'd behaved too horrendously for things to be that simple.

"I'm going in the bath," he said again.

I wanted to stop him, to pull him back, demand more, explain. But explain what? I didn't have a leg to stand on. I had no right to make demands on him. I was worthless; I was shit.

I wanted to cry again, but this time the tears refused to come.

Ø

Andrew went to bed after his bath. I could've joined him, I suppose, but it would've felt wrong. I felt as if I didn't deserve to be in bed beside him.

So I just sat there, staring at the tv without seeing what was on, and forcing the cold fish and chips down my throat. Unsurprisingly, I no longer had an appetite. But I tried to eat anyway, simply because there was nothing else to do.

Ø

The next two days plodded along at a miserable pace, for me anyway. Andrew and I continued our lives seemingly on parallel lines. We were talking, but only just. Things were noticeably different between us, though. It was like Ben had forged a chasm between us that would never be bridged. We were still together, though, Andrew and I. At least that was something, I guess.

But it bugged me. Seriously bugged me.

I know I had no room to talk. It was my fault, anyway. But if Andrew had screamed and shouted at me, it would've made me feel better. Funny as it sounds.

On Wednesday, I'd had enough. Three days after the encounter at Frenzy, with Ben.

Andrew came in from work, quite early at eight-thirty, and I just said, "We have to talk."

My voice was all deep and dramatic. I was scared, though. Scared at what I was getting myself into. I was the guilty party in all of this. It felt as though I were looking down into a bottomless, black abyss.

"Do we?" said Andrew, nonchalantly.

"Yeah. Andrew. I can't go on like this. I need to talk about it."

"What is there to say?"

"Stop being so bloody cool about it all. I know what I did was wrong. I know I hurt you. I didn't mean to."

"I know you didn't. And I know you're sorry. And I forgive you."

"That's not good enough!" I erupted.

"You don't want me to forgive you?"

"Of course I do, Andrew."

"Then what is it you're trying to say?"

"I don't know. Just...this is doing my head in. I hate myself for what I've done. I feel like I deserve to be punished more than you're punishing me."

"I don't want to punish you, Mark."

"Then what do you want?"

"To move on from this. Close the door on it and just get on with our lives."

"How can you say that? We have to talk this through, Andrew. We can't pretend it didn't happen."

"That's not what I'm doing. I know it happened. And like I told you, I know you're sorry."

"But don't you want to know why I did it?"

"No."

"Why?"

"I've already explained that. I don't want to dwell on it."

"I love you, Andrew."

"I know that."

But it didn't sound like he believed it. I stood up. I grabbed his arms. "Andrew, talk to me! Shout at me! Hit me! Do something, will you?" Tears crept into my voice.

"You're being stupid, Mark," he said woodenly.

"Just give me a fucking reaction, will you, Andrew? Please!" And then out of frustration, I slapped him. Hard.

Andrew's head jerked to one side and he put a hand to his cheek. He didn't say anything immediately. When he did, it was, "Are you happy now?"

I trembled, and started crying. I couldn't believe I'd hit him. Couldn't believe it. "I'm...Andrew..."

"All right," he said, voice low. "All right, Mark. Let's talk, shall we? Let's talk about what you've done, Mark. Not what I've done. What you've done. Stop fucking transferring your own shit on me. If you think provoking me will make you feel better, you're wrong, it won't. This is just you misplacing your own guilt. You're the one who shagged around behind my back. You're the one who fucked off with some other arse-hole, not me. And you stand there mouthing off at me, slapping me, getting all aggressive with me, when I've done nothing at all, Mark, nothing at all to hurt or degrade you."

"Andrew, I didn't mean to hit you. I just want to explain."

"Go on then. Explain. Tell me. I'm right here, all ears. Waiting."

"I didn't mean to hurt you. I didn't want to hurt you."

"No? Well, tough shit. You *have* hurt me. Is this really what you want to hear, Mark, that you have hurt me? You've hurt me badly, Mark."

My heart felt fractured at the sound of those words. I started to sob. "Andrew, I had a moment of weakness."

"I thought what we had was stronger than any of that. Obviously not. But you know what? I don't blame you altogether. I don't even blame that little Ben bastard. I blame London; the London gay scene."

That confused me. "How come?"

"You're naive, Mark. And the scene preys on that. It gets you in its clutches."

"That's crazy, Andrew. The scene isn't a monster. It's just a place. It was me who slept with Ben. The scene didn't force me into it. I was in control."

"Then that's even worse, isn't it?"

"Yes. After the way I've behaved, I wouldn't blame you if you threw me out."

"I'm not going to throw you out, Mark. You need me."

I started to get a little annoyed. I know I had no right to; no place to. But I did. Andrew was making me sound like a stupid child. "I'm not a little kid," I said.

"Then don't act like one. I mean, we've been here nearly a year now and you haven't even bothered looking for a proper job. A job you want to do."

"That isn't the issue here, Andrew. I wanted to talk about what I'd done with Ben."

"Well, since we're rowing anyway, we might as well go the whole hog, don't you think?"

He spoke poisonously and I realised I was seeing a side of Andrew that I hadn't known was there. He was like some sort of distorted father figure.

"This Ben," said Andrew, thoughtful now. "Did he ever come round here? Did you ever do it in our bed, Mark?"

"No!" I blurted, horrified that he'd even suggested that. "It was only this one time I went with him. I swear!"

"And how many others have there been? Eh, Mark? I mean, you're out at JayJay's every weekend. And I know you're not working all the time. How many other casual shags have you had?"

I hesitated, remembering Elysium, the anonymous bloke I'd been with while off my face on E. But that little pause, that little gap in the conversation, was death for me. Andrew knew instantly. He could read me like a book, he really could.

"Oh, great," he said, folding his arms. He seemed to tilt backwards. "There's been someone else, hasn't there? At least one other person."

"No..." I trailed. But what was the use? Andrew knew.

"Who?" he said. I saw tears well up in his eyes. "Who else, Mark?"

"Just...it was just this guy. I don't even remember his name, or what he looked like."

"When?"

"At Elysium. The night I was on that Ecstasy. When I went out with Christian. You were ill and..."

Andrew's horror spread across his face like a virus. "But that was ages ago," he said. "Ages ago. Before...shit, it was before Christmas!" Andrew's eyes widened. And then he seemed to fold, and become smaller.

I nodded, hanging my head in shame. I said, "It was meaningless."

"If it was so meaningless," began Andrew, "why didn't you tell me about it? Why didn't you admit that you'd made a mistake. That's what hurts me most about all of this, babe. You didn't even come and tell me. Just covered it up, hoped it would go away. Or even worse, hoped you could still get away with it and that I'd never know."

"No! Andrew, believe me, I never thought of it like that. I always regretted what I'd done."

"But you did it again, didn't you? You did it again with Ben."

"And that was all. That was all. I swear, Andrew."

"Mark. How can I believe a thing you say? I mean, our whole time in London together could just be built on lies for all I know. Don't you see what you've done, what you've caused? You've blown a massive hole in everything we ever had. It puts everything into question, doesn't it?"

"It doesn't have to. I love you."

"Do you?"

"Yes! How can you even think I don't?"

"Oh, it's pretty easy from where I'm standing. If you love someone, do you go shagging around?"

"I never shagged around!"

"You just told me you did it twice!"

"Those were accidents."

"There you go again, Mark, contradicting yourself. They weren't accidents, you said so. 'I was in control', that's what you said. And were you?"

I nodded, weakly. "I suppose so, yeah."

"You suppose so. There you go then."

"I don't want this to ruin us."

"Why? You're obviously not totally happy with me. Otherwise why did you go and seek solace in another man's arms, eh?"

"I wasn't trying to seek solace. It was just sex."

"And sex with me isn't good enough?"

"It is!"

"Clearly it isn't. I mean, was it good? The sex? What was Ben like, eh? You fucked him, for God's sake. Was it good?"

"It was, as it goes," I said quietly. I wasn't trying to hurt him by saying that, I was trying to be honest, and if I'd told Andrew that sex with Ben had been shit, it would've sounded like a lie, anyway.

"Oh. Well, thank you."

"Andrew! I didn't mean he was better than you! God, no! It was just different that's all."

"You're just like all the others, aren't you, Mark? Just one of those stupid sex addict scene queens. It's people like you who give gays a bad name, who make us all out to be promiscuous arse-holes."

"I'm not promiscuous!"

"Not yet, maybe. But it looks like you're going that way, doesn't it? What's next? Drug dealer? Rentboy? You'll be just like Christian!"

"Stop saying those things!"

"Why? Truth hurts does it, Mark?"

He was being really nasty now; really hateful. But I knew in my heart that this monster I was seeing was my own creation. He'd insisted that he'd forgiven me, but no, I had to keep chipping away at him. And now I'd opened the can of worms, he was feeding them to me. I knew I'd behaved horribly, I knew that. But even so, Andrew was being too harsh; too mean. He was making me out to be a real worthless sack of shit, when all I'd really done was made a mistake.

"I know I shouldn't have gone with Ben or that other guy. I knew that..."

"But you did it anyway, didn't you?" Tears were trickling down Andrew's face, staining it. I wanted to hold him, but didn't dare make a move.

"It's London," said Andrew. "See what it's doing to us? I knew it was a bad idea to come here."

"It's not London! Stop saying that? Look at your job, Andrew! Look how you're excelling at it! You wouldn't have that if it wasn't for London, would you?"

"Fuck the job!" he roared in a sudden burst of angry emotion. "The job doesn't matter. All that matters to me is us. No, correction. All that *mattered*. Past tense."

I was shocked. My whole body turned as cold as a corpse in a morgue. "What are you saying, Andrew? That...that we're finished?"

He looked away from me, unable to meet my eyes.

"Andrew?" I choked the name out. Oh, no, I thought. Oh no, oh no, oh no... "Andrew? Are you finishing us?"

"I don't know. I don't know what to do."

"But..." I couldn't find any words. I couldn't believe what had happened. Okay, I'd made a mistake. Maybe two mistakes. But didn't everyone deserve a second chance? I hadn't realised Andrew could be so ruthless. I said, "I thought you'd forgiven me."

He whirled. "That's when I thought it had only been that Ben. But there's been others."

"Only one!"

"How do I know that? You could have men all over London for all I know. I mean, I'm always at work, aren't I? Who could blame you if you got a little bored and needed a bit of extra excitement in the sack, eh?"

The sarcasm in his voice was searing and painful.

"You're just trying to hurt me now."

"Isn't that what you deserve?"

"I said I was sorry!"

"I know."

We were silent then. Not looking at each other. I felt, bizarrely, as if we were two dolls in a Wendy house. Trapped there; trapped and in pain. What had I started? What terrible force had I unleashed on us both?

I should've just left it, I told myself. I should've just left Andrew to deal with it on his own, to make his way through it by himself. That's what he'd wanted. But I'd only stirred things up with this horrible forced confrontation.

Stuff was pouring out of him now. Stuff he'd wanted to keep locked up. If I'd left things, let him deal with it in his own way, I wouldn't have opened the floodgate on his anger and upset.

But it was too late now.

"I'm going to go for a walk, Andrew. I think we both should. I think we both need some fresh air. We can go together, Andrew. Please?" The last word fluttered in the air, like a dying moth.

"No, Mark," he said, solemnly. "I don't think that'd be a very good idea."

"Why? Andrew...don't finish us. Please, don't finish us."

"I don't want to."

"Well then."

Still, neither of us could bring ourselves to look one another in the eye. We were more distant in that moment than we'd ever been.

"Then I'm going, even if you're not," I said, giving it one last try, one final attempt to get him to accompany me. If he did that, then I'd know there was hope. Even if it was just a little bit; just a little chance that things would be all right and we'd be better; that we'd get through this torture.

Torture that I'd brought about, in more ways than one.

You started this, Mark. You pushed the button for all of this. You started this game.

Oh, if only that was all it was! A game. Just a stupid little game.

But perhaps it was. For in every game, there are winners and there are losers.

I have become the loser, I told myself, hysterical with self-loathing. But also, in some strange way, I had become the winner. And this is what I have won, I thought. The chance to be alone forever and ever and ever.

Alone.

Such a frightening word.

"I've got to get out of here," I said. "Please come with me, Andrew."

"I think we should have a bit of time alone right now, Mark."

There it was again; that word; that evil, frightening, chilling word: Alone. I felt as if I were being suffocated by it.

Alone alone alone alone...

Come, Mark, whispered the darkest, sickest thoughts in my head. Come and be alone. Be alone for ever. Without Andrew. Without love. Without hope.

The destructive voices got louder and more insistent, as if the terrible consequences of my curiosities just weren't enough.

What did they say, curiosity killed the cat?

I thought, Oh my God, I'm never going to be happy with what I've got. When will what I've got just be enough?

When I believed I was straight, that wasn't enough, I harped on (...something's missing something's missing...)like a pathetic child. Now I knew I was gay, had found my soulmate, and I was killing it. Why?

I turned on Andrew. "Well, you're probably right, Andrew. Perhaps I'm not mature enough for you, pehaps I'm just a silly little naive boy as you said. Perhaps I'm just not good enough for you, Mr Perfect. Yeah, perhaps we should see other people after all. Obviously, things just aren't the same around here anymore. You don't even respect me."

"*Respect* you? Fuck me, Mark, I don't think you can lay that one on me..."

I wouldn't let him finish, I was salivating. I was incensed. I hated him. I needed him. I loved him. "It's just fucking double standards, Andrew. You're up your own arse! Who are you to judge me, anyway? It's all right for you, you've been out long enough to know the score. You've done everything, haven't you, Andrew? You've been there, got the T-shirt. But little me, I've got to take your word for it that this is the best. Like I fucking know! How would you feel if you were me? I've only just come out and already you want to put me in a cage!"

I knew I'd gone too far. It was a gamble, and one I wasn't sure I wanted to risk.

I pulled my jacket on. Andrew's face was stunned. I couldn't even tell how he was feeling, he was so immobile. If I'd thought I'd hurt him before, this was the ultimate insult.

I tried to move closer to him; I reached my hand out to touch his face, as if this way I could take back the caustic comments. He jerked my hand away. I had to say something to take this whole mess away. To just erase it from our lives. The actions - the thoughtless actions - and the cruel words. "It's not like other people don't have open relationships," I said to him. "Even if they love each other. Look at George and Peter! They're always doing it! And they're still together, aren't they? There must be dozens of couples we know who have open relationships."

"I don't care about any others," said Andrew, his voice a mere whisper. "I don't care about George and Peter. I don't..." The sentence dawdled away, unfinished.

I said, "But I'm sure, if you told me we could - see other people, I mean - you know it wouldn't mean we didn't love each other. Everyone's doing it," I said again, as if this somehow justified the idea of an open relationship, something that I had always loathed, and still loathed.

So why was I suggesting it now? I knew, deep down, that it was something I didn't really want.

"I mean...I'd probably hate it," I continued. "I'd probably hate it and come back to what we had anyway, so it's not like..."

"God," scoffed Andrew, "you're imploring me as if I have the overall say on what you do with your life! Look at you, Mark, what's happened to you?"

I looked back at him. I felt like a school-boy asking for more pocket money.

He carried on. "I don't own you, Mark. I'm not your fucking jailor. But neither do I want a contaminated piece of shit."

Rage grew inside me once more. I hissed, "Fuck you, I don't owe you anything. If you'd have loved me, like you say you love me, you wouldn't have put conditions on me. You wouldn't have expected me to be like you. You've made your mistakes, too, Andrew. You've had to learn for yourself. I thought we were equals. If you had even tried to understand how I might feel so naive and young and inexperienced and curious, we may have never gotten into this fucking mess in the first place. You've pushed me into it."

Andrew seemed weary now. He said, "I don't want to do this anymore. I need to be on my own. I didn't realise you hated me so much. I told you I forgave you, but no, you kept on and on and on. And now you're telling me you want to see other people. I can't believe how we've come to this, and I never thought we would. So perhaps I'm the one who's naive, Mark. Not you." He turned to face the window, waiting for the door to close behind me.

"Andrew?" I said.

"I thought you were going out, Mark," he said. His voice was monotone, without feeling. It frightened me. I suppose you didn't get many chances with people like Andrew. It wasn't that I'd been unfaithful that had hurt him so much as the way I'd treated our relationship.

He turned to look at me.

"Seriously, Mark, think carefully. Relationships are hard work. But nothing beats what we've got, or what we had, at least. And the sad thing is, you have no benchmark so you just don't realise it. Ask yourself this: will it be worth it when you do realise, or will it be too late then?"

Ø

It was probably wrong of me to go. Shouldn't I have stayed to battle it out, to make him see sense, to forge our love again so we could get on with our lives? But I didn't (couldn't?) stay in that flat for another second. There seemed to be no reasoning with Andrew at that moment; no reasoning with myself, either. The only sensible thing seemed for us both to take a bit of time out and talk again once we'd mellowed.

But once you'd opened a floodgate, how did you close it?

"See you later," I told Andrew, and I kissed him quickly on the cheek.

It was like kissing stone.

I shut the flat's door quietly and walked downstairs. It was raining outside, just a thin drizzle, and it stung my face. But at least it hid the tears that were streaming down my cheeks.

I wished I could kill Ben. Oh, what I would've done to him. Yes, I know it was easy to blame Ben; it was easy to say it was his fault, that if he hadn't spilled the beans at Frenzy everything in the garden would be rosy.

No. I had played the game; rolled the dice...and now taken the forfeit card.

Go straight to jail. Do not pass boyfriend's flat. Do not collect love and forgiveness.

I crossed the road at Oxford Street, headed down Dean Street, on my way to Soho.

How stupid and pathetic Old Compton Street seemed to me now. Superficial and ridiculous. I watched the gays walk up and down, laughing with friends, all carefree and happy and jovial, probably on their way out to some bizarre mid-week club.

I don't want this life! I thought, a detestable lump forming in my throat. I don't want to be on my own, without Andrew, feeling hateful and guilty and ashamed and dirty.

Grace's words rose up in my head, like the memory of a long-dead lover:

Then why the hell did you go with this...this Ben, or whatever his name is?

Why, indeed? Oh, how many times had I asked myself that question and was still unable to offer up a decent answer?

There were answers, yes. But none of them could be called 'decent'.

I thought about escaping, running off and starting anew. Ben had said I was good at running away. Maybe I should put that into practice.

But then I would have to do something else, and what would that be? There were no other lives out there for me. I was just going to have to stagger on through this one.

And then a thought dropped into my head so shocking I scarcely believed it. A thought I hadn't had in a long, long while. Since my old life.

I wish I wasn't gay.

It was nonsense to think like that. Pure nonsense.

I walked up to Bar UK, nodding hello to the menacing-looking bouncer that stood at the door. Chatter and laughter spilled out from inside, along with the camp High NRG tunes that the jukebox continuously spewed out.

I thought about going inside. About standing on my own in there.

Then I remembered that time, months ago now, when Andrew and I had had that other row. Seemed small and petty compared to what was going on in our lives now. I remembered that guy (Tony? Or was it Johnny?) who'd offered me money for sex.

"You get a lot of rent..in here".

It was always the same, wasn't it? All built on shit. And you can't build on shit, that was the whole point.

So I ran.

I ran away from the doorway to Bar UK, I ran down Old Compton Street, out of Soho. The only thing that mattered to me was getting away from the scene, away from it all.

I walked down Tottenham Court Road, crying harder now, more bitterly. The rain had increased, getting heavier, drenching my jacket. I trod in a puddle and the water sank through my trainers, soaking my feet and making them ache.

I don't remember how long I walked for exactly, but eventually, I came to a pub. The King Arthur, it was called, at the top of Great Portland Street.

I could see through the brightly lit windows and the doorway that it was clearly a straight pub. Good.

I walked inside.

I went to the bar man and ordered a pint. He was fairly old, in his fifties probably. Bald, tattooed, black short-sleeved polo shirt. He reminded me of Bert, the barman at my local at home in Buckinghamshire.

As I thought of Bert, I was amazed to find myself close to tears. Sentimental dickhead, I silently scolded myself.

I thought of Lyar. Thought of Grace. Even thought of Nick. Oh, how easy everything had been then. Before Andrew. Before the thoughts of being gay had made themselves real.

The jukebox was playing good old-fashioned rock music. It made a change from the campy Europop shit they were always churning out in gay places. I was sick of them; sick of it all.

Shit, I told myself. Nothing but false, superficial shit.

I sipped my lager, looking around the bright, rustic pub. Seeing all the couples: boys and girls; men and women. Some with teenage kids. A father and his son. A couple of lads my age playing darts, some at the pool table. How much more secure it all seemed. How much more real. All those people would all go home to their families, or to their girlfriends or boyfriends.

And what did I have to go back to? My personal life had been blown to smithereens, and my social life was just a horrible patchwork of hollow and illusiory gay bars and clubs.

I looked once more around the King Arthur, and I thought, But I don't belong here, either.

It was true. I'd shut myself out. Oh, being gay had cost me so much! I'd closed myself out of the safety and the reality of a heterosexual world just to immerse myself in selfishness and deceit.

London could be the making of us, Andrew.

What a joke.

The barman placed another pint of lager in front of me. I had just finished the first.

"From a secret admirer," he said, nodding to the other side of the bar, where a pretty young blonde girl sat, about eighteen I guessed.

She was with a friend who had short black hair. The first girl, the blonde, winked at me, and then giggled to her companion. I nodded back with a half-smile. Considering the mood I was in, she was lucky to get even that.

It was like the night I'd first met Grace and her sister Anita. My brother eyeing them up, then going over and introducing himself.

What say we head over there, eh? Get us each a bit.

Even though he was married at the time.

So wasn't that proof that the straight world was just as morally corrupt as the gay world could sometimes be?

Again, I thought, I don't belong here. I shouldn't be here, accepting drinks from pretty young girls who fancy me. That's not who I am anymore.

And it was then that I knew I had to go back.

Go back to Soho. Back to Old Compton Street.

It was my destiny; my fate. And I had to embrace it.

I drank half of the pint that had been bought for me, nodded my thanks to the two girls and then went back outside. The rain had stopped now, but a bitterly chill wind cut through the air. I'd only had a pint and a half but I still felt ever-so-slightly tipsy. I hadn't eaten anything all day, mind.

I went to Bar UK after all. It felt less shallow than when I'd almost gone in there earlier. But there was still a creepiness to it. And eyes everywhere, cruises galore. I kept my head lowered as I walked to the bar and ordered a bottle of Hooch. Eyes were the key. The doorway through which people felt they could approach you. And in some cases, try and buy you.

"You get a lot of 'rent'...in here".

I brushed the memory of that encounter away.

In my wallet, I had thirty quid. Some of the money was from my wages, the rest of it was some cash that Andrew had given me a few days ago to get some shopping in. I'd never gotten round to it.

I finished my Hooch and bought a whiskey to chase it down with.

I knew I was being irresponsible, but I was past caring. I wanted to drown my sorrows good and proper.

I decided to get drunk.

Ø

A couple of Hoochs later, I was slumped forward over the bar a bit, eyes half-closed. I thought of Andrew, but then the tears started to come, so I tried to forget. Everything felt weird and half-real. It seemed like a long, long time ago that we'd had that huge argument. I could hardly even remember what it was about by my third (fourth?) Hooch.

Someone tapped me on the shoulder. I turned on my bar stool. I felt wobbly, but still sober enough to respond coherently.

A man stood in front of me. Quite tall. He was wearing a white tank-top, and on his head a black baseball cap with the Adidas logo.

"Are you all right?" he said. His eyes were warm. Inviting.

I nodded, and managed a smile. Because of the alcohol, I felt loose and uninhibited.

"I was watching you over there," said the man. "Knocking them back a bit, aren't you?"

I shrugged. "Free country, ain't it?" I said. My voice slurred, but only very slightly.

Still, I think Baseball Cap noticed it.

"I'm John," he said, and we shook hands.

"Mark."

"Don't you think you've had enough?"

Normally, the comment would have pissed me off. But I was more than half-pissed, anyway, so I just said, "You're probably right, yeah."

"What's the matter?"

I shrugged.

"Come on, there must be something up for you to be drinking like that. And it can't be easy on your wallet, either. Drinks aren't exactly the cheapest of things around here."

"No."

"So what happened."

I sighed deeply. "I had a row with my boyfriend."

"Ah. Something serious?"

Miserably, I nodded. "I...I cheated on him with someone else." Helplessly, the tears started, cascading down my cheeks. Like acid, they seemed to burn, as if they would eat away at my flesh until I was nothing.

"Hey..." said John. "Oh, hey...Mark come on. Don't cry."

I threw my arms around him, and I pretended that he was Andrew. "I've been so horrible!" I blurted over the chugging sounds of The Vengaboys.

I know I wouldn't have done it had I not been looped.

"Shhh," said John. "Listen, you shouldn't be here. You should be with your boyfriend. Look, I'll get you a taxi. Don't worry, I'll pay, Mark. Okay? You shouldn't have come here. And alcohol won't help."

I nodded my agreement against his shoulder.

"Come on. Come outside. Get a bit of fresh air and then get in a cab."

"I don't want to go back," I said.

"Come outside, Mark."

I did as I was told. I got off the bar stool, stumbled a little and then steadied myself on John's shoulder. I followed him outside. He took my hand, leading me through the crowd.

Outside, the air was fresh and cool. "He all right?" the bouncer said to John as we went past him.

"He'll be fine."

"I don't want to go back to the flat," I said. "Please don't make me go back, John. Not tonight." The thought of going to Newman Street, of seeing Andrew, the icy indifference in his blue eyes, made me feel ill. I'd have to face my guilty conscience again, and that was something I really didn't want to do.

What a coward I was.

"Why?"

"I can't face him."

"It will all still be there tomorrow, Mark."

He was right, but seized by the alcohol, I said, "Couldn't I just go back to your place? I'll be no trouble. Just until tomorrow."

"Mark..."

"Please, John?"

He thought for a minute, looked up at the sky as if asking the thousands of stars if I could be trusted. "I've only just met you, Mark," he said.

"I swear I'll be no trouble. John, don't make me go home. I know I've only just met you, and I know I'm a bit drunk..."

"A *bit* drunk!"

"All right, so I'm pissed. So? I'm not totally gone. Please? I'll leave first thing in the morning. Andrew doesn't want to see me tonight, anyway. And he'll probably kill me if I turn up like this."

"Mm," said John. He shook his head. "All right, Mark. You can crash at mine for the night. I've got a futon, it's no problem. But tomorrow, first thing, you call your bloke and tell him where you are. Okay?"

"I promise. Thank you, John."

"I better not regret this," he said.

Ø

We got a taxi from the depot at the bottom of Old Compton Street. John lived in Camden, in a nice one-bedroom flat. It was a bit similar to our flat, actually. Bit bigger, maybe.

"I'll get you a coffee," he said. "Make yourself at home in the living- room."

"Thanks."

I sat down on the sofa. Inside the flat, for some reason I felt even more drunk than when we'd left Bar UK.

I looked around the living room. Books were everywhere, and a stack of CDs by the big stereo. There was a load of electrical stuff over by the large wide-screen TV, and next to that a state-of-the-art PC.

John came through with the coffee and a plate of dry toast. He handed a mug of coffee to me, and the toast. "Oh, no thanks," I said. "I'm not hungry."

"Eat it. It'll sober you up."

I took a bite, and thought I was going to throw up. I retched. "I can't stomach it," I said.

"Maybe later then."

I sipped the milky coffee. John took out a packet of fags. "Menthol?" he said, proffering the packet.

I'd never smoked menthol cigarettes before. "Thank you," I said, and took one.

"How are you feeling now?"

"Pissed as a fart."

"It'll pass soon. We'll just finish these coffees and then I'll unroll the futon for you."

The door that led through to the bedroom was open and I noticed the large, comfortable-looking king-size bed.

"I don't have to sleep on the futon if you don't want me to," I said, absently.

"Yes you do," he said, gently but firmly.

"John," I murmured. "I could get in with you..."

"You're drunk, Mark. Stop it."

"Don't you fancy me?"

"Yes. Very much. And I'd love to sleep with you. But you're smashed. You don't know what you're saying. And judging from what you've told me so far, and the way you've acted back at the bar, you're in love with your boyfriend. So just shut up, and go to sleep, okay?"

There was a harshness to his words, and they seemed to sober me up a bit more. I felt fogged, but at the same time my mind had sharpened.

"I'm sorry," I told him.

"I know you are. And you're going to be even sorrier tomorrow. So just drink your coffee and get some sleep, all right?"

I nodded and smoked some more of the menthol cigarette.

It was disgusting.

After a few moments silence, John said, "It's gonna be okay tomorrow, Mark. It's gonna be okay with your boyfriend."

I looked at him, tried for a smile but it came out as a sort of grimace. Would it be okay? Would it really?

I hoped so, of course I did. But with my life, it always seems that when things can get no worse, they suddenly do.

Ø

Unsurprisingly, I had a hangover when I woke up. I was still fully-clothed. At first I couldn't remember anything that had happened, but then I sat up, looked around the flat's living room, and it all came flooding back.

I just thought, O-oh.

I remembered the argument. I remembered it all too vividly.

And now here was I, in some bloke's flat that I didn't even know. (Could've been a pervert for all I knew...what sort of man takes back drunken guys they don't even know, anyway?).

But slapping Andrew was the thing that stood out most in my mind. How could I have done that?

Please don't finish us, Andrew.

I don't want to.

"Oh, you're up," said a voice behind me. It was John. He was wearing a white towelling dressing gown.

I squinted up at him. "My head hurts," I whimpered.

"Quelle surprise," he said. "Here. Get that down you." He handed me a mug of milky tea. "I'll make another one for myself."

"Thanks," I mumbled, sipping the hot liquid. I sat in silence for a bit as John went back to the kitchen to fix a drink for himself. When he returned, I said, "What time is it?"

"Nearly ten."

"Shit," I said. Andrew, I thought. I must call Andrew. He'll be worried out of his mind.

"Can I use your phone?" I said.

"Of course. Here." From the coffee table he picked up the white cordless and handed it to me. I dialled the number of the flat, but got only the answering machine. Andrew must have been at work. For a second I considered calling Dimensions.

But say what?

I decided it would be better for me to see Andrew on a face-to-face basis.

"No answer?" said John.

I shook my head. "He's at work. I'll go and talk to him."

I stood up and put down the mug of tea. John said, "Have you got enough money to get back?"

"Yeah. Thanks, John. Thanks for letting me stay here. I'm sorry...sorry if I made a fool of myself."

"Forget about it. You were drunk."

I nodded.

"I hope you sort it out with your boyfriend, Mark. You seem like a nice guy."

"Yeah. So nice I played around behind his back."

"Mistakes happen. You'll both get over it."

"I hope so," I said. "I really do."

Ø

I left John's flat after we exchanged numbers. He'd asked me to call him to let him know how things went, but I doubted if I would. As I caught the tube at Camden station, I doubted very much if I'd ever see him again.

When I got to Tottenham Court Road, my stomach felt as though it had a bowling ball inside it. My mouth was dry as a desert. I lit a cigarette, and gagged on it. I was bricking it as I walked to Newman Street.

I got to our building, unlocked the three doors on my way up to the flat. Even though I knew Andrew was at work, I still felt as sick as if I were about to have another confrontation with him.

I went inside.

Silence met me. A horrible, dusty silence. The flat felt of nothing.

I went into the living room, as slowly and carefully as a burglar wondering what to steal.

The flat looked the same as it always did. Except something felt a bit odd and off-centre about it.

I looked around. Everything in order, everything where it usually was...

And then I saw the note.

A folded piece of paper resting on top of the television. My name was written on top of it in Andrew's writing.

With a barely steady hand, I unfolded the note and started to read.

Dearest Mark,

I'm writing this note because it feels easier than talking to you face-to-face. I know that might sound cowardly, but after last night's argument I really don't think I can trust myself to be around you. Plus, this way gives me more space to think and to get across exactly how I'm feeling without things escalating into a mindless row.

First off, let me say how much you have hurt me. It was bad enough when I found out that you'd slept with Ben, the humiliation I suffered at the club in front of all those people was awful. Then when you told me about that other guy, it really was like you'd taken a shotgun and blown away a huge part of my life. How could you do it, Mark?

As I said to you last night, I think the London scene is, at least partly, to blame for what's happened. You would never have done something like this back home.

Or maybe you did. After these recent revelations, I just don't know what to believe about our relationship. Was it just me believing that everything we had was perfect? Maybe you had other ideas about us.

I don't want this to be the end of us, Mark, I really don't. But the way I'm feeling right now, I can't see any alternative other than for us to go our separate ways. Perhaps it's time for us both to move on. I just don't feel like I know you anymore.

And for that reason, I've decided to move out for a bit. I've got a few days' holiday so you won't be able to get hold of me at work. I really think it's for the best if we don't see other for a while. I need some space to get my head around what's happened and to decide what to do next. I have to think on what you said, about an open relationship. Is that what you really want? If it is, Mark, I don't think I could handle it. I really don't.

The rent on the flat is all up to date and I've left you some cash in case you need anything.

I'm sorry if this letter has sounded harsh, Mark, but you have to understand how badly you've hurt me.

I'll be in touch soon.

Love,
Andrew.

I read it once more. It was so awful. So cold. I started to cry. But not hysterically. The tears just trickled down my cheeks. I looked around the flat, and wanted to burn it to the ground. I'd lost him. I'd lost him!

My own fault, my own stupid, stupid fault!

Perhaps it's time for us both to move on.

No, Andrew. No! Please, no!

"I love you," I said aloud. But what did it matter? Who was I saying it to? Myself probably. Someone who'd behaved like I had was nothing but selfish.

On a shelf near the television was a framed photograph of me and Andrew, taken at our surprise leaving party at Medusa's. We had our arms around each other's shoulders, these big fat cheesy grins on our faces. It was a picture of two people in love.

And now? Now what did we have? What did I have? An empty flat and a goodbye note from my boyfriend.

It was all too much.

Wiping away the tears with the back of my hand, I picked up the framed photograph and hurled it violently against the wall.

12 **Andrew**

I moved in with Rebecca and her girlfriend Louise. They lived in Muswell Hill. I had a week off work, so that gave me enough time to get my head around what to do next.

I had no idea, see.

Like I'd told Mark in that letter, I didn't want us to finish. I loved him. I still loved him even after the things he'd done, the way he'd betrayed me. But even when you love someone, it doesn't necessarily mean that the right thing is to stay with them. Mark had cheated on me at least twice. Who's to say that he wouldn't do it again? The bottom line in all of it was that I didn't know if I'd ever be able to trust him again.

Rebecca was one of the few people I told about the bust-up. We'd sat up all night talking about it. I'd told her everything. She couldn't believe it at first. "This is Mark we're talking about?" she'd said. "Mark...your boyfriend?"

"Yes."

"I can't believe it, Andrew. God! I mean...I mean, he never ever struck me as the sort of guy who'd do that. And to you, too! No offence, darling, but he must be a couple of sandwiches short of a picnic to mess around on you."

"I know. Rebecca, I don't want to break up with him. But I don't think there's any other way. I feel like everything's been destroyed.

Wiped out, just like that."

Rebecca said that it hadn't really. "You're just feeling that way now. Don't make any rash decisions. You don't want to turn your back on two -nearly three - years in a split second, Andrew. Believe me."

"It's London," I told her. "I know it is. Look at Mark when we were back home. He was so sweet, a bit naive, maybe, but he was decent; a good bloke. And now look at him. Bedding every bloke who looks twice at him."

"Don't exaggerate."

"Maybe it's not such an exaggeration, Bec. Maybe Mark hasn't told me the full story of what he gets up to when I'm at work."

"Oh, I think he has. There's no point in keeping anything else from you, is there? Not now, not after this."

"I guess."

"I think you were right to take some time out though, Andrew."

"Yeah?"

"Yeah. It'll stop you from ending it completely. I don't think that's what you want, is it?"

"I told you, no it isn't. But there doesn't seem to be any choice, Rebecca."

"There's always a choice, Andrew," she said.

Ø

I didn't do much in the next two days. Brooded around the flat. Rebecca and Louise went to work during the day, leaving me to sit around and think about Mark. A couple of times I wanted to call him, but I stopped myself. The mean, low-minded part of my personality thought, let him stew in it.

It was good getting away from work for a while, though. The stress of running Dimensions was the last thing I needed.

I made myself useful at Rebecca's. Tidied up, did the washing, got the shopping in and all that. I couldn't get Mark out of my head, though. I thought a lot about his coming-out, about when I first met him, the shy, innocent guy who couldn't deal with the fact that he was attracted to men. He'd seemed so vulnerable back then, like he needed someone to look after him, to look out for him.

But I guess that's what we all need. That's what everyone in the world's crying out for, I suppose, for someone to look after them. Even if they don't always admit it.

I kept my mobile phone switched off the day after I went to Rebecca's. I really didn't want to speak to Mark. I think part of me was punishing him. I know I said I didn't want to punish him, but it seemed a bit unfair that I was going through emotional hell when he was pretty much getting away scot-free.

Well, no. He wasn't really, was he? Mark must have been feeling like shit, too.

But he deserved to.

Two days after moving in with Rebecca and Louise, there was a phone call from Daniel. Other than Rebecca and Martyn, he was the only person at Dimensions who knew where I was staying. I felt a bit like some sort of James Bond-style spy camping out from the enemy.

Except I didn't want Mark to be my enemy.

"Hi, boss," said Daniel on the phone. It was a Friday.

"Daniel. How's it going?"

"Busy. But don't worry about that. You enjoy your holiday, okay?"

The way he spoke made me sound like some type of invalid. "Not exactly a holiday, is it, though?" I said. I'd told Daniel about what had happened between Mark and I. Only briefly, mind. I knew he and Mark were good friends and I didn't want to go into too much detail in case things got back to my estranged boyfriend.

"Well...you know what I mean." He sounded embarrassed.

"So what can I do for you?" I said. I hoped he wouldn't be on the phone too long. I wasn't exactly in a talking sort of mood.

"Mark dropped in to see me a while ago. Andrew...he's in a bit of a state. Red eyes from crying. I think he'd had a drink or two, actually."

"Oh," I said. I tried to sound as casual as possible, but it was difficult. My heart was breaking. I just wanted to go to Mark then, wrap my arms around him and tell him it was all right. But I couldn't. I couldn't. "What did he say to you?"

"Just that he feels terrible. He asked me where you were staying. He really wants to see you, Andrew."

"You didn't tell him where I was, did you, Dan?"

"Of course I didn't. But I wanted to, Andrew. I really wanted to. But you asked me not to so I haven't. But I think you should talk to him. He looks like a total wreck."

"It's too soon, Daniel," I said. I was determined to be resolute about it all.

"When won't it be? There's never going to be an easy time to deal with it. And the longer you leave it, the worse it'll get."

"I know."

A short pause followed, then Daniel said, "I don't want you two to break up, Andrew."

"I don't want us to either."

"Then..."

"You don't understand," I interrupted. He didn't. Daniel's longest relationship had lasted for only two months. Mark and I had been going nearly three years, as Rebecca had pointed out. How could Daniel ever understand that?

"The thing is, Andrew," he began, somewhat tentatively, I thought. "Mark...he seemed really close to...well, close to the edge."

"The edge of what?" I frowned into the receiver.

"You know? The edge of despair or something. You don't think he'll...well, try and do something to himself, do you?"

"No. Mark isn't the type." But the words rang hollowly in my head. I tried to dismiss Daniel's worries as an example of his usual over-reactions. But somehow, I couldn't.

But surely...surely Mark wasn't the suicidal kind.

Until now, maybe?

No.

Daniel said, "I told him to take a holiday."

I snorted. "Mark can't afford a holiday." Helplessly, I thought, maybe one of his fancy men'll treat him.

Perhaps that was unfair. But perhaps not.

"I know. But he said if you won't speak to him at the moment, he can't stand being in London. He's going to go back home for the weekend. To see his mum. That's what he told me, anyway."

Home, I thought, picturing the town where I'd lived for three years. I thought of Medusa's, of our old flat, of Mark.

"Why don't you go with him?" asked Daniel.

"I can't."

"Don't be so stubborn."

"Daniel! You know what Mark did to me. He's turned my life into shit."

Daniel said nothing.

"Sorry," I told him flatly. "I didn't mean to snap."

"Yes you did. But it's okay."

I thought for a moment. "I'm not going with him," I said. "But I promise I'll speak to him when he gets back. Yeah?"

"Don't do it for me, Andrew."

"I'm not. I'm doing it for me. Not even for Mark. For me."

PART IV
Drowned Worlds

1 Mark

Homecoming.

What a nice word that is. But my homecoming felt like something horrible. It felt like a sort of failure. London had beaten me. I thought I'd been able to take it on single-handedly and come up smiling. No. London had sucked me up, chewed on me for a bit, then spat out the bones. And then it had laughed as I got on the train back to the world I thought I'd said goodbye to forever.

London was dead to me without Andrew. It seemed utterly pointless. The bright lights; the big city...it was worth nothing to me. I'd destroyed it for myself.

Ben, you bastard!

There I go again. Blaming someone else. What a nice person I am.

It had sort of been Daniel's idea for me to go home. He'd told me I'd looked awful, that I should get away. "Not without Andrew," I said. "I really want to talk to him. Where is he? Daniel, you must know!"

But Daniel's face had crunched up on itself and he'd said nothing. He knew, but obviously Andrew had sworn him to secrecy. That felt awful. It was like everyone was laughing at me behind my back.

Sing-songing, we know something you don't know!

Still, I probably deserved to be kept in the dark.

"I think you need a break," Daniel had told me. "You should go somewhere for the weekend."

"Like where?"

He'd suggested Brighton. "Brighton?" I laughed. "What the hell am I going to do there?"

That was when I'd come up with the idea of going home for a weekend. Daniel was right. It would be good for me to leave the gay scene for a little while.

"And I'll talk to Andrew while you're gone," he'd added, then he'd hugged me. "It'll be fine, Mark. Andrew just needs time to cool off. You'll see."

So there I was. Back on the train, a rucksack of clothes on my back, and eyes hidden behind dark sunglasses. My eyes had been red for the last few days, the result of too much crying.

I'd called Grace and had asked if I could stay at hers. She'd said no problem. I didn't want to go and stay at my mum's. Besides, I knew I wouldn't be welcome. Not really, not properly. Not the way a son should be.

The train journey took about forty-five minutes. As I sat there, in a window seat, holding an unlit cigarette that I wasn't smoking in my hand, I prayed for forgetfulness. But it didn't come. I was forced to roll over in my head the dreadful events of the last two weeks.

When I arrived, I got on the bus that took me to Grace's.

How grey the town seemed. And empty. And quiet. A year since I'd been in that town, almost a year, anyway. But it felt like forever. It had died the day I left for a life of wild abandon in London, and now that I'd left London that had died, too. So what did I have left?

Grace buzzed me up to the flat, and when she opened the door, I just hugged her and cried into her shoulder. We stayed like that for some time as I just let all my pain out.

When I'd stopped, she took me inside and poured me a whiskey. "Down it in one," she said. "It'll make you feel better."

I did as I was told, wincing at the sharp taste.

"Where's Jason?" I said.

"Round his mum's. He's taken Rupert with him. Given me a bit of a break so we can talk. You didn't say much on the phone."

"Andrew's moved out," I blurted, and the tears started to come again. "Oh, Grace! I've been such a bastard to him!"

"He's moved out? Where?"

"I don't know. He won't tell me. His mobile's always switched off so I can't contact him. I've left so many messages. Grace, I don't know what to do. I feel like I've got nothing left."

"Of course you have!" she said. "Andrew just needs some time to get over this, I'm sure."

"That's what everyone keeps telling me. But I just find it so hard to believe. Grace, I think this is the end of us."

"Don't say that."

"I just can't see any hope for us."

"But Mark, you two have been *together* for so long. And that's rare in the gay world, isn't it? You know how transient gay relationships are. You and Andrew have been together for almost three years."

"I know."

"So you've obviously got something going for you. Something strong. Just a little...I don't know, one-night stand surely isn't enough to throw away three years of happiness for?"

"But it wasn't just a one-night stand. There was...someone else, too. Before Ben."

Grace's jaw dropped. Her eyes bulged. "Mark?"

I told her about that night at Elysium; the drugs and the anonymous sex.

"Oh, Mark," she sighed. She seemed pained.

"Andrew warned me it would happen. He told me how London had affected *him*."

"It's got nothing to do with London!" she exclaimed. "London's just a city."

"And I'm just a bastard."

"Quit wallowing in it," she said. "Have you told your mum what's happened?"

"No."

"Why not?"

I thought of what Mum had told me when I said I was moving to London.

You're lucky to have him, Mark. You know that, don't you?

"She'd go mental, Grace. You know how fond of Andrew she is. And I screwed everything up."

"Yes. You did, Mark. But going over and over it isn't going to change what you've done. You should be focusing on making it up to Andrew, on making amends. You have to save the relationship, Mark. No one's going to do it for you."

"I don't know how to make amends. I've tried everything. I've apologised until I'm blue in the face. He says he can't trust me again."

"He says that *now*."

I nodded. Then said, "Do you know what I was thinking? I'm as bad as Nick, aren't I? Look what he did with Anita. And that's just what I've done."

"Nick's a different story altogether," said Grace.

"Is he?"

She nodded, and then shook her head. "Look, why are we talking about him? Nick isn't important. Andrew is. Listen. The thing is to let him cool off, then when he comes to you - which he will - you can prove to him that you can be trusted. Fight for him, Mark. Get him to see that you don't have to split up."

"It's all easy to say, Grace. But you didn't see him. When we had that row...when we blew up at each other. God...he was so different."

"What do you expect?"

What, indeed? I thought.

We talked some more after that, basically just saying the same things but in different words.

Jason came home an hour later, along with baby Rupert in one of those rucksack things that babies fit into. He was such a sweet little thing. And Jason and Grace...well, they'd taken to being parents like ducks to water. How safe and secure it all seemed. Like the people in that pub, the King Arthur. And I realised that a tiny part of me was actually jealous of what Grace and Jason had. Their lives were sorted and settled. What was mine like? Just a shambles; a complete and utter mess.

I left them to it at about five, and decided to go and see Mum. Dad would probably be home, too. The thought unnerved me a little, but I knew, despite everything, it would be good to see him.

I didn't get the bus home, but walked instead. Grace's flat was in the high street, above a pet shop, so it was pretty much nearby to everything.

Including Medusa's. It was Saturday, and the place would be pumping later on. It looked so small to me now, compared to the daunting capacities of JayJay's or Elysium or Frenzy.

But it had been ours.

As I walked past the club, memories slipped in and out of my mind; memories of my first encounter with Andrew; with a homosexual.

"Catching flies? Sorry, mate. We had the exterminators in last week".

I moved away from Medusa's before the tears started again.

The blacked-out windows of the club looked like blind eyes. But they seemed to be laughing at me.

"Ha! So we weren't good enough for you, eh? Had to go and try and be a big shot in London, did you, Mark? And look what it's got you! Haaaaaaaaaaaa!"

I'm really cracking up, I told myself, and walked on. I felt like I was stumbling through some sort of freaky funhouse where bad memories assaulted me at every turn.

And it was when I popped into the corner shop for a packet of fags that I bumped straight into another unpleasant blast from the past.

Chris Snowdon.

Chris had been the singer, and founder member, of my band Lyar.

He'd also been in on my brother's sick attempts to 'cure' me from being gay, by shutting me in his flat with two whores to fuck.

He was standing by the magazines, flicking through a copy of Select. He didn't look up as I went into the shop, so he didn't see me straightaway. It was amazing, the fact that I hadn't laid eyes on him for nearly three years, and he still looked exactly the same. It was like looking through a window into yesterday.

I went to the counter. "Twenty Silk Cut, please," I said, speaking loudly. I wanted Chris to see me. I was curious as to what his reaction would be.

I got my fags, turned and said, "Chris!" like I hadn't seen him there.

He turned his head, then when he saw who it was, he sneered horribly, looked me up and down as if I was dirt. Then he closed the magazine, turned and left the shop.

Well, of course I wasn't having that.

I dashed out after him. "Oi! I was talking to you!" He didn't turn to acknowledge my outburst. He just kept walking away from me, head down. "Chris! Look at me! I'm talking to you!"

I felt so enraged. All these emotions filled my body and brain, colliding with one another. Anger, humiliation, sorrow.

"Chris! Look at me!"

I ran up behind him and shoved him in the back. He was a big bloke, mind you. But fat with it. Sluggish.

Now, he stopped. He turned. His eyes were like pebbles at the bottom of a cold river. "Fuck off, Mark," he growled.

"Can't even look me in the eye, can you?" I said.

He turned and went to walk away from me. I grabbed his shoulder and pulled him round with a hefty swing of my arm.

Now his eyes blazed. For a second, I thought he was going to hit me. "Freak!" he barked. "Fucking subhuman!"

"You got a problem, Chris?" I said. I thought we were going to have a fight right there, I really did. Right on the cold grey streets. I steeled myself.

"Have I got a problem? Have I got a problem? You bet your fucking arse I have, freak."

"What did you call me?"

"Freak." He hissed the word now. His thin, spiteful lips curled into a smile of malice. "Do you know what I do now, Mark?" he asked. "Do you know what I do for a living?"

I shrugged at the bizarre question. "I don't know. Work in a warehouse. Still?"

"No, Mark. No, I don't do anything. I'm on the dole. On the fucking dole like a loser..."

"You *are* a loser, Chris."

"Maybe I am. Maybe I'm on the goddamn scrapheap of life. But you know what, Mark? You put me there. You." His eyes glittered with hate.

"What? What are you on about?"

"We could've been so good, Mark. We could've been so bloody good! We could've made it! We almost did make it!"

I smiled, sarcastically. "Oh, that's it, is it? You're jealous, are you? Jealous because Andrew got me and not you? Why, Chris. I didn't know you cared."

"I ain't no queer, you little shit!" he spat, disgusted. An old lady on the other side of the road stared at us. "Christ, you make me puke," continued Chris. "I meant that Lyar could've made it, could've made it to the top. Till we lost our faggot drummer."

I laughed, bitterly; ironically. "Oh, I get it. So because I'm gay I wrecked our chances of making it, did I? Don't make me laugh. I wasn't the hysterical bigot who threw me out of the group. So you're on the scrapheap? It's not my bloody fault, Chris. It's yours. Yours and yours alone!"

"I was going to get married!" he seethed. "I was engaged! Yeah, didn't know that, did you? But when Lyar split, so did fucking Gloria. The bitch. Didn't want to go out with a failed pop singer, did she?"

"S'pose she's got some taste after all then," I said.

Chris's eyes narrowed with malevolence. "I hope you die, Mark. I hope you get fucking AIDS and die. You freak. Subhuman, that's what you are. That's what all you shit-stabbers are like. Subhuman."

"Go to Hell," I muttered, and then I turned and walked away. There was just no reasoning with people like that, no reasoning at all. Shit for brains, and no mistake.

But his words had no real effect on me, not in a hurtful sense. Chris was just a lot of hot air. He wouldn't do anything to me, I knew that. Despite all his bluster, he was a wimp.

"Freak!" he shouted after me. "Dirty queer! Polluter! Don't get too close to Mark, everyone. Unless you want AIDS!"

Vile, wasn't it?

But I had far bigger concerns than Chris the Partisan.

As I headed to my parents' house, I thought of Daniel and all that had gone on outside Dimensions. Those morons, attacking, physically and verbally. They were just like Chris, those idiots.

So you don't think you get stuff like that in London? That London's some sort of idyllic, poof's paradise?

I got home. It didn't feel like home anymore, though.

Butterflies danced in my stomach as I saw Dad's van parked outside. He was home. The old man was home.

Jesus.

As I mounted the steps, as I lifted on the old Victorian knocker, I couldn't help remember the day I came out.

Generations of my family had lived in this small terraced house. I wondered if any others had been gay. If years and years and years ago, there'd been other young men here, distant relatives of mine, who'd harboured secret homosexual feelings. Who knew?

The idea seemed sort of humorous.

Wouldn't it be weird if somewhere, buried in history, I did have gay relations?

Eventually, Dad answered the door. I almost flinched.

It was nothing like the Prodigal Son returning home to his

delighted father. We stared each other out for a good few seconds before anyone dared say anything.

I was the first to speak. "Hello, Dad."

"Son." He opened the door wider, and let me in. "Didn't expect to see you," he said. His words were blunt.

"Just a flying visit," I told him. "Had a spare weekend, so I thought I'd pop down. Haven't been back here for a while."

"No. D'you want a cuppa? Or a beer. There's a coupla cans in the fridge."

"Yeah, wouldn't say no. Ta."

Beer would calm my nerves. Good.

I followed him into the kitchen and as we walked past the open living room door, Dad poked his head in and said, "Mark's here."

"Mark!" shrilled Mum's disembodied voice. A few seconds later, she came out. She was beaming, and held her arms out. I enfolded her in a huge hug and tried not to cry.

We all went into the kitchen together, a happy little family.

Yeah, right.

Dad got me a beer out of the fridge and one for himself. "This is a surprise!" gushed Mum. "Why didn't you call and let us know you were coming down?"

"Like you say, I wanted it to be a surprise."

Dad said, "I'll leave you both to it. Footie's on in a bit."

He left the room, Mum and I both watched him go in silence. See? He was still cold towards me, even now. He still couldn't accept it.

His loss, though.

"Be patient with him, love," Mum said quietly. "It's gonna take time."

"It's been ages already."

She just looked at me, pained. "I'm sorry," she said, as if it was all her fault.

"Don't apologise, Mum." I smiled.

"So where's Andrew? He not with you?"

My heart turned cold. Something inside me broke. After a pause, I said, "He's...he's working. Couldn't get the time off."

"Oh dear. That is a shame. I would like to have seen him."

"Yeah..." I trailed, and I looked at my mother, at the joy and delight in her eyes at seeing her youngest son after all this time, and it was just too much for me. I broke down, my face crumpling and the tears streaming hot and painful down my cheeks. I sat down at the small kitchen table and put my head in my hands, softly weeping for the love I'd as good as thrown away.

"Mark! What is it?" Mum sat down next to me and put her thin arm around my shoulders. She held me against her and I cried like a little boy into her cardigan. I couldn't speak for ages. I thought of Andrew, and Chris, and Grace, and Ben and Daniel. Thought of Newman Street, and JayJay's and Old Compton Street.

"Mark, tell me. What's wrong? Mark?"

But her words, the sound of her voice, only made me cry harder. I just wept against her tiny frame and she said nothing. The only sound was my ragged breathing and the noise of the televised football match leaking through from the living room where my dad sat, oblivious to the pain I was suffering.

"Oh, Mum...Mum I don't believe what I've done!" I blurted when I'd composed myself a little.

"What? Oh, Mark it can't be that bad. Tell me. Did you and Andrew have an argument? Is that why he's not with you?"

I nodded against her bony shoulder.

"Oh, Mark. You'll both make it up. You know you will."

"Not this time, Mum. I don't think we will. It's so awful. I've been so awful. So horrible to him." I cried a bit more. Mum stood up and pulled off some kitchen roll. She handed it to me and I dried the tears. I sniffed loudly. I only hoped Dad wouldn't come through for another beer or something. I didn't want him to see me crying, especially over this. His poof son bawling like a little girl in her mother's arms. Yeah, that'd be all he'd want to see.

"Why?" said Mum. "Mark, what happened? Why have you been so awful?"

How could I explain? How could I? Mum would never understand the gay scene, the way it is there, the way things are.

"I had an affair," I said. I felt like I was deflating, or sinking into quicksand. Helpless and out of control. "I slept with someone else."

Silence. At first. Then, "Oh, Mark..." The way she said my name, drawing it out in a hideous gasp, made me feel ill.

"I know," I said, sniffing and wiping my eyes some more. "I know. But it was just this one time, Mum. And I was drunk."

Okay, so I had to be a bit economical with the truth. But I couldn't tell her the full story. She'd be furious probably. As I'd said to Grace, she was so fond of Andrew.

I looked into her eyes and wanted to throw up at the disappointment I saw in them. She'd never expected something like that of me.

I'd let her down. I'd let Andrew down. And most of all, I'd let myself down.

"You were drunk," she said, processing that information. "But...it still doesn't make it all right, does it? Eh?" She spoke softly; soothing her baby boy.

"No. No, it doesn't, Mum. I know that. But I'm so sorry about the whole thing. And now Andrew's moved out, I feel so alone. And it's all my fault! I'm not trying to hide from that fact, but I don't know what to do!"

"Andrew will come around, Mark," was all Mum said. "He will."

It's what everyone had been telling me. Everyone.

"I don't know, Mum. I don't know."

"He knows you're sorry, Mark. He knows you love him. He knows you won't do it again. You...won't do it again, will you?" She added this last bit almost cautiously, as if warning me.

"No! Of course I won't! I wouldn't dream of doing it again. I love Andrew! I do."

"I know you do. And he knows that, too. You just have to have faith."

"What if that isn't enough?"

"It will be, love," she said. "It will have to be. It's all you've got."

It was always weird, when she went all insightful like that, and at other times seem so ignorant of the real world. It was as if she had a split personality, able to dip between one place and the other almost seamlessly.

We talked some more about it after those fateful words.

You just have to have faith. It's all you've got.

Mum was understanding. I'd tried to tell her about the London gay scene, about how selfish and devious it could sometimes seem. She'd just nodded and sipped her tea, as if she understood. But I don't think she could have really. Straights rarely do. They try and pretend they get what it's all about, and sometimes they probably do think they've got the whole queer biosphere sussed. But they haven't. They can't, see. How can you understand something you'll never know? It's impossible.

At one point, I'd said to her, "What if people can't change, Mum? What if I do it again, somewhere down the line? What if this...this faithlessness runs in my blood and I end up cheating again?"

"That's nonsense talk, Mark. You won't do that. You love Andrew too much. Okay, you're young, and you made a mistake. A stupid mistake. That doesn't mean you'll do it again."

"Nick did it," I muttered under my breath. "Look what happened with Anita. Look what he did to Saffron. Exactly what I did to Andrew. You know what he'd said to me when I told him Anita was pregnant with his baby? He'd said, 'I didn't think I'd be caught out'. Mum...what if I didn't get caught? I'd've probably kept on doing it, kept on...playing away from home."

"Nick made a mistake, just like you did, Mark. And Nick's changed."

I eyed her sceptically.

She thought for a moment, then she stood. "Look...I wasn't going

254

to show you this, Mark. Not yet, anyway. But...maybe now it's what you need to see. Maybe you'll feel better once you've seen it."

Confusion spun in my head like a dervish. "Mum...what are you talking about?"

"Just wait there a second."

She went from the room, leaving me at the small table, my unfinished beer in front of me. I was puzzled. I felt like she was about to bring down some great family heirloom or something.

I lit a cigarette and listened absently to the drone of the football match that still oozed from the livingroom. I'd been in that house for almost an hour and Dad hadn't come back to see me. But I was glad. Emotions were running too high as it was, without some homophobic show-down to add to it.

Mum returned a couple of minutes later. "Here," she said, and she placed a brown envelope on the table in front of me.

One word was written on it.

Mark.

Horrifyingly, I was reminded of the note Andrew had left me a few days ago on top of the television.

"I just don't think I can trust myself around you right now. How could you do it?"

The words rang through my head as if in some hateful echo chamber.

"What is it?" I said.

"Open it, Mark."

I did and found a single A4 sheet of paper covered with tiny neat writing in blue biro.

Dear Mark, it began.

"What is it?" I repeated.

"It's a letter for you."

"Who from?"

"Just read it and see," said Mum. Commanded, actually. It was her best order-giving voice, the one she'd used when I was little and would pull my sister's hair until she cried.

I started to read.

Dear Mark,

What can I say? I know you're probably going to destroy this letter when Mum tells you who it's from, but please don't. Not until you've heard what I have to say.

I'm sorry. That's the bottom line, Mark. I'm sorry for what I've done. To tell you the truth, I really don't know why I did it. Being inside has made me think a lot about it. About what you are. About what I am, too. I was wrong to attack you because you're different, I know that. I think I probably reacted out of shock or something. Or maybe after Dad had that heart attack it just sort of triggered something dark inside me. I don't think I'll ever know the true reason; I don't think any of us will. But I'm sorry, Mark. You have to believe that. I'm sorry.

You probably don't believe it, though, do you? I know what you probably think. That I'm just saying I'm sorry, telling you what you want to hear so that everyone else will believe I'm sorry, too. You probably think it's just a front so I can get out of prison.

But, Mark, that isn't the case. I'm sorry I hurt you. You're my little brother, after all. And I can't imagine what it's like for you to be gay. I can't begin to imagine, and I won't pretend I can. I don't want to be a hypocrite.

There are a few gays in prison with me, Mark. And I suppose that's something that's made me see things in a new light. It's not like I've found myself or anything like that, or that I'm on the turn. But I know that queers are normal fellas. Pretty much, anyway. The idea of men sleeping with men still turns my stomach, but if I try not to think about that part of it, it's okay. I don't know if that makes much sense to you, Mark. But I hope so.

I've taken up a creative writing course while I've been in here. And I'm seeing a counsellor, too. That's helped me a lot. It's helped me to accept what you are better, and also to feel remorse for what I did to you. Once again, Mark, I can't say how sorry I am.

I hopefully should be getting out of here soon. I've started to behave myself, and I think I've learned my lesson. I hope I'll be able to see you once I'm out, but I'd understand if you didn't want that, or if it took some time before you felt ready to see me again.

Write back if you can. Mum says you've moved to London and I'd like to know how you're getting on there. But again, I understand if you feel you couldn't tell me.

I can't think of anything more right now, but if you'd like, I could write again. Please don't hate me Mark. Hate what I once was, yes. But don't hate the person I am now, the person I've become. Please, Mark. Please.

Your brother,
Nick.

"I don't believe him," I said when I'd finished reading. I felt hard and bitter. I folded the letter back up, put it in the envelope and calmly handed it to Mum.

"Mark...why not?"

"Exactly the reasons he says there, Mum. He's not sorry at all. He's just making out he is for everyone else. If he got out of prison, Mum, the first thing he'd do when we're alone is try and kill me again."

"That's unfair, Mark," she said, crossly. "He's different. You haven't seen him. It has been a long time. He's like a model prisoner now."

"A model prisoner? Mum, if he was such a model prisoner, why isn't he out by now? Two years he got sent down for. Two years. But everyone said he wouldn't even have to serve half of that. But he's still there, isn't he?"

"Yes," she said. "But there was a bit of trouble at first. He didn't settle down very well. It's prison, Mark. Not a holiday camp. You don't adjust straightaway. And yes, he used to get into fights a bit, the odd scrap at first. But he's changed in the last year. Really, he has. It won't be long before he's out of there for good, I know it."

"People like Nick don't change, Mum."

"How can you be so closed-minded, Mark? You of all people."

The words dug into my brain and made me stop and think for a moment.

"Do you think *you* can change, Mark? Do you think you'll be cheating on Andrew forever?"

"I don't know."

"Of course you won't. I can see it in you, boy. You've learned from your mistake. Just like Nick has. Just like he told you in that letter."

"You've read it, too?"

"He asked me not to. But I had to see for myself, see if he had changed. I didn't want him handing you some poisonpen thing. But I was pleasantly surprised. And so should you be."

"It's different for you, though, Mum. You don't know what it was like, what he did to me, how awful it was."

"Maybe not. But what about how awful it was for me, to see my sons, my pride and joy, doing that to one another."

"I didn't do anything."

"I know you didn't. I know that. But from Nick's point of view, he just thought you were trying to hurt us all in some way. I know that sounds stupid, but at first, that's what I thought, too."

"You did?"

"Yes. I know that's not the case now, though. I know you've not changed as a person. You're still my baby boy, Mark." As she said this, tears started to roll silently down her cheeks. "Just because you're the way you are...it makes no difference to me. Not any more. Not even to Nick now. Even Dad's much better, you have to agree. He wouldn't even have you in the house at first, after he got out of hospital. Do you remember?"

I nodded, remembering the pain. It sliced through my heart like bread knives with serrated edges.

"I need to go now, Mum," I said. "Grace is expecting me round for dinner."

"Why can't you stay here? We were going to have fish and chips later."

I thought about it for a second. I thought and thought and thought. The house felt contaminated with spirits from the past, though. It was haunted by pain and sorrow and violence.

"I can't, Mum."

"Mark, why? This is your home..."

"Not anymore, Mum. My home's in London now. With Andrew." The mention of his name made my heart contract with misery. "There's too many bad memories here for me now, Mum. It's too...too hard to stay here."

"Please don't go."

"I must. But I'll see you tomorrow. Yeah? I'll drop round before I go back to London, to say goodbye."

She stopped, considered everything. She looked into my eyes and they seemed to pierce right through me to another world; a world of cold wind and ghosts.

She knew I was right.

"I understand," she said. "But don't go back without seeing me and your dad first, will you?"

"I promise I'll say goodbye before I leave."

We hugged goodbye. As I turned to go out of the kitchen door, Mum handed me the letter from Nick. "Don't write him off just yet, Mark. And think about what I said, won't you?"

There it was again; that wise and worldly side to her that surfaced so very rarely. I took the brown envelope and put it in my pocket. "All right, Mum," I said. I kissed her on the cheek and went to leave the house. Before doing so, I popped my head round the door of the front room. "See ya, Dad."

He looked up from his position on the sofa where he'd been doing the newspaper's crossword. "'Bye, son. Take care, all right?"

I nodded. And then I left.

Ø

When I got back to Grace's she'd prepared the table for dinner. On the stereo, Shirley Bassey was singing I Who Have Nothing. How ironic it was.

We had dinner that night, Grace, Jason and I, after Rupert had been put down to sleep for the night. Grace made a really nice meal: sweet and sour chicken.

That night, as I slept, I dreamed of Nick.

Ø

Next morning, I didn't feel like hanging around so decided to get straight back to London. I missed the place. Crazy, or what? But yeah, I did miss it.

I went and said goodbye to Mum as I'd promised. Dad was out at the time, on some emergency job. Probably for the best.

There were tears in Mum's eyes as I hugged her goodbye. She told me that things with Andrew would be fine, but I still had to wonder.

I got back to London at around mid-day. It was foolish of me, but when I went up to the Newman Street flat, half of me expected him to be there, arms wide open, heart full of forgiveness.

But the flat was empty.

I wanted to break down then, but I rallied.

There was a red light blinking on the answering machine, telling me I had three new messages. I wondered how many people had tried to contact me.

Maybe Andrew!

Hope blossomed inside me once more.

But the messages weren't from Andrew. The first was from Daniel, asking if I'd got back yet. The second was from George, inviting me to a party the next Friday. And the third...the third was weird. A computerised voice told me it had been left at seven twenty-nine the previous evening.

It was a woman, asking for Andrew, and at first I was puzzled as to who it could be. But as I listened to the rest of the message, I realised who it was, and my first emotion was one of complete and total surprise.

"Andrew...Andrew, are you there? Pick up if you're there. Andrew, it's Mum. Listen...I know it's been a while. But I need you to contact me as soon as possible. Something's...something's happened. Please contact me. It's urgent."

There was a click and a beep as the message ended.

2 Andrew

I'd chosen to go back to work on Sunday. Funny that. I had avoided the Saturday rush, but Rebecca had said she could manage. I didn't know if Mark was going to be back on either Sunday or Monday, but I knew that whichever day it was, he'd come straight round to Dimensions to see me. I wasn't a workaholic or anything that extreme, but Mark knew I couldn't stay away from Dimensions for long. In the time I'd been the manager of the place, it had become my baby. And mothers can't keep away from their babies for long, can they?

Mothers.

There was something else about mothers that Sunday.

I got into work early, at seven, ready to open up at nine. I wanted to get the feel of the place back before the hungry gay masses surged in.

Daniel turned up at around half-eight. He said to me, "Remember what you promised?"

I nodded. "Sure, sure. I'll speak to him. Do you know when he gets back to London?"

Daniel shook his head. "No. All he said was that he was going home for the weekend. I left a message on his - sorry, your - answering machine, asking. But he hasn't got back to me yet."

"Mm," was all I could say. To be quite honest, the idea of seeing

Mark again sent goosebumps rippling across my flesh.

But it sort of still felt too soon. Daniel was right, though, when he said it'd get worse the longer I left it. So I supposed it was a matter of now...or never.

But I didn't have to wait to go and see him. He turned up at Dimensions at about one-ish. He seemed a bit anxious. Not all subdued and nervous as I'd expected him to be around me. He was wearing his old leather jacket, and his hair was all messy.

It looked like he'd run all the way.

I was sitting at the bar at the time, going over some figures.

Mark stalled when I looked up and then he did seem slightly nervous to approach. But there was a look in his eyes, a look I couldn't quite put my finger on. Something in his expression seemed to override everything that had gone on between us for the last couple of weeks. As if there were a different issue here; a deeper issue, one of more importance.

"Hi," I said. I kept my voice flat. But he looked gorgeous, all worried and slightly out of breath. Gorgeous.

"Hi," he said. "Andrew..."

"Yeah?" I raised my eyebrows.

"I just got back. Been back home for the weekend."

"Oh, really? How is everyone?"

"Fine. They're fine, yeah."

"How's your mum?"

"She's good. She asked about you."

"And did you tell her why I wasn't there?"

"Yes, I did."

"And what did she say?"

"That I'm a stupid bastard."

"I see."

"Here," said Mark, and he handed me a small, folded piece of paper. "There was a message on the machine for you. It's from your mum."

My face paled and my heart seemed to shrink and stop pumping blood. A message from my mother? Since moving to London, I'd only spoken to her once, and that had just been to give her the phone number of the Newman Street place after we'd moved from Camberwell.

She'd left a message for me?

Something is wrong, I thought at once.

I took the paper from Mark and said, "Oh. Thanks." I tried to sound as casual as possible, but I felt faint and sick.

A message from my mother?

Why?

"Well..." began Mark, awkwardly. "I guess...I'll see you later then shall I?"

"Maybe, yeah. But...I'm quite busy. I don't know. I'll see, yeah?" I couldn't concentrate on Mark at that moment. I could only think of my mother and what the hell that bitch could possibly want.

Mark nodded, smiled slightly, and then turned around to leave Dimensions. I didn't watch him go, I just stared at the piece of paper he'd given me with parts of my mother's message on it.

Ø

Downstairs in the office, I dialled the number with a barely steady hand. I knew something awful was waiting for me around the corner; something out of sight that would pounce on me in just a few seconds.

But it was a man's voice that answered. "Dad?" I said.

"No. Is this Andrew?" The voice was deep; grave with concern.

But if it wasn't my father then who was it?

"Yes. This is Andrew. Who's this?"

"Hang on a minute, Andrew. I'll get your mother." There was a soft click as the phone on the other end was set down.

My mind was whirling. What was going on? Who had that

strange man been? Where was my mother...?

She came on about a minute later. "Andrew. Thank goodness you called me." It was Mum all right, but there was something in her voice I didn't like, something way way off. She sounded distant and tiny and unsure of herself. It was not what I was used to from her. Not by a long shot.

"Mum!" I exclaimed. "What's going on?"

"Andrew, something's happened." Her voice sounded strange and uneven. There was something else about it too, something familiar that - And then it hit me, smack in the head. She was crying. Only softly. The sniffly, weepy sort of crying. But she was still crying.

"Mum, what's happened? Tell me!" My voice strained.

"Andrew, your father's dead."

Dead.

The world blew up. That's what it was like. Boom! Over. Everything.

There was a silence between my mother and I for what felt like an age.

Finally, I said, "When?" My voice was as flat and cold as a tombstone. Shock, I think. I was numb.

My father was dead.

Dad was dead.

Dad!

Like some great and terrible film shown on a projector in an empty classroom, childhood memories filtered through my mind. Christmases, birthdays, family holidays. My father and I playing football together; him showing me how to ride my first bike without stabilisers.

That's how it had been when I'd been a little boy. When I'd grown up, Dad and I had grown apart. And then, of course, I'd moved away and hadn't seen him for years.

But when I made that call to Mum on that fateful Sunday afternoon, I only thought of the good times with him. Funny, isn't it, the way your mind works in a time of crisis, a time of tragedy.

Yeah, very funny. Ha ha.

"Friday," my mother told me. "It was a heart attack, Andy. He...he died on the way to the hospital." She stopped there, crying harder. Her use of the word 'Andy' dug into my head. It was what my parents - especially my dad - had called me when I was young. It had stopped once I hit ten.

"Andrew, come home. Please. I know we've had our differences but...I need you with me. The funeral..." Again, she trailed off into tears.

"No, no. Of course I'll come home, Mum. I'll come straightaway."

"Thank you, Andrew. It would mean a lot to me."

It would mean a lot to her! I thought, anger surfacing in spite of it all. My father was dead for Christ's sake! She almost made it sound as though she were inconveniencing me.

"Who was that I spoke to just now?" I asked.

"Rob. He came straightaway."

Uncle Rob. My mum's half-brother. I hadn't seen him for ages.

"Oh."

"What time do you think you'll be here?"

"I don't know. I'll leave now. Should take me about an hour, maybe two."

"Okay. Andrew, there's so much to organise, to sort out. I can't..." She sounded almost hysterical now.

I couldn't fully react to the news. It hadn't sunk in.

"I'll sort it out, Mum. Don't worry I'm gonna be there for you."

How awful it was. I thought, Listen to us. It takes the death of my father to bring us together.

There was something inherently sickening about that.

When I put the phone down, I started shivering in the small office.

Dad was dead.

No.

No!

But the cold, hard fact remained.

I went upstairs. My mind felt closed off; I felt closed off. It was as if I'd been removed from everything around me and placed in another zone.

I was sweating a cold sweat.

"Andrew?" said Daniel. He was frowning; brow furrowed in concern. "What's the matter?" He gave a nervous, brittle chuckle. "You look like you've come back from the dead."

Not a good choice of words.

I couldn't say anything at first and Daniel noticed straightaway that there was something seriously wrong. "Andrew?" he said again.

I was blunt. "My dad's dead." The words swirled through the café like a winter wind.

Daniel's jaw dropped. "Ohmygod!" he blurted. "Andrew! I'm so sorry! God! God!"

I nodded. But still the total impact of what had happened refused to hit me.

Daniel threw his arms around me. "Oh, Andrew, that's just awful."

"I have to go home," I said woodenly. "My mum's in bits. I'll have to sort out everything. The funeral..."

The word was like a key unlocking a door.

The tears came. They really came.

Dad was dead.

I put my head in my hands and sobbed.

"Oh, shit," gasped Daniel. "Andrew, sit down. Here." He guided my shivering body to one of the bar stools. To Yvonne, who was at the bar, he said, "Yvonne, get some water, will ya?"

"What happened?"

"Andrew's just had some really bad news."

Yvonne got the water, but I didn't touch any of it; I couldn't. Daniel was saying all these comforting things, but they went straight over my head.

Dad was dead. Dad was gone.

Dad!

Ø

I never thought I'd have to go back to that house again, back to Milton Keynes. All right, so it was inevitable that my parents would one day die and eventually - like now - I'd have to return.

I guess I just hadn't thought that far ahead.

But it was here now; a gruesome reality; and it had to be dealt with.

I wondered, as I got into the taxi that would take me home, what my mother would look like now, after all this time. It was difficult to imagine. And even more difficult to imagine was my mother in her new role of widow.

Then I thought of my father, lying cold and lifeless on some slab in the morgue of Milton Keynes General Hospital.

I was going home.

And Dad was dead.

So he'd never know then. Never found out about me, about his only child.

Had Mum ever told him? I wondered.

The idea seemed impossible, absurd. I couldn't imagine Mum sitting Dad down with a nice cup of tea and saying, "Darling, there's something you really should know about Andrew..."

I got out of the taxi, at the end of the street where I'd been raised. Bury Avenue.

I didn't ask the cab to stop at number thirty-eight. Why? Maybe to give me time to run, to get away, turn back and high-tail it straight back to London, into Mark's arms...

Oh, yeah. Mark.

I'd told him about Dad. On the phone, though, from Rebecca's, where all my stuff was.

He'd cried, and said he'd like to come with me. He said I'd need some support.

Well, that much was true. But Mark? Bring him home to meet Mum? Take him to the funeral?

No way. That would be like the final insult for my mother, letting her meet my boyfriend - my estranged boyfriend, no less - just after her world had caved in. Perhaps, caved in for the second time in her life.

Because isn't that how parents were supposed to feel when their child comes out as gay? Like they've lost someone, like they're grieving.

Is that how Mum felt about me?

Steeling myself, I walked down Bury Avenue, on my way to number thirty-eight.

Talk about the Lonely Mile.

I tried to imagine what to expect from her, from everything here, and found that I couldn't.

The street was so quiet, so suburban. Pretty different from the screaming noise and fluorescent chaos that was London.

I got to the house. It had been painted white since I last saw it. Dad probably did it.

But Dad was dead.

I knocked on the door and waited. And waited.

It seemed a long time before someone answered, and in that short space my head went mad with visions of Dad in a morgue, Dad in a coffin, burials and cremations.

It was Uncle Rob who answered. He looked no different. I hadn't seen him for about eight years, and there he was exactly the same, except maybe a little less hair. He was wearing grey trousers and a white, open-necked shirt with short sleeves. His eyes were reddened from tears, which surprised me a bit. He and my dad had never exactly been close. But maybe seeing his half-sister in such a terrible state had more to do with it.

"Andrew," he said. He held out his hand and, grimly, I shook it. "I'm very sorry about your father."

"Thanks," I said.

"Your mother's in the living room," he said. I nodded, and

followed him through. How weird it was, being back in that house. The smell of it was the same. It smelt of childhood.

But the place looked pretty different. I wondered how many times my parents had decorated since I'd left.

I went into the living room. Mum was on the armchair, wearing jeans and an old grey jumper. She had no make-up on. Her hair was shorter than I'd remembered.

Her eyes were red and puffy. She looked like a withered old crone. It was truly shocking.

"Mum," I said.

She looked at me, as if seeing someone she only vaguely recognised. Yet I was her son. Her son.

I went over to her and we hugged. But it was a hug that lacked any emotion whatsoever. An obligatory hug.

She started to cry against my shoulder. "What am I going to do now?" she whimpered. Uncle Rob stood in the doorway like a spare part.

I could think of nothing to say. My mind felt like a blank piece of paper. It was dreadful.

"I'll arrange the funeral," I said, because there seemed to be nothing else to say.

"He wanted to be buried," Uncle Rob said from his position in the doorway, and at the sound of that awful word buried Mum started to cry again.

"Right," I said. I kept my arm around Mum who was sniffling.

"It was so sudden," she said.

"Yes."

Uncle Rob said, "I'll put the kettle on. Andrew? Do you want a cuppa?"

"Thanks."

He left the room. Mum turned her face to mine. She said, "He was talking about you, Andrew, Dad was. The day before he...died. He wanted to know why you never visited."

"You know why, Mum."

She nodded. "Yes. That was for the best, though. You know how bad his heart was. You know how worried I've always been about it."

I nodded. She was right. Dad had had a congenital heart defect. A hole in the heart. He could have had surgery for it, but had always turned it down. I never knew why, though. I'd never known why he wouldn't have it fixed. He knew he would have died a relatively young man if he'd just left it. But that's what he'd done.

Left it. Left it to kill him.

Forty-nine, he'd been. So much life to him still.

"I'm glad you came back home," said Mum. But it seemed ridiculous to call that house home. It hadn't been home to me for such a long time.

"I had to."

She nodded. "How's life in London?"

"Yeah, fine," I said. "Fine." That's all I wanted to tell her. I knew she didn't really care about my life. She was just trying to distract herself from all that had happened.

I glanced around the living room. It was all tidy and neat, everything in place. There used to be a framed photograph of me on the fireplace. Me aged sixteen, just after I'd finished school.

But the photograph was no longer there.

A queer, Andrew! You're a bloody queer! I didn't raise you like that, to be a queer!

Words from the past, hateful and stinging. But now, with my mother looking so tiny and fragile, it was difficult to imagine that it was her mouth they'd come from, all that time ago.

How different I was now. How much had changed. Back then, she'd been like some great, almighty giant, casting out her scruffy little nineteen-year-old queerboy son. And I'd left, because I'd been weak and she had been strong.

But now I was the strong one, and I had to be strong for her.

Ø

Of all the things that had so far happened that year, I would never have guessed I'd be having to organise my own father's funeral.

I felt like I had stopped having a dad when I'd left, five years ago.

And now I really didn't have a dad.

He was gone forever.

Organising a funeral took a lot of work. It was painful. I kept Mum at my side while I sorted it all out. I wanted to make sure that everything was just the way he would've wanted. But I hadn't known who he'd been when he'd died, so that part had to be down to Mum.

There was so much to do, to get sorted out. Coffin, flowers, the service, the guests. It didn't take long, though, just a couple of days.

He'd died on the Friday, and would be buried on the Wednesday. The speed with which everything was sorted out amazed me. I suppose you can't muck around, though, can you, when somebody dies.

My father.

Mum and I went to see his body in the Chapel of Rest. At first I didn't think I'd be able to go through with it. Somehow, it seemed wrong. When you consider how long I hadn't seen him, or even had any contact with the man

But Mum was in no state to go in on her own, so I had to accompany her.

He looked so still, lying there, like a statue made of porcelain. He was wearing a dark blue suit, and he still had his wedding ring on. That was one of his wishes, to be buried with it.

I wanted to touch him, but didn't dare. I felt almost as if I had no right to do it.

He'd never known about me.

I wondered quite a bit about that. I wondered if he could've guessed, even if Mum hadn't told him. I half-wanted to ask Mum if she'd told him, and what she'd thought about me all this time. But I couldn't, could I? It would've been so inappropriate to do so, at such a time.

Perhaps one day I would, though. Dad dying might bring my mother and I closer together.

As I looked at my father's still and lifeless form, I wished I'd gotten to know him more. We'd never really got on during my awkward teenage years, but perhaps we would've done now. It would've been good, to have had a father who cared where I lived and how I behaved.

But that could never have been. And now, never would be.

Ø

The thick grey sky was a quilt of gloom that hung over the gathering in the cemetery.

I stared at the long wooden box that contained my dad, willing the tears to come, to flow down my cheeks in a relentless waterfall. But my eyes remained dry.

I looked around at my family and the friends of my father who circled me, huddled together as if keeping out the darkness of death that was so evident.

Poor Dad.

The words of the vicar drifted across the bleak atmosphere, gliding high into the clouds like an invisible crow. I did not hear them and I did not care.

Dad was dead.

Even then, with the proof stretched out before me like that, I couldn't believe it was true. It was like my mind had abandoned me once again, refusing to accept the reality.

Dad was dead.

I surveyed the collection of mourners. Most of my family, people I hadn't seen for years, were gathered in the pit of the cemetery

I saw my Aunt Anna hovering uncertainly with her husband Pete.

Two of my cousins, Geoff and Jeremy, stared at the gaping hole in the ground, as if wondering what it could be for. My mother's best friend, Nicola, wheel-chair bound after a car accident some years back, sat with tear-reddened eyes.

And Mum herself stood beside me, dark glasses hiding her own eyes, swaying slightly as if she were made of tissue. She was pale; submissive and trembling.

A thin breeze filtered through the silent gathering; it ruffled through my hair, as if it had fingers to inspect my head with.

The breeze felt cruel and unwanted, wrapping around every sinew in my body.

"Ashes to ashes," the vicar was saying. "And dust to dust."

I adjusted the dark glasses on my face.

I longed for it to be a month ago, before all this. Back when I was happy with Mark, when we had each other, and life had been good. Now Mark and I had split up, and my father was dead.

What a difference a few weeks can make to a life. Look at my dad. He'd only been forty-nine. He had ages, years ahead of him. So much still to do, to see.

And what of me? I hadn't even seen him for five years, maybe more. It's difficult to remember the last time I had seen him, even spoken to him.

Now I would never see him again.

And for what? Because I was gay. Because I was different.

How unfair it all seemed. How bloody unfair!

And what of Mark? What about him? The man I loved. I'd lost him, too. He felt as closed off and unreachable to me now as my poor dead father.

But he isn't, Andrew, I told myself. Mark isn't unreachable or closed off. Mark's there, waiting for you, waiting for forgiveness and love.

I watched from behind the dark wall of my sunglasses as my father's coffin was lowered into the earth.

My mother wailed hysterically. "Alun!" she cried. "Don't leave me!"

I held her close against me. She was shaking violently, her body quivering against mine like a dying bird.

Would that be what Mark would say?

Andrew! Don't leave me!

As inappropriate as that thought might have been, it came nonetheless.

Life's too short.

That's what I'd said to Mark the day I'd told him I'd taken the job in London.

Life's too short.

I clasped my mother's hand as she threw a single red rose into the grave, on top of my father's coffin.

After that, I threw in a handful of earth. It landed with a horrible rattling sound.

Andrew! Don't leave me!

My father's face filled my head. And those childhood memories returned, heavy and lasting.

I thought of Mark, back in London, all alone.

And it was then that I knew what had to be done. I knew what I had to do.

I have a boyfriend, I thought. He isn't dead; he isn't buried. He's alive and he's waiting for me and he loves me.

I straightened my shoulders.

I couldn't go backwards in time, back to when my father had been alive. I couldn't go back and explain to him what I was, and that it was nothing terrible, that I was a good person no matter which gender I was attracted to.

But I could go to Mark.

Rest in peace, Dad, I thought. Sleep well.

27 **Mark**

It was Friday. I'd been at Dimensions, having a heart-to-heart with Daniel.

When I got in, at two o'clock in the afternoon, Andrew was waiting for me on the settee.

I couldn't believe he was there. Could not believe it. It was so weird. Good, but weird, and just a little frightening.

He was wearing jeans, a jumper and his leather jacket. He looked exhausted.

"Hi," I said, softly. I didn't know where to put myself; didn't know what to say, do, or even where to look.

"Hello," said Andrew. He looked up, smiled wearily. His eyes were baggy and red. He did not stand.

"Are...you okay?" I asked softly. Over the last couple of days I hadn't been able to get him off my mind. No change there, though. But his father had died, hadn't he? Andrew's father. And that meant he'd had to go home to Milton Keynes, back to see his mother, too. His mother. The woman who threw him out when she found out he was gay. God. What that must have been like for him! And he'd had to go through it alone.

Alone.

I'd offered him my support, of course I had. Said I'd go with him. I guess I wasn't exactly surprised when he turned my offer down.

In fact, I'd sort of resigned myself to the fact that we were through, that Andrew wanted to end it. So really, all things considered, I was going through a bereavement of my own.

But there he was, back in the Newman Street flat, like nothing had happened; nothing had changed.

"How...when was the funeral?" I asked.

"Wednesday. But I had to stay a bit longer. Make sure Mum was all right."

"How's she coping?"

"As well as can be expected, I guess. It was so sudden. She's probably still in shock."

Cautiously, I went on. "And you?"

"I'm handling it okay, yeah."

"Andrew..." I trailed. I wanted to say something. Throw my arms around him. Sob into his shoulder. Tell him I was sorry and I wanted it all back, how we were. But for a start, that seemed selfish considering what he'd just been through. And secondly, I'd tried all that, hadn't I? And it hadn't worked at all. So perhaps I needed to think of a different tactic.

If there was still any hope of saving our relationship.

"Flat looks tidy," Andrew said.

"Ta."

How absurd it was, this small talk. Maddening. When there was so much else that needed to be said, to be discussed. It was like we were hiding behind everything else.

"How's work?" he asked.

"All right, I guess."

"Mark..."

"Yes."

He looked at me, wet his lips, and swallowed. The silence in the air was thick and awful. "I missed you."

"You did?" I said, somehow guardedly.

He nodded.

"Yeah, Mark. Yeah, I missed you. But..." He stopped there, and looked away. He ran a hand through his hair.

Suddenly, I felt like a trespasser.

I tried to focus my mind, to make things clear. But nothing was clear. I wondered if Andrew was going to make everything all right, and we could start again, together. Oh, what a wonderful word that was.

Together.

Far better than alone.

Andrew, I thought. Oh, Andrew, let's be together again.

"Andrew?" I said. I spoke carefully, gingerly. I felt like a skater on black ice. I was treading on danger. But I had to say those words, because they needed to be said. But what now?

Wasn't that always the question in my life?

What now?

Andrew looked at me, and his eyes, too, seemed like ice. At first, anyway. But the ice soon melted, and left something there. But I couldn't quite see what that something was.

"Mark," he said.

That was all for a few moments. I stayed by the living room door. Not moving. Hardly even daring to breathe, lest it stop whatever Andrew had been about to start.

When he spoke, he sounded strangely elderly. "To find peace with ourselves, Mark, in this life, we have to let things that hurt stop. To let them become history. The past. Do you understand?"

"I...I don't know." I was confused. What did he mean?

He said, "I've learned a lot these last couple of days, while I've been back home. And one of those things is that holding on to bad stuff, to bad memories, stops us from getting on with our lives.

"There's something else there, too. Something else I've come to realise while I've been...away."

"Yeah?"

Andrew sighed. He seemed so fatigued.

"I've been too hard on you, Mark."

"No - "

"Let me finish. I was just so shocked that you did what you did..."

"Sorry..."

"Mark, stop it. There's been enough grovelling around here."

I nodded.

Andrew went on. "You were right what you said. I've been there, done it, got the T-shirt. But you...you hadn't even had sex with anyone else until we came here, to London. I suppose it was - maybe - a type of learning experience?"

I nodded.

"I mean, I'm still not totally over it, Mark. I'm trying, though, and I think I'm getting somewhere with it. But I have been a bit...well, heavy-handed."

I nodded again.

"And all that business you said about open relationships, seeing other people - it's not what you really want is it?"

"No! No, Andrew, it's not. I just said that because I was - because I was - "

"Scared?" he supplied. "Trying to justify yourself, even though you knew you were wrong?"

"Yes! That's exactly it!"

Andrew sighed. He smiled, sadly, but happily at the same time. "It's important to leave things behind, Mark. It's important to let stuff become history. Otherwise what hope is there for any kind of future?"

"So...what are you saying?"

"I'm saying that my father is dead. My father is history. And I have to let go of him, or I won't be able to get on with my life. And there are other things that need to be let go of, aren't there?" His eyes were probing and somehow accusing. It was like he was waiting for me to tell him something.

What will he say next? I thought. What will his next words be?

So you and I are history, Mark? I have to move on?

No!

"Andrew?" I said, my voice a mere tremble. His name sounded curiously ancient, as it quivered free from my throat.

He got to his feet. He was like a giant, and I a tiny ant.

Waiting to be crushed.

Oh, Ben, what you did to us! I thought. What you did!

Andrew said, "I still love you, Mark. Of course I do. It's only a very tiny thing inside me that tells me I should hate you, that we should be over. That we should be history."

I nodded. I couldn't speak. The lump in my throat, formed by fear and hurt, blocked any chance of speech.

"You were weak and you were thoughtless," he went on, "and it would be easy for me to hate you for that, to close you off and never see you again. It would be too easy, Mark. Do you know what I mean? And yes, maybe I did jump off at the deep end. A bit."

I nodded, dumbstruck.

"But I can't just shrug off what you've done, either, Mark. I can't. It still hurts me. It still really hurts me. But I know that you're hurting too, aren't you, Mark?"

"Yes," I told him. "Yes, Andrew. You don't know how much I'm hurting."

"Oh, I think I do."

I nodded again.

"I was wrong to run to Rebecca's, Mark. I was wrong to hide from what had happened, to hide from you. So now I want us to make things right. For a relationship to work, for any relationship to work - gay or straight - there has to be trust, Mark. And you abused my trust."

"I'm sorry."

"I know you are. So stop saying that. And let me finish. There has to be trust, Mark. Trust is like the keystone of any partnership. But there also has to be forgiveness. There has to be."

I nodded, and a seed of hope was planted inside me.

My eyes grew wide.

"There's still a fair way to go, though, Mark. But we've got too much going for us for me to just dismiss it like that, to throw us away."

"Yes," I said.

Andrew took a step towards me. Just a couple of inches apart we were, but it seemed like a lifetime before he got to me. He smiled. And I realised I was looking at the old Andrew; the Andrew I loved and who loved me back.

The Andrew that was mine.

"Come on, Mark," he said softly, a smile touching his mouth. "Let's talk."

He held out his hand.

And I took it.